▼   ▼   ▼   ▼   ▼

As Vidar spoke its name, the monster showed itself. First the huge, horned head, black with streaks of blood-red. The slitted, yellow eyes, the darting tongue. Then its sleek, scaly coils, unwinding along the cavern floor.

It was the one living thing that even Odin had backed down from. And Vidar and his companions had taken shelter in its lair!

The massive head rose, loomed. The red-streaked maw opened, revealing rows of long, sharp teeth. Suddenly, the long, pink tongue flickered out from between its jaws. And Vidar knew he only had a moment to act.

Vidar didn't hesitate. He darted forward, but as he did so, he slipped on serpent's venom. He tried to keep his feet, but to no avail. As he picked himself up, too late to help, the serpent catapulted forward, snatching one of his comrades up in its jaws. Vidar was about to pick up a sword when he saw something even deadlier. The stalactite that the serpent had dislodged. Vidar lunged for it...

★

"Exciting...races along to a wild climax."
—*Kliatt* on *The Hammer and the Horn*

Also by Michael Jan Friedman

The Glove of Maiden's Hair
The Hammer and the Horn
The Seekers and the Sword

Published by
POPULAR LIBRARY

The Fortress and The Fire

MICHAEL JAN FRIEDMAN

POPULAR LIBRARY

An Imprint of Warner Books, Inc.

A Warner Communications Company

POPULAR LIBRARY EDITION

Popular Library®, the fanciful P design, and Questar® are
registered trademarks of Warner Books, Inc.

Cover illustration by Kevin Johnson

Popular Library books are published by
Warner Books, Inc.
666 Fifth Avenue
New York, N.Y. 10103

 A Warner Communications Company

Printed in the United States of America

First Printing: April, 1988

10 9 8 7 6 5 4 3 2 1

For Fara and Eric,
who taught me how to play again

The Fortress and The Fire

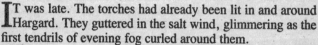

I

IT was late. The torches had already been lit in and around Hargard. They guttered in the salt wind, glimmering as the first tendrils of evening fog curled around them.

The wind was in his face now too, cold and wet with spray. It felt good to have a fresh horse beneath him. It felt good to gaze upon the dark, elvish sea, still embroidered with a border of the sun's last gold. It reminded Vidar of old times. Days when he and his brothers would hunt in Alfheim's forests, riding through sun and shadow, breathing rich scents of oak and elm ... nights when they would wrestle in the feast-hall at Hargard, while the hearth flames leaped and the lords of the *lyos* cheered.

It recalled simpler days, when they raced along this very road, and Hermod would always win because the horses loved him best ...

Life was much too complicated now. His brothers were gone, Asgard fallen and rebuilt. Odin had come back from the dead to haunt them. Vali and Modi and half their armies were lost—perhaps in M'thrund, as the traitor Hoenir had confessed with his dying breath.

An invasion of Odin's making might even now be descending on Alfheim, Asaheim, or nowhere at all, depending on which theory one subscribed to.

What to do? Try to invade M'thrund, on the chance that Hoenir had given them the truth—and that Vali had survived the trap that must have awaited him there?

Or lie still, waiting for Odin to make his next move?

The hooves of Vidar's gelding clattered against the stones of the sea road. Birds flew beside him on updrafts, screeching, then dove past the cliff's edge to seek their dinners. The sound of waves crashing far below was a steady pulse in the air and in the earth, more felt than heard.

Some of the elves had already spoken in favor of waiting —wary of leaving Alfheim defenseless while they went off in search of Vali. But Vidar was restless. The sooner they found their lost armies, the sooner they might find Odin.

He turned away from the sea as the road twisted, guiding him toward the gates of Hargard. His warrior's braid tapped against his back in time with his horse's gait, as it had in the days before Ragnarok. He'd bound his hair up days ago, to keep it out of his eyes while he was riding.

His beard had grown too. It was full and barbaric now, wilder than it had ever been. If someone from Earth—Midgard—had seen him, they might not have recognized him. After all, he hadn't looked this way in well over a thousand years.

Hargard loomed before him, a low black keep wrapped about itself on the brink of the cliff. The sentries on the wall called out and he waved. It only took them a moment to recognize him in the firelight.

The gates opened and he urged his horse inside. In the courtyard, a groom trotted out to meet him. He dismounted and gave over the reins.

After so many days of riding, it felt awkward to walk. Nor was he eager to give up the broad sky for these walls of dark stone.

But it was time. High time. These last few miles, he'd promised himself that he would get it over with. Quickly. Then he'd take a bath and sleep for a while.

At the entrance to the keep itself, the elves on either side watched him pass. Their hard, green eyes glinted, but they made no sign of welcome. Nor had he expected any. No one was eager to guest the Aesir—especially one of Odin's sons.

Once within, he found the stairs and took them two at a

time. When he reached the third floor, he saw the knot of guards outside Magni's door.

As luck would have it, Ullir was one of them. He at least would give him a proper welcome.

The blondbeard came forward, smiling, and grasped Vidar's hand. "Well met, my lord. I trust the road was good to you."

"When there was a road," said Vidar. "But yes—we accomplished what we set out to do. H'limif and V'ili are still out there, finishing up." Vidar glanced at Magni's door. "They didn't really need me anymore, so I came on ahead."

"No signs of unwelcome company?"

"None," said Vidar. "And now the *lyos* have been alerted. If Ygg does launch a sneak attack, through some gate we don't know about, there are lines of communication. We'll find out in time to do something about it."

Ullir nodded. "There's some comfort in that, I suppose. Not much, but some."

"Aye," said Vidar. He glanced again at the door. "And our prisoner?"

"Quiet," said Ullir. "For the most part. But he's asked after his children. And you."

Vidar frowned. "Very well then. He need not ask any longer."

The other guards—all Aesirmen like Ullir—stepped aside as Vidar approached. He went up to the door, knocked. When he heard no answer, he opened it and went inside.

The Lord of Alfheim was sitting by the fire, his chair tipped back, his foot braced against the stones of the hearth. He didn't turn around when Vidar entered.

"Took you long enough," said Magni. His voice was little more than a whisper.

Vidar hung his cloak on a peg. He found a chair by the window, where a square of darkness was crowded into the aperture. From there, he could see Magni's face in profile, lit by the flickering light of the flames. There was a silver goblet full of mead in his hands.

"I came as soon as I could," said Vidar.

Magni grunted.

"I heard that you asked for me."

"Aye," said Thor's son. "I asked for you." His voice was louder now, but hollow. Vidar could hear the madness in it, could almost reach out and touch it. It burned in the one eye that he could see, reflecting firelight.

Magni raised the goblet. He took a long draught, then wiped the foam from his honey-red beard with the back of his hand.

A smile formed on his lips. "They despise me, don't they?"

Vidar shrugged, and Magni turned toward him as if attracted by the movement. His face was almost beautiful. It was his mother's face. But now there were dark hollows under the eyes, and a mad light within them.

"Can you blame them?" asked Vidar. He wanted to be gentle, but he knew that Magni would hate it. So he spoke plainly. "You sold out their world from under them. Sold *them* out. What did you expect?"

The smile faded. What replaced it was pitiful, and Vidar had to look away. This was what he had dreaded all the way back to Hargard.

Watching his nephew was like standing at the edge of a chasm. How deep was this madness? Deep enough.

Magni let his knee bend and the front legs of his chair came to rest against the floor. When he spoke again, the hollowness hurt.

"There must have been women, Uncle. Women you truly loved."

"Aye," Vidar said. "A few."

He looked up and saw Magni's eyes. They were red sparks, painfully bright. But there was a clarity in them that had not been there before.

"Then perhaps you will understand," said Magni. He licked his lips. "She was life itself, Vidar. Nothing less. Maybe you found peace in that world of yours, away from Vali and Asgard. But not me. For a long time, I only drifted, trying not to remember Ragnarok." The delicate brow furrowed. "Then came Am'bi. Like a gift. And if I knew then that she would die some day, it didn't make it any easier when the time came."

He turned back toward the fire. Perhaps he saw her there. Perhaps he saw other things—the children he'd set against one another, the land he'd torn in two.

"How can I tell you, Vidar? She was my light. My light. When it went out, I was lost. It was as if I'd never ruled in Alfheim at all, as if I'd only been the mouth through which she spoke—the hand that carried out her judgments. I was in a strange place suddenly, an alien kingdom. But I didn't want to lose it. It was all I had. That and the children she'd given me. So I clutched Alfheim as hard as I could." His free hand became a fist. "And the more it slipped away, the tighter I held on to it."

Silence for a moment. Within it, Vidar could feel the waves washing up against Hargard. A bird shrieked, breaking the spell.

"Skir'nir said that there were injustices."

Magni grunted. "Injustices? Yes. Perhaps. But Skir'nir was my wisest child. He knew me better than the children of my blood. Why did he not counsel me? Why did he stand against me at court, then go up into the hills and turn the lords there against me as well?"

"He said that you were . . . unapproachable."

Magni's head came up suddenly. "Unapproachable? Is that the word he used?"

"No," said Vidar. He'd gone too far to stop now. "The word he used was *insane*."

Magni seemed to flinch at that—or was it only the dance of firelight on his face? After a moment, he shrugged.

"I was." He laughed, carelessly. "If there hadn't been a madness in me, would I have allied myself with Odin? *Trusted him?*" Magni shook his head. "But it all seemed to make sense at the time. Lots of sense. I thought that Skir'nir was plotting my downfall. I knew the mood of the people, and how much they loved him. And I knew where a great many of them would place their loyalties."

Magni pulled at his mead, wiped his mouth again. But flecks of foam still clung to his beard.

"Then Odin appeared. Offered me armies, to keep hold of my kingdom. A return to the ancient ways, to the Asgard of old. In my . . . my madness, I concede it . . . I clutched at that straw. I didn't want to give up Alfheim, Vidar. And the promise of that other time, before Ragnarok . . . before the family was destroyed . . . it sounds empty now. But it was so real then." Magni winced.

"He's persuasive," said Vidar, because it seemed that he should say something. "We all know that."

Magni held the lip of his goblet against his chin for a moment. "I could have stood against him. I could have. But it had been ingrained in me since birth—Odin the Invincible, Odin the All-Knowing. The All-Powerful. You remember the time we rode into Jotunheim and took those horses from Hrungnir?"

"Yes," said Vidar. "I remember."

"I gave Odin first pick of them. Because one did not take chances with him. Wasn't that always the way? We were taught to fear him. Even his kin. *Especially* his kin."

Magni's face puckered. "So when he came to me, I didn't think to say no. For if he achieved his victory—and I'd defied him . . ." His voice trailed off.

"Then he never told you what he intended?" asked Vidar. "The annihilation of the nine worlds, the unmaking of his creations?"

Magni turned back toward him. He shifted in his chair so that they faced one another. His brow was knotted over the bridge of his nose, and suddenly there was a lot of Thor in him.

"You sound as if you spoke with him too, Jawbreaker."

"I did," said Vidar.

Magni regarded him. "And is that what he talked about? Destruction?"

"Aye," said Vidar, falling again into the archaic speech

patterns of his youth. "Complete destruction. A surrender to the Ginnungagap."

Magni started to laugh, then cut himself short when he saw the look on Vidar's face. "You're serious," he said.

"Dead serious."

"But why?"

Vidar searched his nephew's face for evidence of dissembling, but he couldn't find any. The surprise, the concern—they seemed genuine. And the madness—that seemed genuine too.

"Why?" echoed Vidar. "Why not? He spent some time in Niflheim, he said. Learned that all his empire building had been folly. And now he wants to tear it down, in his cosmic embarrassment."

Magni just stared at him. Perhaps he searched Vidar's face even as Vidar had searched his. Paranoia, mistrust . . . they came with the genes, didn't they?

A moment later, it seemed that Magni had found whatever truth he'd been seeking. He took a deep breath, let it out slowly. He glared at things beyond Vidar, beyond this room. His fingers closed into fists and his knuckles turned white.

The goblet in his hand crumpled, shrieking in protest. The mead boiled up, ran out between his fingers, and formed a puddle on the floor.

"I was a fool," said Magni. "A bigger fool than I'd thought."

Vidar didn't say anything. Odin had made fools of them all with regularity. No need to rub it in.

Magni cursed, helpless in his frustration. He tossed the twisted goblet aside and it clattered against the stones. "He *used* me."

"At least you're still alive," said Vidar. "Be glad of that. Hoenir gave his life for his folly."

Magni's eyes focused again. He met Vidar's gaze.

"Yes—poor Hoenir," he said. "But he gave Odin away before he died—didn't he?"

"You know that?" asked Vidar. He was only mildly surprised.

"I overheard my guards out there. Only they call Odin something else—Ygg. Wasn't that the name of one of his battle masks?"

"Yes. It's the name he went by in Utgard."

"I see," said Magni. "You'll have to tell me sometime about what went on in Utgard." He paused. "Are you going after Vali now? In M'thrund?"

Vidar nodded. "In fact, that's what I came to talk to you about."

Magni chuckled. He stood and went to the window. "You need to know where the gate is."

"Aye," said Vidar. "Some of the Aesirmen here told me of Vali's ancient attempts to conquer M'thrund. They said that the gate Vali created was in Alfheim—so if the *thrund* ever tried to counterattack, Alfheim would have served as a buffer. To protect Asgard."

Magni nodded. "Vali was always that way. Ready to sacrifice anything for his city. Anyone." He turned. "And what about you, Vidar?"

"What *about* me?"

Vidar's heart sank when he saw Magni's far-off look. The madness was there again—even worse than before.

"You were always the first one to leap into the breech, Uncle. They called you the bravest—next to Thor, of course. Asgard's staunchest defender." His eyes narrowed. "But you left Asgard, didn't you? Just as I did. So why are you back? What are you fighting for now?"

"For Midgard," said Vidar. Once, not so long ago, that had been the whole truth. Before he'd told B'rannit the *dwarvin*-queen that he would challenge Vali for his throne—and halt the pattern of conquest that Odin had created before Vidar was born. "Only for Midgard," he lied.

"To keep it safe from Odin."

"Aye."

"And you would give much to accomplish that."

Vidar eyed him. "What are you getting at? You want something in return for the whereabouts of the gate?"

Magni's nostrils flared. "I do."

"All right—what?"

"Redemption. A chance at Odin."

"You mean," said Vidar, "you want to come along. To M'thrund."

Magni held out his fists. "I don't want to be shunned, Vidar. Not by my own children. And Modi—my brother— is among those who followed Vali. If I could but find Odin ... I'd make him pay for what he's done to me." Magni shuddered suddenly with anger. "I'd make him pay, Vidar."

As Vidar watched his nephew's features twist, his stomach clenched. Hadn't he left Asgard even as Magni had, with the vision of Ragnarok seared into his memory? Hadn't he sought forgetfulness on Earth, even as Magni had in Alfheim?

But for this tug of fate or that, couldn't it as easily have been him standing here in Magni's place, raging at his shame and his helplessness?

Part of Vidar was tempted to give Magni his chance—to take him along to M'thrund. But the other part remembered that Magni was of Odin's blood, and treachery came too easily to this family. Even if Magni was sincere, he was also mad. It was too big a risk.

Vidar shook his head from side to side. "I can't do it, nephew." He shrugged. "We'll have to find the gate some other way. There must be accounts around here somewhere of the invasions into M'thrund."

Magni's jaw fell. "You would deny me this, Vidar?" His voice was tight, reedy.

"I have no choice," said Vidar.

Magni's eyes grew fierce. "Then be damned," he rasped. He lifted his finger and it shook as he pointed it at Vidar. "Be damned along with your bloody father. You're two of a kind, Vidar—you don't care who gets trampled, as long as it's not you."

Vidar frowned. "What would *you* do, Magni—if our situations were reversed?"

That took him by surprise. Slowly, his features softened.

And Vidar pressed his advantage quickly—before Magni's mood could shift again.

"That gate is more than a way to get to Vali—and perhaps Odin. It's a way for Odin to get to us. Would you plunge Alfheim into danger a second time—knowing you could have prevented it? Would you betray your children all over again?"

Magni's face seemed to drain of all emotion. He swallowed.

"Or will you seize this chance—and prove you're not a traitor?"

For a time, there was only the crackling of the fire. Then Magni spoke.

"All right," he said softly. "I'll tell."

II

"BOTH of you have fought well for me," said Odin. "You have learned my laws, you have proven yourselves equally. But now your father is dead and his throne sits empty. One of you must fill it—but which one?"

The twin brothers Agnar and Geirrod stood before Odin in the hall called Valhalla, where the warriors from Midgard honed their skills between battles. And they sorrowed at the news of their father's death, for they had only been youths when Odin brought them to Asgard, and they had not seen their father since.

"Well?" asked the Valfather. "Who shall rule?"

Agnar spoke first. "Your pardon, my lord, but my brother and I have always shared what was ours. When we were infants, we shared a wet nurse. When we were ten, we shared a horse. And here in Valhalla, we have shared the bounty of your table."

"Aye," said Geirrod. "We can as easily share our father's kingdom."

Odin nodded. "Then share it you will. Just don't forget your yearly tribute to me—a hundred warriors, tall and fit. No runts."

The brothers said that they would not forget, and they were returned to Midgard.

But when they reached their father's kingdom, they were dismayed by what had befallen it. No longer was it steeped in wealth. For to make up for the loss of so many warriors —a full hundred a year, even as Odin had said—the king had been forced to hire mercenaries at great expense.

And even mercenaries had not been enough to guard the kingdom. Little by little, the neighboring lords had whittled away at its borders, until the kingdom was only half its former size.

Seeing this, Geirrod was no longer as well disposed toward sharing. "There is little enough here," he told himself, "without having to haggle over it with someone else. Greed came to fester in him, blackening his heart.

And before they reached their father's hall, he had slain his brother Agnar.

"Bandits," he told the people as he carried his brother's body into the hall. "And I could not save him."

Many believed Geirrod, for they remembered the brothers' love for one another. Some, on the other hand, did not. As Geirrod ascended the throne, there were grumblings. Rumors.

But he stilled them. He fought his encroaching neighbors as he'd fought hrimthursar for Odin—bravely, and without stint. Soon, he won back his father's lands—and more. For he conquered those about him, and demanded their tribute, and gathered wealth such as his father had never seen. And with this, he was open-handed—giving his best warriors gold and silver armlets, rings and necklaces, and well-wrought swords.

All who served Geirrod came to love him, forgetting the stories of how he'd slain his own brother.

But not everyone let the rumors gather dust. Geirrod's neighbors remembered them. And when they sent their own youths to Odin in Asgard, they carried the tales with them.

So it was that ten years after Geirrod's return—ten years to the day, my lord—there came a wayfarer to his feast-hall. The traveler wore a hooded cloak, and it was the color of the night sky. When the dogs at the door saw this hooded one coming, they whimpered and crept away into the corners of the room.

Right up to the king's seat came the stranger.

"Who are you?" asked Geirrod, "that you come into my hall unannounced? I don't mind entertaining my guests, but I like them to have some manners."

"My name is Grimnir," said the wayfarer. "And I have come to see the kings of this land."

"There is but one king here," said Geirrod.

The stranger peered at him from within his hood. "I thought there were two kings—and I came from afar to witness this, for it is a great curiosity."

"There would have been two," said Geirrod, trying to contain his anger—for he was sure that this Grimnir was goading him. "But my brother died."

"Ah, yes," said the stranger. "Now that you mention it, I have heard that story as well." His voice dropped, so that no one could hear him but Geirrod. "But I have it told two ways. Which version, I wonder, is the truth?"

"The truth," said Geirrod, "can be a costly thing, way-farer."

"As well I know," said Grimnir. "Yet I seek it, and I am willing to pay the price."

He looked about the feast-hall, until his eyes fell on the firepit and the spit above it.

"For the truth," he said, "I will give you more than gold

and silver. I will hang eight days and eight nights on that cooking spit. And I will not say a word about your cruelty for putting me there."

Geirrod smiled. His black heart swelled at the prospect of such sport. And before he could think about it, he had admitted to his brother's murder.

"Now," he said, "the spit. And there you'll dangle like a pig, until the flames singe your behind and blacken your flesh."

Geirrod's retainers were shocked. But none dared raise his voice against his lord. The wayfarer was tied to the spit.

And a strange thing happened. The flames died down, as if they had no wish to burn this Grimnir. Geirrod ordered more logs and dung thrown into the firepit, so that his visitor could be punished for his impudence. But even with all that, the flames never touched him.

Had Geirrod been less consumed by anger, and by the guilt he was only now beginning to feel, perhaps he would have guessed that his visitor was no mortal. But he could not find it in his heart to let Grimnir off the spit.

For eight days and eight nights, the stranger hung over the open fire. On the ninth day, Geirrod's son—named Agnar like his long-dead uncle—took pity on Grimnir. While everyone else was feasting and drinking, young Agnar got hold of a horn full of mead.

Concealing it under his tunic, he brought it to the stranger.

"Here," he whispered, and held the horn to Grimnir's lips. "I cannot watch while my father punishes you. After all, you haven't done anything wrong—at least, not that I can tell."

Grimnir drank. When the horn was empty, he licked his lips.

"Come closer, boy," he said.

Unafraid, Agnar came closer.

"Soon, you will be the king," said the stranger. "And now I'll tell you what a king must know. . .

"There are nine worlds, boy. The Aesir live in Asaheim, ruled by Lord Odin; the elves in Alfheim; the hrimthursar in

Jotunheim; the Vanir in Vanaheim and men in Midgard. The dark elves dwell in Svartheim. In Utgard, all live together—men, elves, and thursar. Then there's Niflheim, populated by monsters, and Nidavellir, where nothing lives at all.

"There are three great weapons, boy. They are Mjollnir, the hammer of Thor; Angrum, the sword of Vanir-born Frey; and Gjallarhorn, which is Heimdall's alone to sound.

"There are nine sons to fight for Odin, boy. Remember them well. They are Bragi and Heimdall, Thor and Vidar, Hod and Baldur and Vali, Hermod and Tyr."

"But who are you," asked the boy, "that you should know all this?"

"I have many names, young king. I am called Grim One and Traveler, Battleglad and Deathworker, Lord of the Ravens and Most High. I am Pain to my enemies and Justice to my friends. But you may call me Odin."

Then the stranger turned away from Agnar, and as he did this his bonds fell away, and he swung out to the edge of the firepit. Geirrod gasped, for he saw now past his anger, and realized that it was one of the Aesir he had tortured.

Geirrod's heart sank in his chest.

"Once," said the stranger, "you told me you would share everything with your brother. Now it is time to share one more thing with him."

The wayfarer threw his hood back.

The king had been sitting with his sword in his lap, half in its sheath and half out. When he saw who his visitor was, he got up quickly to pray for forgiveness with both hands. But in his haste, he dropped his sword.

The weapon's hilt hit the floor, so that it stood point-up for a moment. Geirrod stumbled in trying to avoid it, but the blade seemed to know where he would fall. A piercing cry rang throughout the hall—and in that moment, the death of Geirrod's brother was avenged.

Sin Skolding
Namforsen, 532 A.D.

III

MORNING. Someone was knocking.

Vidar propped himself up on one elbow and said, "Come in."

The door shook impatiently. "I cannot," said his caller. "It is locked."

He recognized the feminine voice. It seemed to have a note of urgency in it. Wrapping his blankets around him, Vidar crossed the cold stones of the floor on bare feet.

When he opened the door, he saw that Sif had been crying. And she was not someone who cried easily.

"What is it?" he asked her.

"It is G'lann, my lord." She took a ragged breath, let it out. "He..." But she had to bite her lip to keep it from trembling.

"Is he all right?"

"All right?" she echoed. "He is unhurt. But he is anything but all right."

She looked so frazzled, so helpless. Vidar wanted to embrace her. But then his blanket would have fallen.

"Eric is not back yet, nor is Skir'nir. And I needed someone to..."

"Easy," he told her. "Come in out of the hallway and talk to me. Slowly. While I get dressed."

It was only then that she took stock of what Vidar was wearing—and she blushed as she turned away.

"I said come in."

Still averting her eyes, she headed for the hearth, settled into a chair before it. Her copper hair thrust out from her braid in disarray. It was still wet with the fog she must have ridden through. Perhaps she'd returned to Hargard only moments ago.

Vidar crossed the room again to get some clothes. He dropped the blanket, rummaged through a drawer.

"G'lann," he prompted.

"Aye," she said, a little calmer now. "I met him on the way back. Within sight of Hargard. Neither of us had found any evidence of an invasion."

"Nor did I," said Vidar, drawing on a pair of sturdy, elvish breeches.

"But G'lann had not come home empty-handed. He'd come across one of our beautiful white horses, whose breed our father stole from Jotunheim. And my brother was eager to show him to me, so we stopped in a clearing not far from here, and G'lann had his warriors bring the beast on ahead.

"It was a stallion—Hild was his name—and he was more splendid than ever. He'd run wild, it seemed, ever since Hargard had fallen to Skir'nir. There was an air of arrogance about him, of recklessness, and burrs in his long, tangled mane.

"But when he got near to G'lann, he screamed and reared, pawing at the air with his hooves. If there hadn't been a rope on him, and some sturdy elves to hold it, he would surely have bolted.

"G'lann had always loved our father's horses, for they were clever beasts as well as beautiful, and he prided himself on his way with them. So when Hild showed such fear of him, he was naturally hurt. 'What is it?' he asked, as if Hild could answer. 'What's the matter?' And then he saw where the horse's dark eyes were riveted—on the sword at his hip.

"Slowly, he drew the blade out. And the beast stopped screaming. He came down on his forehooves, suddenly tame. But he trembled, kinsman. Oh, how he trembled."

She paused then, as if suddenly lost in thought.

Vidar turned the sleeves of a blue, woolen tunic inside out. "Go on," he told her.

Sif went on.

"G'lann took a step toward the horse, another. The blade gleamed in the scattered sunlight, and the runes on it seemed to move. To writhe. I started to protest, for I had a vague sense that something terrible was happening, was about to happen. But a look from G'lann silenced me. 'Quiet, little sister,' he seemed to say. 'I will not harm him. I only want him to see what he's afraid of.' So I did not stop him. Not even when he lifted the sword level with the horse's eyes."

Vidar tugged on one boot, then the other.

"'Is this what makes you shy away so?' asked G'lann. 'See—it is but a sword. You've seen swords before.' But the trembling only got worse, and that seemed to anger G'lann. 'Stop it,' he said, his own voice trembling slightly —but only slightly. 'Stop it, Hild.'

"But the beast would not—could not stop. Deep in its throat, it whimpered. It was a pitiful sound, one that reached into the hearts of all of us. And into G'lann as well."

Vidar saw her shoulders slump.

"Too late, I saw the flash of emotion that ravaged his face. With a strangled . . . sound . . . he drew the sword back and brought it forward again. Edge first. It was like a dream that moved too quickly. The blade disappeared between the horse's head and his shoulders. For a moment, nothing happened. The beast's eyes were as wide as before, his carriage as rigid. Then his head toppled and blood spurted out, painting the grass at our feet. His legs folded and were buried beneath the sleek, white torso.

"And standing behind Hild, still holding the blade in the deathstroke position, G'lann gazed at his handiwork. His eyes, Vidar . . . his eyes were full of horror."

Then Sif's head dropped again, and she shivered.

"The sword," she breathed, for emotion seemed to have robbed her of her voice. "The damned sword . . ."

Vidar came to her, laid his hand on her shoulder. "Where is he now?" he asked.

Sif covered his hand with her own, drawing strength from it. She turned, looked up at him. Her eyes were red-rimmed. "He said he was going to ride out along the sea road. To think." Her nostrils flared. "He didn't look well when he left."

"It's all right," said Vidar. "I'll find him."

Sif shook her head.

"He said he wanted no company. Not even me. He just wanted to be by himself."

"Nonetheless," said Vidar, "I'll find him."

"He will be dangerous," said Sif.

"I know," said Vidar.

Sif thought for a moment, released his hand, stood. "Then I'll go with you. Try again to talk to him."

"No," said Vidar. "He'll use your love for him against you. Let me face him by myself. I know what must be done."

She seemed to see the wisdom in that. Reluctantly, she nodded.

"And afterward," he told her, "there will be much for us to discuss."

Sif nodded again. But she was so preoccupied by her fear for G'lann, she didn't ask what "much" might be.

This time, the wind was at his back. Sunlight glittered like dragon scales on the water.

It was too bad, this business with the sword. For a couple of reasons.

First, because G'lann had shown such aptitude as a *lifling*. With a little help from Vidar, he'd unlocked Angrum's secrets in only a few weeks—not bad for someone without any prior training. Or, for that matter, with only half a helping of Aesir blood.

Second, because it meant that someone else would have to carry the sword now. And barring Magni, for obvious reasons, Vidar was the only pedigreed Odinson around.

Perhaps he should have seen this coming, laid claim to the sword from the beginning. Or at least insisted that G'lann leave it at home when he struck out for the hinterlands. Far from Vidar's guidance, the blade must have been too much for him. It must have whispered of blood and fury, for those were the reasons that Frey had paid to have it made. It must have cried out in his dreams of the fires in which it had been forged . . .

The cries of the seabirds were faint with distance. They foraged far from shore, wheeling and dipping in long, languorous curves.

A couple of hours must have gone by before he spotted G'lann. Magni's son was headed toward him, returning from wherever it was he'd gone. Even from far off, Vidar could see that he rode one of Magni's white horses, a descendant of the beasts that had been won that day in Jotunheim.

The gap between them closed. And for the first time, Vidar noticed a dark smudge on the horizon. A storm coming, but not for a while yet. It seemed to gather behind the lordling like an army of dark spirits.

Vidar reined in a bit, and they came together. Slowly. G'lann's pale golden hair was wild. His coarse features had settled into wariness.

"Fancy meeting you here," said Vidar.

"Who sent you?" asked G'lann. "My sister?"

"She told me what happened, if that's what you mean."

The elf chuckled. "And now what? You've come to slap my wrist?"

Vidar drew his sword out. He held it up, where G'lann could see it.

"The armorer said that this was one of yours. I thought you might like it better than that monster you've got now."

G'lann's eyes narrowed. "Give it up?" He shook his head from side to side. "I found it, Vidar. It's mine. Alfheim's. Though I confess I wondered when you would try to claim it for yourself."

"That's not you talking, G'lann. It's the sword. It's made a murderer out of you already, and it'll only get worse. Give it to me and free yourself—now, before it takes another life."

"I thought you hated swords," said G'lann.

"I do. But I can't let that thing run loose. I should have asked you for it back there in the mountains, but I didn't. So I'm asking now."

"No," said G'lann. "I've too much invested in this. I risked my life for it—or did you forget?"

Vidar frowned. "Don't you feel it? It's changed you. Sif told me that, G'lann—and who knows you better than she does?"

G'lann spat. "She's but a child. If she could hold it as I've held it, strike with it as I've struck . . . then she'd know."

He dragged the blade free, held it aloft. "Beautiful, isn't it, Vidar?" The runes that ran its length glittered in the sunlight. "And useful." His mouth twisted into a grotesque smile as he dismounted.

"G'lann, it's got hold of you. Who's the master—you? Or *it*?"

"Shall I show you how useful?"

G'lann lowered the point of the blade to the ground. His brow beetled in concentration. He tapped the roadstones once, lightly.

Suddenly, there was a fiery crevice a yard long, extending in Vidar's direction from the point of the blade. The riderless white horse nickered and retreated, and Vidar's would have too, but he forced it to hold to its place.

"I guess you've forgotten the beast you slew," he told G'lann. "But who's next? One of the humans camped there outside Hargard—someone who looks at you funny?"

G'lann didn't look up. He was fascinated by Angrum's power. He tapped again and the road split further, as long now as a man was tall. The flames ate at the edges of the opening.

"Or one of your *lyos*, your advisers, trying to talk some sense into you? Var'kald, perhaps, or H'limif?"

A third tap, and a fourth. The crack lengthened, deepened, approached the place from which Vidar would not move. It opened like a grave before him, making a ripping sound as it came.

"Maybe Sif, G'lann. Will the sword thirst for her next?"

The elf's face was awash with sweat, but he was smiling, and he seemed not to hear. He tapped again, and the crack advanced, blazing. Vidar's' mount took a step backward. It bellowed. It tried to toss its head, but Vidar held it steady.

"Or is it your father it wants? Your treacherous, backstabbing slug of a father?"

G'lann looked up. There was murder in his eyes. He lifted the blade off the ground and leveled it at Vidar. Cords of muscle stood out in his neck.

"Go ahead," said Vidar. "If that's what the *sword* needs to be happy."

He could see the struggle going on behind G'lann's face, past the smoke that rose from the flames. Anger crossed it, then shock, then anger again. He trembled, paralyzed by the forces that fought for control of him.

Then, suddenly, he slumped, fell to one knee, and thrust the sword from him. Angrum clattered on the stones—a hollow sound, as if it were disappointed.

Vidar got down from his horse. He walked around the crevice to where the sword lay, picked it up. He left the ordinary sword on the ground in its place.

G'lann looked up at him. He glared as he took the proffered weapon.

"You're welcome," said Vidar.

G'lann rose, thrusting the plain blade into his sheath.

"But how did you know," he asked, "that I wouldn't kill you?"

Vidar shrugged. "It was a little bit of a gamble."

G'lann considered Frey's sword. There was a sullen greed for it in his eyes, but also disgust. He spat.

"We should have left it where we found it. Or tossed it into the sea. It's evil, kinsman. Evil."

Vidar hefted it. He regarded the intricate runes, the carved hilt. He could feel the power in it, waiting for *him* now.

"Perhaps," said Vidar. "Let's go."

They rode back together, leaving the flaming fissure behind them. Up ahead, the dark edge to the horizon grew mountainous, and the wind, changing direction, brought the scent of lightning.

Before they reached the castle, they could hear the thunder.

IV

NO one in Asgard had hair like Sif's. It was long and thick, a torrent of gold. Thor loved to run his fingers through it, enjoying its glitter like a dark elf sifting his wealth in some underground lair. For hours he could sit, feeling no need to speak, while Sif carefully combed each strand. The way the light struck that hair was fascinating to him; the way it fell about Sif's shoulders was a source of constant amazement.

So you can imagine how he felt when he woke one day to find it all gone. He bolted out of bed, crying out for vengeance, and his cries woke Sif.

"What is it?" she asked him. "Your eyes are bulging out of your head, Thor, as if you'd just seen a giant in our bedroom."

"Your hair!" bellowed Thor. "It's been cut like a field of ripe wheat!"

Panicky, Sif felt her head—and found only tufts of what had once been so plentiful. "Aiee!" she screamed. "Gone! All gone!" She reached for her mirror, held it up to her face, and shrieked again. "How can I go out into Asgard looking like this?" she moaned. "The Aesir will say that my husband did this to me, out of jealousy, so that no one else could look on me with desire!"

"They wouldn't dare!" said Thor, shaking his fists in frustrated anger. "I'll find the one who did this to you—I swear it. And when I do, I'll make him sorry he ever laid eyes on you!"

Attracted by all the commotion, Thor's sons appeared in the doorway. Modi, the elder of the two, rubbed the sleep from his eyes. Magni, the younger, looked white as a ghost —for he'd never seen Thor turn purple with rage before. The Thunderer was not accustomed to venting his anger in his own hall.

Sif ran to the children and embraced them. "Do not be frightened," she said. "Despite what I look like, I'm still the same mother that you've always known. And Thor's still your father, even if you've never seen him quite so angry."

"Why is he angry, Mother?" asked little Magni.

"Because someone stole my hair, child," said Sif. "But don't worry. When Thor discovers who did it, he'll crush his thieving hands."

"And his head!" raged Thor. "And his legs!"

"But who would want your hair, Mother?" asked Modi.

"Someone who hates us," said Sif. "Some maker of mischief."

"And his neck!" roared Thor. "And his ribs!"

And with that, he grabbed his hammer Mjollnir, vowing to tear down all Asgard if he had to—but he would find the one who'd shorn Sif of her locks.

It was still early. The Aesir were only just waking. But Thor knew that they would be on their way to the court at Gladsheim soon, and that they must pass over the river to get there. So he went down to the bridge that girded the river and stood astride it—so that no one could pass without confronting him.

The first one who came to cross the bridge was Hod, his half-brother and the son of Odin.

"Not another step," cried Thor. "And don't try to go

around me. I'm looking for the one who stole Sif's hair, and I'll tear down all of Asgard to find him."

Hod had seen the damage that Mjollnir could do, but he spoke up, unafraid. "What's all that got to do with me?" he asked. His voice was like the wind in a dead man's mouth. "I know nothing of your wife's hair, though it's as splendid as the sunrise on a field of swords. Now let me pass, Thor, or I'll tell all of Gladsheim that you've gone insane."

Thor scowled and bellowed and threatened, but there was nothing more he could get out of Hod. Reluctantly, he let him pass.

The next one who came to cross the bridge was Vali, his half-brother and the son of Odin.

"Not another step," vowed Thor, and the streets on either side of the river echoed with it. "And don't try to go around me. I seek the one who stole Sif's hair, and I'll tear down all of Asgard to find him."

Vali knew the damage that Mjollnir could do, but he spoke up, unafraid. "Why come shaking your hammer at me?" he asked, his eyes as hard and sharp as an eagle's when he sights his prey. "I know nothing of your Sif's hair, though it's as golden as the sunlight on a sea of burnished shields. Now let me pass, brother, or I'll inform all of Gladsheim that you've lost your wits."

Thor raged and cursed and raised his hammer, but there was nothing more he could get out of Vali. In the end, he had no choice but to let him go by.

Then came Baldur—the beloved, the shining—his half-brother and the son of Odin.

"Not another step," shouted Thor. "Not one! And don't try to go around me, either. I'm looking for the thief who took my wife's hair, and I'll tear down all of Asgard to find him."

Baldur was well aware of Mjollnir's capacity for destruction. He'd seen giants fall prey to it more than once. But he spoke up, unafraid.

"Why do you stand here," he asked, "blocking my way?" He smiled, and his smile was as gentle as the warm, summer wind. "I didn't steal your Sif's hair, though it's as bright as the sunset in a nest of clouds. But I saw your son Magni yesterday, with a scissors in his little hands—and he was telling the other children how he'd make a gift to you of his mother's tresses. For—he said—you loved nothing better in all the nine worlds."

"Magni?" asked Thor, slack-jawed.

"Aye," said Baldur. "Magni." And he laughed.

Thor slumped against the side of the bridge, cradling Mjollnir in his mighty arms.

"Younglings," he murmured, shaking his head. "Who can begin to understand them?"

Sin Skolding
Saeverstod, A.D. 522

V

SKIR'NIR returned with the storm at his back. He was tired and wet, but he agreed to speak with Vidar and the others before he took his rest.

They sat at a long darkwood table in Magni's feast-hall, dwarfed by the size of the place. The long windows in the western wall showed a sky that was dark even at midday. A couple of birds trilled in the rafters, disturbed by the hiss of rain on the roof.

Skir'nir had much the same to report as the rest of them. No invaders—no sign of them. And the wounds that the war had opened were beginning to heal. The *lyos* were starting to trust one another again, forgetting their enmities in the face of the threat posed by Ygg.

G'lann began to say something about the incident with the horse, but his brother stopped him. "It's all right," he said. Apparently, he'd heard about it already.

Then it was Vidar's turn to speak. He told them all what he had learned from Magni. They weighed his words.

"What would you have us do?" asked G'lann. "Marshal our armies? Lead them into M'thrund?"

"No," said Vidar. "I'm not willing to march into M'thrund just yet."

"You fear that Ygg—Odin—may be waiting for us?" asked Sif.

"More than that. I fear that he may not be in M'thrund at all. Nor Vali either."

The windows filled suddenly with light. A moment later, thunder rolled, sending the birds into a panic overhead.

"I see," said Skir'nir, smiling a little at the theatrics. "You mistrust our sources. Even as I do."

"Aye," said Vidar. "Hoenir may have been lying to us— even with his dying breath. It seems unlikely, but there's no knowing the depth of his loyalty to Odin. And Magni says that Odin came from M'thrund when he visited him here at Hargard—but Magni's proven himself mad as well as treacherous. And then, of course, there's the possibility that both of them believe what they told us—but were themselves deceived by Odin."

Skir'nir nodded. "And there's no way of knowing for certain."

Vidar leaned forward. "There's one way. I can see for myself."

"Go to M'thrund?" asked Sif. "*Without* an army?"

"Exactly. Then, if it turns out that either Vali or Odin are there, we can return *with* an army."

G'lann rubbed his hands together, slowly. "It will be dangerous," he said. He looked as if he would have liked to go along. But he wouldn't, Vidar knew. Not if it meant getting close to the sword again. "Only Magni remembers the last time the Aesir set foot in M'thrund."

"And he's already told me what he remembers—what the *thrund* are like, how to reach the walled city where their rulers live. Surely, if some new influence had turned up at court—or if an army as large as Vali's has been taken prisoner—there will be some news of it."

Sif frowned. "And whom do you propose to take along on such a mission?"

"No one," said Vidar. Again, the lightning flared. This time, the thunder was like a whip cracking in the sky.

"*We* must stay," she said. "Alfheim needs us, for we are all that holds it together. But Eric will want to go. And no doubt, your other comrades as well."

"There's no need," said Vidar. "I'll be able to move more freely on my own."

A smile pulled at the corner of Skir'nir's mouth. "You are strange, Vidar, for an Aesirman. Your kinsmen have always loved to surround themselves with retainers. You refuse them at every turn." His voice grew just a bit softer. "You cannot carry the nine worlds on your shoulders, my lord. Sometimes even you may need help—or did you forget the condition you were in when we met?"

Vidar shook his head. "I haven't forgotten. It's just that I've got too many damned ghosts. I don't need to see anyone else cut down for my sake."

The elf shrugged. "As you wish," he said. "Though you are not the only one troubled by ghosts."

"When," asked Sif, "do you intend to ride?"

Vidar glanced at the windows. "As soon as this storm dies down." He turned to Skir'nir. "I wouldn't want to catch my death of cold."

The elf nodded. "How practical of you." He stood, pushing his chair back. "And now, if you don't mind, I'd like to get out of these wet clothes myself." He paused. "I'll see you before you go, won't I?"

"Aye," said Vidar. "You'll see me. But there's one more thing we should talk about."

"What's that?" asked G'lann.

Vidar met his gaze. "Your father."

G'lann's eyes grew hard, angry. Sif turned away. Skir'nir laughed softly.

"He turned us against one another," said G'lann. "Turned us into murderers of our own kind."

"Would you have us forgive him now?" asked Skir'nir. "After all that?"

"No," said Vidar. "Not forgive him. Just see him, as I did. See what's become of him. Then you can do as you like."

G'lann scowled. "I do as I like now." And having said that, he left the hall.

Lightning seared the sky. Skir'nir turned, drawn by it. The sound that came after made the stones shiver.

He looked at Vidar. "Sorry," he said. He frowned. "Perhaps in time. But not now."

The cries of the frightened birds echoed about them.

On his way out, he stopped by his sister. Put his hands on her shoulders.

"Coming?" he asked.

"Not yet," she said.

The elf nodded, left her alone with Vidar in Magni's feasting place.

When he was gone, Sif heaved a sign. "If it were Odin sitting up there, would you go to him? Let him worm his way back into your confidence?"

Vidar pondered that for a moment. "I don't know."

Sif looked at him, listened to the storm.

"For your sake," she said finally. "I'll see him."

They came to him while the storm was in its fullest fury. Perhaps he might have expected it.

"Sif told you," he said.

Eric shrugged. N'arri might have said something, if he hadn't lost his tongue to Odin's tortures. Finally, it was Ullir who answered for all of them.

"Could we have let you go alone?"

"Aye," said Vidar. "Could have—and will."

"But why?" asked Eric. "One would think by now that we'd have proven something to you." The boy looked older by the day—but then, he'd seen a long lifetime's worth since he'd left his father's kingdom in Utgard.

"Proven?" asked Vidar. He tried to muster up some anger, but to no avail. "Proven what? That you're mortal? Did you forget how close you came to death after we stole that ship in Ilior?"

"But I didn't die—did I?" Eric wasn't giving an inch.

Vidar scowled. He turned to N'arri. "And you! Don't you ever learn? If you hadn't followed me into Indilthrar, you'd still have your tongue."

N'arri looked amused. His dark elf eyes were fierce, defiant—as mocking as those of any elf bred in Alfheim.

"He pledged his sword to you," said Eric. "And you accepted it."

It was no more than the truth. Stymied there, Vidar looked to Ullir. "You, at least, should know better. You've got a family, Ullir. I can't let you reave your wife of her husband—or your children of their father."

"What kind of father would I be," asked the Aesirman, "if I turned away from the best chance to defend my home?" His eyes narrowed in imitation of Vidar. "Or did you think that we were doing this just for you?"

Vidar shook his head. "No. I won't allow it. What good would it do for all of us to get caught?"

"Perhaps we won't get caught at all," said Eric, "if we watch each other's back."

"Four heads are better than one," added Ullir. "Or don't they have sayings like that back in Midgard?"

Vidar sighed out of frustration. "You're all pretty cock-sure of yourselves, aren't you? But this is no game. It's Odin we're dealing with—and he may have his back to the wall this time."

"We know that," said Eric. "We've known all along."

"Nor are we the only ones who would like to have come

along," said Ullir. "N'arri had his hands full dissuading all the other *dwarvin* who followed you out of Utgard."

Vidar grunted. "Really? Then why is it I can't dissuade you three?"

N'arri hooked his thumbs into his belt and spread his feet a littler wider.

"Face it, my lord," said Ullir. "You're stuck with us."

Vidar regarded them. Finally, he nodded. "Perhaps I am at that. Truth be told, I guess I'm glad for the company."

He looked at N'arri. "But you'll have a hard time passing for a native in M'thrund—unless we make some changes."

The elf's brows knit.

And despite what lay ahead of them, Vidar couldn't help but laugh.

The storm broke sometime that night. In the morning, they took the sea road east toward Dindamoron, beneath a sky full of golden tatters. Here, the drop to the sea was gentler and the road led them inland a bit.

"I hope that Magni told us the truth," said Eric after a while. "About the *thrund*, I mean." He glanced back at N'arri, who'd been scowling ever since they bleached his hair and brows. Accustomed to the caverns of Utgard, the dark elf wore a hood to shade his eyes—bit it hid neither his hair nor his displeasure. "It would be a pity," Eric continued, "if N'arri's sacrifice were all for nothing."

"We heard that," said Ullir from behind. "You'd frown too if you'd woken up and seen a *lyos*'s face in your bathing water."

It was true. But for their coloring, the *lyos* and the *dwarvin* were indistinguishable. And with his hair lightened, N'arri could easily have passed for an elf of Alfheim.

"What's so terrible about the way the *lyos* look?" asked Eric. "Isn't Sif as fair as they come?"

Ullir chuckled. "It's the Aesir in her, lad."

N'arri spurred his horse and came up on Vidar's other flank. With his free hand, he pulled at the garb they'd fitted him with at Hargard. Then he wrinkled his face in disgust.

"N'arri doesn't seem to care much for the wardrobe either," observed Vidar.

"He's not happy without those mournful, dark weeds of his," said Eric. "And the *dwarvin* don't normally wear so much jewelry."

"Aye," said Vidar. "But the *thrund* do—at least, as Magni remembers them."

N'arri made a gesture of disgust. As the road narrowed, he fell back again alongside Ullir.

"Don't let them mock you," called Ullir, so that they could all hear. "Seems to me I heard a story about someone dressing up like a courtesan back at Indilthrar."

Vidar turned toward Eric accusingly. The boy held his hand up, an expression of exaggerated innocence on his face.

But when Vidar swiveled to get a look at N'arri, the elf's grin gave him away. He tried to picture N'arri telling a tale like that one without a tongue.

"If you think N'arri's bleach job is the worst of it," said Vidar, "you're mistaken."

That got everyone's attention.

"What do you mean?" asked Eric, cocking an eyebrow.

Vidar laughed, and patted the pouch at his belt.

"I mean," he said, "that we're all about to get that much-sought-after Coppertone tan."

"Coppertone?" asked Ullir. "Tan?"

"Aye," said Vidar. "It seems the *thrund* have a ruddy kind of skin. So the *lyos* mixed me up some berry juice—to use as a dye. They tell me that Vali's spies used it, back when he went after M'thrund. And they say that the stuff won't come off, either. Not for a good, long time." ·

There was some grumbling at that, and a couple of mock protests.

"Of course," said Vidar, "you could stay as you are—and hope that the *thrund* have forgotten the Aesir invaders."

Quickly, the grumbling stopped.

"Just make sure," said Ullir, "that there is enough to go around."

They rode all the rest of that day, taking their meals on horseback. As the sun lowered behind them, casting their shadows out ahead like beasts in flight, they came in sight of the plateau. It jutted out into the sea, a sweep of land some fifty feet lower than the highway.

"This must be it," said Vidar, and the others followed him as he turned off the road. The way down was thick with weeds, but wide enough for them to descend two abreast. And when they reached the table of land itself, they found large patches of exposed rock where they could dismount, sure of the footing.

Vidar surveyed the place in the ruddy light. It was large enough to have served as a staging ground for Vali's invasions—yet easy enough to defend. If the *thrund* had chosen to strike back at Vali, they would have had to survive a hail of arrows from above—and then fight their way up from the plateau. All in all, no simple task. And this was the only gate they might have used, the only one Vali opened in his lust for conquest.

But that had been long ago. The gate lay unguarded now, sealed up—or so Magni had said—on the M'thrund side. Nor was there any reason for the elves to fear an attack here, as long as Vali left the *thrund* alone.

Vidar scanned the side of the cliff. It was overgrown, thick with a lush covering of broad-leafed creepers. Somewhere in that confusion of greenery lay the way between worlds.

"What now?" asked Ullir. He stretched, raising his arms up and out. "Try to find the gate before it gets dark altogether? Or wait until morning?"

"I'm for morning," said Eric. He glanced at Vidar, then shrugged. "But of course, it's up to you."

N'arri was moving along the cliff face, probing here and there among the creepers. He alone could work in the dark as easily as in the light, having been bred underground.

Vidar frowned. He was eager to discover what had happened to Vali—and to Modi. To get them out of M'thrund, if there was anything left of them to get out. To find Odin, perhaps, as well.

But if he had waited this long, he could wait overnight. There was no telling what they'd run into on the other side of the gate, and some sleep couldn't hurt their cause.

"Morning then," he said. "But we start looking for the gate at first light."

N'arri whistled. When he'd gotten their attention, he put his arms out and fell backward. The wall of leaves devoured him without a trace.

A moment later, he emerged, grinning and brushing leaves off his tunic. Vidar chuckled. "Looks like our friend N'arri has already found it."

Vidar woke with a start. His pulse was pounding hard in his neck. He was sweating. He could feel it evaporating from his skin in the breeze off the sea.

The waves surged against the rock, boiled, and retreated. Surged, boiled, and retreated.

A nightmare?

He didn't think so.

Then what?

He had a sudden urge to get up, to walk. He stood, rearranging his cloak so that it draped over his shoulders, and waded through the tall weeds to the edge of the cliff.

For a time, he just stood there, breathing, bathing in the cleansing breeze. The sea was black and infinite, except where it churned white at the base of the rocks. He lost himself in it.

"Vidar?"

He turned and saw Eric. In his reverie, he'd failed to hear the boy approach.

"Is something wrong?"

Vidar shrugged.

"I woke," said Eric, "and saw you standing here. I thought perhaps you'd seen someone, the way you're holding that sword . . ."

Vidar looked down, saw Angrum in his hand. Turned it over so that it caught the light of moon and stars.

When had he taken it out?

Deliberately, he slid it back into its sheath.

"Don't say it," Vidar told him. "I'll have to be more careful—I know."

Eric frowned, nodded.

The wind rose, flattening the weeds. It was chill on his skin.

"Come on," said Odin's son. "Or we'll miss our beauty sleep."

"Aye," said Eric. He smiled a little at that. But he still looked uneasy as they turned their backs on the sea.

VI

AS each of them parted the curtain of creepers to enter the gate, it lit the way for the others up ahead. But once N'arri had passed inside, bringing up the rear, the blackness swallowed them for good. Since a torch wouldn't have helped for very long, no one lit one.

Vidar led the way, having had the most experience with such places. The ground before him sloped downward a bit. His gelding nickered and held back, but he pulled it forward by its reins. It wasn't the lack of light alone that daunted the beast, he knew—it was the first faint hum of the Ginnunga-gap. There was no mistaking it, no other sound quite like it.

A few steps more and he could no longer feel the stone walls on either side of him. For that matter, he couldn't feel anything—only the resistance of his frightened horse, though its whinnies had begun to dissolve into the hum.

It was difficult to say at which point he left the unyielding rock of Alfheim behind and entered the space between worlds. He put one foot before the other and trusted that he was moving forward.

Perhaps the worst part was the feeling that there was nothing below to hold him up. That he was falling—would perhaps fall forever.

Vidar had never pretended to understand the workings of the gates, nor how Odin had constructed them. He only knew that in order to go from world to world, one had to pass through the Gap. And that at one time, there'd been nothing *but* the Gap.

Then there had been Asaheim, and Odin, and his brothers Hoenir and Lodur. They wrested Order from the Chaos, linking the nine worlds—only the last of them, Utgard, being the work of Odin's hand.

Now the All-Father wanted to return his nine worlds—and presumably all the others that had been discovered since—to the abyss that had spawned them. Then all would be as it was for Vidar at this moment. Soundless, lightless, nothing that could be touched or felt. The end of things.

It made him cold to even think about it. The Ginnungagap seemed to yawn before him, opening jaws a league wide—no, as wide as the cosmos itself.

He walked on, or at least made the motion of walking. The hum was loud in his ears now, frenetic. He seemed to drift, weightless, as if in deep water. And still he walked, knowing that his feelings could only serve to confuse him here.

Then there was a ragged edge of brightness. Vidar drew his blade. If Odin were here, he'd have no reason to believe that they'd discovered his hiding place—but he was still Odin. He would have protected himself against any and all possibilities. That meant guards on the M'thrund side of the gate. Perhaps just outside the opening.

The hum began to die. A moment later, the ground came

up under Vidar's feet, solid and reassuring. His breath froze white and dissipated on a whisper of wintry air.

Vidar's eyes adjusted to the brightness. Soon he could make out the size and shape of the opening. As he had suspected, it was big enough for only one man. The gate itself was larger, but it had been stuffed up with rocks and timbers and what looked like mortar.

"Doesn't look big enough to fit a horse through." It was Ullir's voice—a whisper just behind him.

"No," said Vidar. "It doesn't."

He led his gelding toward the opening, shading his eyes against the still-too-white light. His sword streamed with it. The horse snorted.

"Here," said Ullir. "Let me take him." He wrested the gelding's reins from Vidar's grasp, allowing him to creep even closer to the aperture. Vidar quieted the blood in his veins, even as Frigga had taught him long ago. He listened carefully, but he heard no sounds from outside. And only Heimdall had boasted a more acute sense of hearing.

Then he raised his head—just enough to peer out.

"Well?" asked Ullir. "Is there anyone out there?"

Vidar stared at the body spread-eagled in the snow, not a man's length from the opening. It was dressed all in black, but for a silver byrnie.

"Aye," he told the Aesirman. "But he's not likely to give us any trouble."

"What do you mean?"

"He's dead." Vidar noted the blood frozen on the *thrund*'s chin. It had turned the snow a rusty red where it must have pooled beside him.

"What's going on?" hissed Eric, for now he'd emerged from the Gap as well.

Ullir explained as N'arri came out on Eric's heels.

Vidar signaled for silence. Again he listened.

Ah—there *was* something after all. A breathing. But ever so shallow.

"Stay here," he told the others. And with that, he slithered through the aperture.

The gate, he found, was set into a sheer rock face that rose steeply into a dense, blue sky. Up top was a convenient perch for anyone who might have wished to keep watch.

Staying close to the gate and what little protection the debris around it afforded him, he took a closer look at the corpse. From this angle, he could see that there was a ragged wound below the *thrund*'s armpit. So he had not just fallen —there'd been violence.

For a moment, he gazed at the upturned face—the copper-colored skin, the angular features. Almost like the Hollywood version of the Noble Red Man, except for the fairness of his hair and the blue of his dead, staring eyes.

Much as Magni had described them.

He looked up again. This time he heard more than breathing. He heard a moan.

Vidar surveyed the wall. About fifty feet to his right, there was a crevice of sorts, half jammed with snow and ice. It seemed to be the only way up.

He took it. There were handholds in the rock, footholds in the ice. And when these were too slippery to be trusted, he dug his blade in and pulled himself up after it.

He was no mountain goat. But in his youth, he'd negotiated the crags of Jotunheim more than once. After a time, he looked out over the top of a great, gray ledge—one that rose gradually into yet higher ground.

And there he saw the corpse's companions. Black and silver, as he had been. Grotesque, bloody, frozen in odd postures. Some of them heaped together like pieces of a puzzle that did not quite fit. There was a little wind up here. It ruffled their hair, seeming to mourn for them.

Was that all he'd heard? The wind?

Then he saw her. She lay apart from the others, near the cliff's edge. She still clutched a sword whose blade had snapped off near the hilt.

Vidar looked around—at the white slopes that led up to black forest, at the river valley that opened up not far from the gate. But there was no sign of those who'd surprised these *thrund*.

He approached the female carefully, lest she find the strength to lash out at him—thinking one of her enemies had returned. But as he got closer, he saw that she was in no shape for that. He knelt beside her, laying down his sword, and inspected her wounds.

Nasty. He grimaced when he saw the holes gouged in her shoulder and thigh. And again at the place where a sword had probed between her ribs.

Her lips were wet with blood. As she labored to breathe, the blood bubbled. She was alive—but only barely.

When he touched her, she shuddered. Her eyes came open. Then, seeing what she might have believed to be a friend, she let them close again.

"Demons . . ." she whispered. The word rattled softly, dangerously in her throat. But it had been clear enough.

"Quiet," said Vidar. He explored her wounds with more than his fingers. Then he split the pain with her, as only a *lifling* could. He shared the white-hot agony of her torn flesh. He drew the ruin into his own body, where it would be felt only over the long course of time. And in return, he gave her some of his own strength.

Finally, having helped her all he could, he wrapped her tightly in her fur cloak. He picked up his sword, stood, sheathed it. Then he pulled a cloak off one of the corpses and wrapped that around her as well.

Weary, he smiled a little. He was pleased with his work. With her features in repose, the *thrund* was pleasant to look upon. It was a strong face, but a fair one.

A scrabbling sound roused him. He whirled and had Angrum out before he realized who'd made it.

N'arri froze halfway out of the crevice, his eyes on the blade. Then he raised his gaze to meet Vidar's.

Odin's son frowned, replaced Angrum in its sheath. "I thought I told you to stay in the cave," he said.

The elf shrugged, climbed the rest of the way up. He surveyed the *thrund,* grimacing.

"Dead," said Vidar. He indicated the female with a tilt of his head. "Except for this one."

N'arri approached her. A couple of feet away, he stopped, as if in awe of the healing power he'd seen save the lives of others. He sank onto his haunches.

The *thrund*'s breath rose like smoke on the air.

"What are we going to do with her?" Vidar asked the question for him.

N'arri turned, nodded.

Vidar rubbed his hands together against the cold. "We can't leave her up here. There will be animals." He glanced warily at the distant treeline. "Not to mention whoever it was that brought her to this state."

The elf grunted in assent.

"You should have stayed in the cave," said Vidar. "Now you're going to have to help me carry her down."

The descent was slow and treacherous, but they got her down safely. Neither Ullir nor Eric questioned the necessity of taking her along. There was simply no other choice.

It took less time to work loose some of the stones that had been used to block up the gate. Soon they'd made a hole big enough for the horses to slip through.

"There is a river valley," said Vidar. He pointed. "Just beyond this ridge. And it leads east—in the direction of Erithain, if I remember Magni's directions at all."

Ullir confirmed it. "Aye. Vali followed a river on *his* way to Erithain. Or so the stories say."

They spurred their mounts up the white-rimmed slope. Vidar clutched the *thrund* to him with one hand, cradling her as best he could. The gelding complained a little, but did as he was directed.

At the top of the ridge, they saw the valley—blinding white with snow, although there were shadows born of gray clouds moving in from the north. A black stitch of river wound its way eastward among the hills, and the land was relatively flat and treeless on either bank.

They came down the other side of the ridge, throwing powder from their hooves. As they reached the river and turned to follow it, the blinding sun was half consumed by the nimbus.

In time, as the sky clouded over, the day grew even colder, and a forest reached down to them on their left. Then the flood widened and there was forest on both sides, leaving only a silty bank for them to travel. The water moved more slowly now, frozen where it pooled among the rocks, reflecting the green depths of the close-growing fir trees.

"These must be the woods," Ullir said after a while, "where Vali's defeat had its beginnings. The *thrund* hid among the trees and cut down the Aesir as they went by."

"There's a comforting thought," said Vidar. He gazed into the dark spaces between the trees, but all he could see was the occasional bird taking flight.

It was late in the afternoon, after the sky had become a dead mass of gray, when the *thrund* began to moan. It was not a good sign.

"Demons," she cried out suddenly, then mumbled something else. "*Jalk!*"—a second cry.

Vidar wrapped the reins about his saddle bow and touched her forehead. It was hot. She was delirious.

"We'll rest," he said abruptly. He waited for Ullir to dismount before he handed her down to him. And before Vidar himself could swing out of the saddle, the blondbeard had set to work on her.

Vidar's first impulse was to protest. He'd begun the healing—and the *lifling* in him wanted to continue it. But Ullir had also been trained in the *lifling* art, and his reserves of vitality were fresher.

As Ullir worked, the others came over to watch. Only once more did she complain of demons. Then she lay silent as the Aesirman's ministrations took effect.

Eric frowned. "Demons? What does she mean by that, I wonder?"

N'arri grunted. He stuck a thumb in his chest.

"You?" asked Eric. He chuckled. "How could that be? She hasn't even seen you yet."

N'arri held his arm up and turned his palm down, parallel to the ground. He looked up at it meaningfully.

"Giants," said Vidar, beginning to understand. He saw the

puzzle piece fall into place. "Of course. Vali's thursar. And his dark elves. The *thrund* might think of them as demons, never having seen their like before."

N'arri looked from his upraised hand to the *thrund* and back again. Then, with his other hand, he made a cutting motion, flinching a little as he did so.

Eric frowned. "Vali's troops made those corpses?"

Ullir brushed a wisp of pale hair from the female's face. Her lips moved without sound.

"That would mean," said the boy, "that they're loose. Or at least some of them are."

N'arri nodded.

"But if they'd gone to all that trouble to cut down its guardians, why not use the gate to escape—to return to Alfheim?"

Vidar shrugged. "It may be that they just failed to recognize it. Or recognizing it, went to tell Vali of it."

Eric's frown deepened. "Perhaps. But wouldn't Vali himself have known where to look for the gate—and headed straight for it?"

"Only," said Vidar, "if he was in familiar territory. He never got a chance to see much of M'thrund, apparently—much to his chagrin."

There was another possibility, of course. Vali could have been slain somewhere along the line. But Vidar didn't mention that one.

Nor was there any point in speculating further—not until they had more to go on.

By the time Ullir cooled the fever, it had begun to snow.

The twilight came early, and with it an angry wind. It drove the snow into their faces until Vidar's beard was stiff with it. Dervishes danced out across the dark expanse of the river, and ghosts seemed to writhe in the hollows between the trees.

They had to go slowly now, for the snow covered the ice that had crusted in the shallows and it was harder than ever to tell what was solid land. As the night deepened, the storm became dreamlike for all its ferocity. The intricate patterns of whirling snow seemed to repeat themselves until the effect became almost hypnotic.

N'arri, who saw best in darkness, led them into the embrace of the woods. They found a place where the boughs sheltered them from the worst of the elements, and tied the horses to the branches of a sturdy pine. They dared not light a fire here among the trees, but they huddled close together and thanked the *lyos* for the thickness of their cloaks.

Vidar and Ullir kept the female between them, lending her their warmth. For a time, Vidar watched her, as the others succumbed to their fatigue. Mostly, she slept soundly. When a word escaped her, it was no longer *demon*, but *jalk*. Only *jalk*.

Whatever that was.

He fell asleep wondering.

The sound of moaning roused him. It was louder than the storm that raged outside their sheltered clearing.

He turned inside his cloak, saw the *thrund*. This time he didn't have to feel her forehead to know how sick she was. The fever had come back stronger than before, and she was writhing under the lash of it.

Ullir woke a moment later.

"Damn," he said. "She's burning up."

"I know," said Vidar, crawling out of his cloak. He knelt by the female's side. Laid his hands on her shuddering form to begin the pain splitting.

But nothing happened. It was as if something was holding him back. As if some niggling thing inside him was hoarding his energy for itself.

He fought it. He struggled to exchange his untainted life force for the fever. Sweat poured down the sides of his face.

The *thrund* shook and groaned in her fever dream.

"What's wrong?" asked Ullir.

"I . . . I don't know," Vidar stammered. "It's not working."

Ullir's brow knotted.

"Here," he said. "Let me try." And he placed his own hands next to Vidar's.

It wasn't easy for Ullir either. He'd imparted some of his energy to the *thrund* only that afternoon. And his blood wasn't pure Aesir to begin with.

But in time, the moaning subsided. Ullir blushed as he absorbed the fever. And the *thrund* lay still again.

"Is she all right?" asked Eric. Vidar turned and saw that N'arri was awake also, his eyes wide and catlike in the dark.

"Aye," said Ullir. "I think so."

Vidar stared at his hands. The power had never failed him since he'd found it as a boy.

Why now?

Unless . . .

He laid his hand upon the hilt, felt the runes carved there. They were warmer than they had a right to be.

With a sudden loathing, he took his hand away.

VII

IN the days when the Aesir still walked the earth, there was a chieftain called Aun, who made his living raiding the lands across the sea. It is said that Aun would set out in early spring and never return until midsummer, when his ship was so full of plunder that it would have sunk under the weight of one more ring.

But one year, the weather blew inland, and Aun could not get his vessel out to sea. Even with all his men at the oars, the headwinds were too strong. And this went on for not one day, but twenty.

Aun didn't know what to do. The raiding season was slipping away. So he asked his councillors what course of action was best.

"You have angered Odin somehow," said his councillors. "He must have a sacrifice, or you'll never leave home again."

"A sacrifice?" echoed Aun. "What kind of sacrifice?"

"One of your men," they said, "must ride Odin's tree."

"You mean," asked Aun, "that I must sacrifice one of my stalwarts? Hang him by the neck and pierce him with a spear?"

"Either that," said his councillors, "or stay home all year."

Aun called for the sacrifice.

Stones were placed in an iron helm. But when all of them had been removed, Aun himself was left holding the black stone.

He looked about at the faces of his men. They were relieved, of course, not to have been chosen for the sacrifice. But they were also reluctant to hang him, for he had been a good leader, and one who'd brought them home safely time and again.

"It's all right," said Aun, seeing how confused they looked. "You need not hang me in truth. All that's required is the spirit of the sacrifice."

So a mock hanging was staged. Aun stood on a tree stump as if he were to be sacrificed after all. But in order not to tempt fate—and the impatience of his men—he took some precautions. A calf's intestines were looped first around his neck, in place of a rope, and then around the branch of a young tree.

For an hour or so, he stood there. But the wind did not change direction. If anything, it grew stronger as it swept inland.

"So much for sacrifices," said Aun, frowning at his councillors. And removing the intestines from his neck, he went back into his hall.

As it happened, one of Odin's sons was trekking up the seacoast that very spring. His name was Tyr, known to his kinsmen as Stalker. As was his habit, he assumed the guise of a warrior whose sword was for hire. And when he heard of Aun's ploy, he came to visit him in his hall.

"What troubles you, my lord?" asked Tyr.

Aun shook his head sadly. "I can see that you are a wise man, and well traveled, for something troubles me indeed. But I doubt that even you can help me. The winds of the sea keep me imprisoned, and the only way I may free myself is by sacrificing a man to Odin. But when I agreed to this and we drew lots, it fell to me to be hanged."

"Obviously," said Tyr, "you did not hang yourself—or you would not be here now to speak of it."

"No," said Aun. "I did not. But I staged a mock hanging —for the spirit of the sacrifice is the important thing."

"Is that true?" asked Tyr.

"So I have heard. Yet when I wrapped a calf's intestines around my neck—so as not to tempt my men—it did no good. Odin was still unappeased and the winds still blew against me."

"I think I have the answer," said Tyr. "Perhaps, as you say, the spirit of the sacrifice is all that's needed. But you must at least use a real rope—and a tree of some consequence. Anything less is an insult to Odin."

Aun looked doubtful. "Are you sure," he asked, "that my men will not take it too seriously? They itch to ride the seas again, you know, and with that rope around my neck . . ."

"Don't worry," said Tyr. "I'm a good friend to have when you're surrounded by enemies. If one of your men even thinks of pushing you off that stump, he will be sorry."

Aun smiled. "You are a good man," he said.

"But I will need a spear," said Tyr.

"A spear?" asked Aun. "Why?"

"I prefer it to a sword," said Tyr, "when I have to keep a crowd away."

"Ah," said Aun. "Of course."

The next day Aun stepped up onto the stump. This time he placed a real rope about his neck. And as he'd feared, his men looked as if they would have liked to tighten it.

"Remember what you said," he told his visitor. "That you would not let them hang me."

Tyr smiled. "Them, no. But I said nothing about me."

Odin's son pushed Aun off the stump then, so that he dangled in the air, clutching at the noose. A moment later he drove his spear through the chieftain's ribs.

"You see?" asked Tyr, turning to Aun's men. "That is how it's done. Now let's have no more nonsense with calf's intestines."

And as luck would have it, the weather turned around the very same day.

Sin Skolding
Rogaland, 337 A.D.

VIII

BY dawn the elements had grown calm. The sky was piled high with clouds, but there was no wind to move them. The shriek of a bird seemed far away, alien in the pristine stillness. Like something heard in one's dreams.

The horses waded through the drifts left by the storm and hugged the edge of the forest, staying away from the uncertain banks of the river as much as possible.

The *thrund* still slept—a proof of Ullir's success the night before. Again, she rode with Vidar, her head resting against his shoulder. Her breathing was even, he noted, and she didn't moan even once.

As the morning wore on, the clouds grew fewer and farther between, revealing great patches of blue sky. By midday, when they stopped to rest the horses and to eat, the sun had become warm enough to melt the snow off the branches.

It was while they chewed their journey bread that the *thrund* came awake. She put out an arm, planted her elbow, and lifted herself onto it. Then she looked around—at the river, at the woods, and at each of her companions. Slowly, she sat up, moving over a bit so that she might rest her back against a tree.

"Welcome to the land of the living," said Ullir.

"Who . . . who are you?" she asked. Her voice was strong for one who'd so recently been close to death.

"Friends," said Vidar.

"Aye," said Eric. "We found you a couple of days west of here."

She tried to say something else, but her throat was parched. She began to cough.

N'arri, who was the closest, offered her some water—though he was careful not to let her get too good a look inside his hood. When she had had her fill and returned the skin to him, he got up and pretended to care for the horses.

She peered at the rest of them as she wiped her mouth with the back of her hand. There was no fear in her eyes—only confusion.

"Where are . . . the others?" she asked.

Vidar met her gaze. The look in them, and the set of her jaw, demanded the truth. No matter how bitter.

"Dead," he told her. "You were the only one alive when we found you."

The *thrund* swallowed. She licked her lips.

"Damn," she said. "Damn them all."

"Who?" asked Vidar.

"The demons." She shook her head, remembering.

"What's your name?" asked Vidar.

She blinked. "Tofa. I am . . . one of Jalk's soldiers."

Ah. So Jalk was a *who*—some kind of military leader. And one of some importance, for her to have cried out to him in her sleep.

Tofa glanced at Eric, looked longingly at his half-eaten graincake.

He smiled when he saw that. "Care for some?" he asked.

She nodded.

He came over, gave her what he had left. She wolfed it down in a matter of moments—another sign that Ullir's work had had the desired effect. The food seemed to make her even stronger.

Wiping her mouth, she asked, "Did you see them? The demons?"

Vidar said that they hadn't.

She grunted at that. "Nor did we."

"Not at all?" asked Eric.

"A glimpse, perhaps—but no more than that." She paused, seeming to gather her strength. "They struck too fast . . . as they always do." Another pause. "That's why no one can say what they look like."

Ullir cast a sidelong glance at Vidar.

Interesting indeed. If Vali's warriors were the demons, and the demons had never been seen . . .

Then none of Vali's forces were in captivity.

Ergo, there had been no trap.

Or had M'thrund *itself* been the trap?

It would have served better than a prison—weakening both Vali and the *thrund*, yet taxing none of Odin's resources. And leaving him free to spin his webs elsewhere.

Aye. It was a possibility.

Tofa, meanwhile, was nibbling on her lower lip. "Jalk must be told of what happened to us. You must take me to him."

Vidar didn't want to let on that he'd never heard of Jalk before, or that he had no idea where to find him. Especially since Tofa seemed to assume that he would.

"We're headed for Erithain," he told her, hoping that it would be answer enough.

"Good," was all she said.

This time, when they mounted the horses, Tofa rode behind Vidar. She refused, she said, to be carried like a baby anymore. And to her credit, she hung on to him better than Vidar had expected.

For a time she was silent. Then she asked his name.

"Vidar," he said, unable to think of a reason to lie about it.

"Vidar," she repeated. "A strange name, but a good one. Strong." She paused, perhaps watching the dark currents of the river. "I am grateful, Vidar. But for your help, I might have died on that ledge."

Not *might have*, he told himself. *Would have*. But he preferred to let her believe her wounds hadn't been that serious. Or else, how would he explain the speed with which they'd healed?

"It was nothing," he said.

"Nonetheless," she told him, "you have my gratitude. I will not forget."

Birds tittered, off in the forest.

"Your friend," she said, "with the hood. Why does he wear it on such a pleasant day?"

"It's not the cold," said Vidar. He glanced at the back of the elf's head. "It's his eyes. They can't stand the sunshine."

"Too bad," said Tofa.

"He doesn't talk, either." Vidar remarked on it before she could. "An accident of birth."

His charge made a clucking sound with her tongue. "Twice afflicted, then. Yet he seems cheerful enough."

"He's that way," said Vidar.

Not long after, the wind picked up again, and the weather grew colder. The sky covered over with a gray haze, so that the sun could only be seen as a vague, pale disk.

Ullir had been riding with Eric and N'arri up ahead. But now he dropped back until he was even with Vidar.

"How do you feel?" he asked Tofa, smiling in his beard.

"Well enough," she said, though Vidar could tell by the sound of her voice that her strength was ebbing.

"Perhaps we'll stop soon," said Vidar.

"Aye," said Ullir. "Perhaps we will."

Suddenly his smile faded.

"Did you hear something?" he asked.

Vidar listened. There were sounds all right—coming from the woods. The sound of branches snapping. Something was making its way through the forest. And quickly.

The sounds were getting louder. And the ground, Vidar thought, was beginning to shudder.

His horse whinnied and wheeled, and he had to tighten his grip on the reins to keep it steady.

Then they saw it—something big. Very big. A flash of white among the trees.

And it seemed to be headed in their direction.

"*Tarsas!*" cried Tofa.

In that moment, the thing came crashing through the undergrowth, churning up the snow.

It had tiny, red eyes and massive shoulders—a white, shaggy behemoth taller than an elk. For a moment it stopped, confused, slashing at the air with cruel, curved horns.

Then it fixed its gaze on the nearest thing to it—Vidar. And it charged.

He dared not meet it. Not with Tofa behind him. Bringing his steed around suddenly, he dug his heels into its flanks. It reared, bolted.

But the beast already had a head of steam up, and it would have skewered them on those horns—if not for Ullir. Somehow, the Aesirman managed to distract it.

The beast took off after him instead—forcing him in the direction of Eric and N'arri. It bellowed its rage, screamed its bloodlust.

The elf drove his horse into the shallows to avoid the thing while Eric rode his into the forest. And in a contest of sheer speed, the monster was no match for Ullir's roan.

Frustrated, it stopped, whirled. Snow flew in all directions. Again it bellowed, and the brittle air of the valley rang with it.

Vidar let Tofa down.

"What are you doing?" she asked. "That's a *tarsas*. A mad *tarsas*. And you have no bow—no spear."

"Trust me," he said.

And as he spurred his gelding forward, he drew Frey's sword.

Tofa was right, he told himself, about the thing being mad. It wasn't about to leave them alone. And while the others might have outrun it, he couldn't—not with Tofa's extra weight.

As he came for it, it drew a bead on him. Its powerful shoulders lowered, drove it forward. In moments it was pounding toward him at full speed.

Someone yelled from off to his right, he thought. Eric perhaps. But he didn't stop to look around. He kept to his collision course.

Then, just as the beast brought its horns up to gore them, Vidar pulled the gelding off to the left—and, leaning out of his saddle, brought Angrum down with all his strength.

The sword cut deep and was torn out of his grasp. Blood spurted, turning the snow a bright red all around them.

Vidar had dealt the animal a mortal stroke. But it didn't know it yet. It kept on going, veering off toward the woods. Finally, it crashed headlong into a tree, shaking the snow loose from its branches. It recoiled from the impact, fell in a heap.

Vidar approached it warily. Its legs were still moving, he saw. But where the sword protruded from the ruin of its skull, its blood was making a steaming pool in the snow.

Then its heart gave out, and its legs did too.

"Damn," said Eric, riding up beside Vidar.

N'arri and Ullir joined them a moment later. The elf whistled as Vidar and the boy dismounted.

"Ugliest thing I ever saw," said Ullir.

Vidar had to agree. The beast had a snout that would have made a warthog sick for jealousy.

As he tugged his blade free from the ruin of the thing's skull, he thought he felt a thrilling in the blade. But no—it was his imagination.

"Look at this," said Eric, kneeling in the snow. He touched his fingers to the creature's hide just behind the shoulder. Then he held them up where the others could see them.

"Blood," said Vidar. "And not from the wound I gave it?"

"No," said Eric. "It was wounded already. Perhaps that's what made it so mad." He probed again. "I think there's a shaft in there, broken off at the surface."

They looked at one another.

"You'd have to be pretty hungry to hunt something that looks like this," said Eric.

Ullir glanced in Tofa's direction. The *thrund* was making her way over to them, but she wasn't close enough yet to overhear anything.

"Vali's troops might be that hungry," he said.

"Aye," said Vidar. "And if that wound's not too old, they might not be far from here."

He peered into the forest, as if Vali's warriors might come charging out at any moment, in hot pursuit of the *tarsas*.

But of course, there was no one there.

They stopped just before dusk and made camp among the trees, for the sky was turning pink and it looked as if it might storm again.

Tofa's fatigue finally overwhelmed her. And no sooner was she asleep than Ullir set to healing her further.

Vidar watched for a moment. Then he left the shelter of the trees, telling the others that he had to refill his water bag, and went down to the river.

When he got to the bank—for at this bend, at least, one could tell the land from the water—he took out the sword.

And drove it into the snowy ground.

And sat before it.

He felt as if a great weight had been lifted from him. For a time, he just enjoyed that feeling of freedom.

Though the river moved like something dark and predatory.

Though the sky stood above him, stained with blood.

He heard footsteps, turned. Saw Ullir in the eerie half-light.

"We wondered what had become of you," said the Aesir-man. "And then it occurred to me that my own water bag might need refilling."

Silence, but for the crawling of the river.

"It stopped me from healing," said Vidar.

"Aye," said Ullir. "I thought that might be it."

Vidar grunted. "Back at the gate, it allowed me to expend my energy on Tofa. But the longer I carry it, the more it calls to me. And it won't stop until I answer it."

He considered the twisted runes of its hilt, the flawless length of its blade.

"I lived with the Gjallarhorn for more than a thousand years, and it never called to me as this does."

"They say the horn is older," said Ullir. "More patient. It's made of the stuff of the Ginnungagap. It can wait."

Vidar took a breath, let it out. It sounded loud in the still, brittle air.

"I know this sounds crazy," he said. "But it seems to know who I am. Exactly who I am—and what I can do. How I can join with it as G'lann could not. And it . . . *desires* that joining."

Ullir shrugged. "Not crazy at all. The sword of Frey was born in blood and fire—just as the hammer was. It yearns to know blood and fire again. To return to the violence that created it. In the hands of one who can unlock its true power."

"In the hands," said Vidar, "of a *lifling*—a healer. There's irony for you."

"Aye," said Ullir. His breath ghosted on the air. "And how much longer do you intend to go on like this? Carrying the blade, but resisting its power?"

"As long as I can," said Vidar. "Forever, if possible."

"Yet you may need it," said the blondbeard. "When we find Odin."

Vidar nodded, scowled. "Aye. I may. It's just that I've lost so much of myself already. Or at least, the self I nurtured in Midgard. The self I like best." He paused. "Some of it was lost at Indilthrar, when I cut down Odin's thursar without thinking twice about it. And more was lost at Ilior, when we waded in elves' blood to steal that ship."

"Perhaps," said Ullir. "But I was there at Indilthrar, and again at Ilior. I saw your face, my lord. It was racked with guilt, tortured by what you had to do. You're no war monger. No one who knows you could believe that."

"Yet I wear a warrior's braid," said Vidar. "Just like in the old days. And I carry a sword with me all the time now, whether it's Angrum or some other." He swallowed. "I'm slipping away, Ullir. I can feel it. I'm being swept out to sea. Caught in the undertow of Odin's war."

He looked down, and saw that his hands had clenched into fists.

"And it makes me angry," he said.

Ullir gazed at him with mild eyes. Almost as mild, Vidar thought, as Baldur's had once been.

"Then let *me* carry the sword," he said.

Vidar looked at him. *"You?"*

Ullir smiled a grim smile. "Why not? I'm *lifling,* even as you are. I can attune to the blade too. And I can begin now, so that I'll be ready when the need arises."

"You don't know what you're asking for," said Vidar.

"I think I do. To relieve you of a burden. To share the task of bringing Odin down as we have shared it—you, Eric, N'arri, and I—since we found ourselves in that cave above Asgard."

It was tempting. To be free of Angrum. To be able to hang on to the person he'd become on Earth—the person he wanted to be.

He didn't want to pick the blade up. To lay it against his hip, where it could whisper to him.

But he couldn't let Ullir carry it for him. Angrum was *his* burden. His alone, as he should have admitted to himself back in the mountains of Alfheim.

"No," he said finally. He stood on stiff legs, drew the sword out of the ground. It made a sucking sound as it came free. "It's mine. I'll carry it."

They regarded one another. And Vidar saw the further question in the Aesirman's eyes.

"And when the time comes," said Vidar, "I'll use it."

But the attunement, he told himself, could wait. At least a little while.

IX

WHEN the lands of Utgard had been made mountainous or flat, according to his whim, and the rivers had been fashioned along with the lakes, Odin set his hand to populating this new world of his.

First, he approached the elves in Alfheim in their forest halls.

"And what will you offer us?" asked the *lyos*.

"Fertile fields and good hunting," said Odin. "Gentle winters and warm rains."

And some of the *lyos* believed him.

Then he approached the men of Midgard, in their places by the sea.

"And what will you offer us?" asked the lords of Earth.

"Freedom from war and strife," said Odin. "Brisk winds and wide waters."

And some men believed him.

Next, he approached the *dwarvin* of Svartheim, in the fireshot gloom where they worked.

"And what will you offer us?" asked the dark elves.

"Caverns cool and dark," said Odin. "Silver in the rocks and gold in the streams."

And some of them believed him.

Finally, he approached the hrimthursar in their slave pens.

"And why should we bear offspring for you?" asked the giants. "What will you offer them in Utgard?"

"Keeps to smash and women to rape, wheat to burn and gold to plunder. A wide world to pillage, in revenge for your servitude."

And it was only the hrimthursar to whom he spoke the truth.

The dark elves were the first to feel Odin's cruelty in Utgard—but that is another tale, too long to tell here. Suffice it to say that none survived.

As for the *lyos* and the men—they were surprised to see one another. Each had thought Utgard would be his alone. Nor did they mix well, the elf with his passions and the Earth dweller with his hard, simple ways. But neither did they take up swords against each other.

And if the land was more barren and the forests thinner than Odin had had them believe, life could have been worse. So they tilled the fields and hunted the forests and dragged the rivers for fish as best they could.

Nor were there giants to make their lives bitter. For back in Asaheim, Odin's hrimthursar slaves bred slowly, like all their kind. It would be a long time before they created the race the Valfather desired of them.

Odin looked upon Utgard and he was disappointed. He had hoped for more amusement from this world.

So he put his hand to Utgard again, and he brought down upon it the winter he had been savoring—the storm that would last a thousand years and more.

The skies turned to iron, the fields to ice. Trees fell beneath the weight of that storm, and the wind turned flesh into something pale and dead. Elves and men alike cried out to Odin, for this was not what he had promised them.

But their cries fell on deaf ears.

Then Baldur saw what had happened to Utgard, and he came to his father in his court at Gladsheim.

"I have been to Utgard," said Baldur. "And I have heard the cries of those who dwell there. They huddle in caves, too cold to hunt, too frightened of the winds to fish the seas. Surely, they will not live long this way."

Odin heard his son, and he saw the wisdom in his words. But more than that, his heart softened—for who could deny Baldur when he spoke so passionately?

"Very well," said the Valfather. "I will cut a swathe through the storm, where the forests will abound with game and the streams will flow with fish."

But that was not enough for Baldur, the best of all the Aesir. "Where you clear a path through the storm," he said, "let me follow. And I will bring beauty to the land—grace to the cruel cliffs and gentleness to the rocky shoreline."

Odin agreed. He could not help it.

So the Lord of the Ravens cut a piece out of the storm, where life might thrive. Those who lived in Utgard came out of their caves to find this belt of life. And where Odin walked, Baldur followed, using the talents of the *gaut*—the creator—to give men and *lyos* something of which to sing. His works were small compared to Odin's, for so was his power. But they lightened the hearts of those who saw them afterward.

Still, Odin had the last word. For years later, when the peoples of Utgard had made peace with their lot, he finally brought them giants.

Sin Skolding
Algron, 355 A.D.

X

IT didn't storm that night after all, but the morning sky was still filled with the threat of it. They broke camp quickly, hoping to get as far as they could that day—for Tofa recognized this place, and said that two full days' ride might bring them to Erithain.

Once again she rode behind Vidar. And her grip was even a little stronger, he thought, than it had been the day before.

Halfway through that bleary forenoon, she commented on the sword.

"I have never seen such a hilt," she said. "Whoever made it had a passion for it. He should have been a soldier instead of a smith."

"Perhaps," said Vidar. "I never met him." Nor was it a lie. He'd never encountered the dark elf Ival'di—only heard about him. "They say he died a long time ago."

"Too bad," said Tofa. "He'd have been proud to see the way you wielded it. It spoke well of the blade's balance—not to mention your own."

He shrugged. "I'd sooner have had a spear in my hand. But there didn't seem to be one available."

She was quiet for a moment. Vidar didn't like that. It meant she was thinking about something, and it was probably the sword she was thinking about.

"And where are you from," she asked finally, "that some of you forge swords like this one, and others of you use them so well?"

"Beyond the mountains," he said. It had worked well

enough when he was sneaking into Asgard. And he didn't know enough about this world's geography to venture anything else.

"I've heard it said," she told him, "that Jalk was born beyond the mountains. Is that what they say where you come from?"

This was dangerous territory, Vidar decided. He figured he'd better change the subject before Tofa came to suspect anything.

"They say many things of Jalk," he answered. "That is but one of them." He guided the gelding past a jagged-looking rock disguised in snow. "But enough of my homeland, and of Jalk. I'd know more about you—and how you came to be a warrior."

Tofa laughed, and for a moment he didn't know why. "I became a warrior," she explained, "*because* of Jalk."

Damn. There was no getting away from that topic, was there?

"The first time I saw him," she said, "I was very small. He had just come back from putting down the island rebellions, and he was riding through the streets of Erithain—triumphant, with his personal guard of twenty behind him. He rode a black stallion, and his cloak was black, and his tunic and his boots. But his helm was silver, and so were his stallion's reins, and the clasp at his throat."

She paused. "I was entranced by the mystery and the beauty of it. I followed them all the way from the city gates to the palace itself. And it was then that I vowed to someday wear the black and silver of the *hjalamar*. To wield a sword in Jalk's name."

"And now," said Vidar, "the dream has been fulfilled." He couldn't keep the irony out of his voice, but she seemed not to notice it.

"Aye," said Tofa. "Fulfilled." She paused again. "Though what happened to my comrades was not part of that dream."

She fell silent then, and Vidar was thankful. It meant that he wouldn't have to weave any more lies for a while.

And while they traveled beneath that lowering sky, he remembered something that had happened not so long ago. On a day that could hardly have been less like this one. A day in summer.

They'd been at the beach since early morning, because Phil had wanted to beat the traffic. It was some holiday weekend—Memorial Day or July Fourth—and the place was mobbed soon after they got there. But no one seemed to mind. Bobby was only about ten then, and he was content to make wet castles out of sand with a green plastic bucket. Mel was a little older, thirteen maybe. She was sitting on the edge of their little encampment, watching boys she knew and boys she didn't getting thrown end over end by the surf.

Dinah and Phil and Alissa and Vidar were playing gin rummy and sipping Piña Coladas. For hours. By the time they broke for lunch, Vidar's back was burnt, and Alissa insisted he put on a T-shirt before it got any worse. He remembered telling her not to mother him, and her pulling the T-shirt down over his head anyway, and how he'd loved her for it. Things were good with Alissa in those days.

Then they'd looked around and realized that Bobby had disappeared, and they'd all set out over the hot sand to look for him. They even recruited Melissa for the search party.

Vidar was the one who found him, because he'd headed straight for the concession building. In front of the picnic tables, he saw a crowd, and some banners, and Bobby—his bucket still in hand.

When he got closer, he saw what the banners said. It was a marine recruitment stunt—some kind of sit-up contest.

There was a guy who looked like a drill sergeant standing with his hands on his hips. He was looking on approvingly as a strapping kid in fatigues—barely old enough to shave —did sit-ups on a mat.

And the drill sergeant was calling out the cadence with three words. "Like a machine. Like a machine. Like a machine." Over and over again.

Vidar watched for a moment, then put his hand on Bobby's shoulder. "Let's go," he told him. "Everybody's looking for you. It's time to eat."

Bobby gazed up at him and said, "Aw, c'mon, can't I watch for a while?"

Vidar had seen that kind of look in a young one's eyes before. He'd seen it in the eyes of the Aesir and in the eyes of men before they marched off to war, and he didn't like seeing it now in Bobby's eyes.

Sure, it was just a sit-up contest on a nice suburban beach. But it was also more than that. It was an enticement. A seduction.

Vidar remembered the words grating in his ears. "Like a machine. Like a machine."

The kid stopped when he reached a thousand. When he got up, the sergeant saluted him, and he saluted back.

"Now," said the sergeant, "anybody else want to try it? Anybody have what it takes to be a marine?"

A teenager stepped forward—a Muscle Beach type, with a tan he'd obviously cultivated with great care—and the sergeant knelt to hold his ankles in place. Then, as the sit-ups started, the sergeant went into his routine.

"Like a machine. Like a machine."

But the machine conked out around four hundred and thirty.

"Anybody else?" bellowed the sergeant.

Bobby stared at the sergeant. He was mesmerized. And there was nothing Vidar could say that would take the edge off this memory. The fine, clean edge of men who could be like machines.

It made Vidar afraid.

And so, he stepped forward.

The sergeant looked him up and down. Curled his lip a little at the longish hair and the beard.

"You sure you're up to it?" he asked.

"I'm up to it," said Vidar.

He sat down on the mat, and the sergeant went to grab his ankles.

"That's okay," he told him. And he began.

After he'd seen about fifty or so, the sergeant must have

decided to suspend his intolerance. Because he started to bark out that phrase.

"Like a machine. Like a machine . . ."

Vidar stopped.

The sergeant stood over him, arms crossed on his chest. He had a broad smile on.

"Had enough?" he asked.

"No," said Vidar. "I just want you to shut up. I'm not a machine. I'm a man."

There were some murmurs in the crowd. Even a couple of small cheers.

The sergeant turned a dark shade of red.

And Vidar started again.

"The first fifty don't count," announced the sergeant, forgetting to smile. "You stopped, mister."

"Okay by me," said Vidar.

And while Bobby watched, he plowed through those sit-ups to the cadence of the surf pounding at the sand. He could feel it through the mat, in his bones and in his blood.

Then someone started to strum a guitar to that rhythm, and before long someone else was singing along. It was a song he'd heard a lot in the sixties, but not since. And it seemed a lot of people remembered the words.

When Vidar glanced up at the sergeant, he saw that he wasn't pleased by all this. It wasn't quite what he'd had in mind. But the young marine that had done the sit-ups, standing just behind the sergeant, seemed to be enjoying himself immensely. He was nodding his head in time to the music, mouthing the words.

After a while, sweat was pouring from Vidar's neck, and the mat was slick with it, and he wished he had a couple fewer Piña Coladas sloshing around inside him. But he couldn't stop. Not with Bobby looking on, only beginning to learn that there was nothing special about men who were like machines. Not with the sergeant getting madder and madder.

And not with the joyous sound that had gone up all around him.

When he reached two thousand sit-ups, he stopped. By then, Bobby's eyes were wide and happy, and he was telling somebody how that was his uncle out there.

With Bobby's help, he got up.

And the sergeant, like it or not, had to present him with a certificate of achievement. Vidar took it and thanked him. And on his way through the backslapping crowd, who hadn't expected to see such a spectacle that day, he gave the certificate to the guy with the guitar.

Afterward, when they hooked up with the others, Dinah lambasted Vidar for letting them go on for so long without telling them he'd found Bobby. She'd said that she was ready to call the police—and that she didn't know which of them, he or Bobby, was the bigger kid.

But Alissa had just smiled.

Vidar sighed. Up ahead, his companions were riding three abreast. Behind him, Tofa had grown weary enough to lay her head against his back—a reminder that she was not completely healed yet.

And why should that memory come to him now, beneath this gray and lowering sky, in a world far removed from that of Piña Coladas and green plastic buckets?

He knew why. It was because he'd have liked to have been there when Jalk rode through Erithain, to shake the little girl that had been Tofa—to tell her that someday she'd watch her friends die on a lonely ledge, almost die herself, as the price of wearing black and silver.

Perhaps she'd have chosen to wear it anyway. But at least she'd have seen the truth behind the splendor. At least she'd have known.

When they stopped at the end of that long, gloomy day, the sky looked full and purplish, near to bursting. One didn't have to be a *stromrad* to know it would snow on them that night.

When Tofa got down from behind Vidar, they saw that she was pale again. Paler than Vidar had expected, even with all the times she'd slumped against him. He caught Ullir's eye, and the Aesirman nodded.

As soon as she was asleep, he'd give her another dose.

While he sat and watched Ullir work, listening to the soughing of the wind in the trees, Vidar thought about B'rannit. Dark and lovely, clear-seeing B'rannit.

What was she doing now? Sitting on her throne in under-G'walin, waiting for the word that they'd won—or lost? Or had she by now entered onto the chessboard herself, as she had—fortunately, for all of them—at Indilthrar?

He wished she were here now, to touch his brow with her slender fingers, to pare his uncertainties down into truths.

But even B'rannit, he realized, could be wrong sometimes. She had said that there were no evil swords—only evil in the hearts of those who used them.

She had not seen Angrum.

As the sword came to mind, his hand was drawn to it, like a moth to a flame. He watched it as if it were something separate and apart from him. It stopped short, hovering over the carved hilt. Then, after a moment, it alighted.

His fingers closed around the weapon. It felt hot to the touch.

Vidar's impulse was to withdraw from it. But he resisted.

No, he told himself. *Ullir was right. I cannot deny its existence, or the need for it. And sometime soon, I'll have to open myself up to it.*

He forced his fingers to remain where they were. To feel Angrum's heat. And yet, he restrained himself from the next step—the attunement.

It wasn't easy. It was the very verge of desire. But he managed.

And that was important to him. For when he did merge with the sword, he wanted to remain its master.

He was awake instantly, as if he'd never been asleep.

It was still dark out. Snow was falling.

At first he thought it was the sword that had woken him, dredging him up from oblivion with its yearning.

Then he caught sight of not one shadowy figure, but two. And a moment later he spied a third. They were making their way through the trees.

He glanced at Ullir, who should have been on watch. But the Aesirman had fallen asleep—having given too much of himself, perhaps, to Tofa.

Vidar's hand slid down his body, seeking the sword. But he was careful not to move anything else. A fourth figure came into view.

Who were they? Vali's warriors? *Thrund?*

He had no time to think about it. They were too close. And he could see swords in their hands.

He found Angrum's hilt, closed his fingers about it, just as one of the intruders came within a sword's length of Tofa. A bird took flight suddenly, discomfited by their passage.

The figure turned, surprised by the movement—and Vidar took advantage of it. Silently rising into a crouch, he drew the sword out. Before the intruder could turn back again, he'd launched himself across the clearing.

The swordsman saw him, uttered half a startled cry, brought his weapon around and down. But Vidar saw it coming. He met it, turned it. Sent it flying into the woods.

In that moment he had a look at his adversary.

The intruder was helmed and cloaked, and both were caked over with snow. From the size of him, Vidar knew he was no thursar. But he couldn't tell much more than that.

His adversary might have run, now that he was weaponless. But he tried to close with Vidar, grab for the sword. Vidar struck him with the flat of his blade—though he seemed to feel Angrum trying to twist edge-wise in his hands—and sent him crashing to earth.

There were curses, sudden shouts. A second swordsman loomed, blade held high. Vidar shuffled to one side to avoid the blow, heard it whistle as it cut the empty air.

As his adversary stumbled past, carried by his momentum, Vidar caught him with his pommel in the side of the head. The swordsman sprawled, lay still.

By that time, his companions were up, weapons in their hands. But as Vidar glanced this way and that, he saw how thick the woods had become with intruders.

He himself seemed to have a clear path into the woods. But the others were surrounded already, pinned together with their backs against one another.

There was no way they could fight their way out of this. But he couldn't leave them—not even if it meant jeopardizing what they'd come here for.

Hoping desperately that these were Vali's warriors after all, he brought his arms up in a gesture of surrender.

"Stop!" he cried. "No more. We yield."

His companions recognized his voice. N'arri, who stood facing him, stared in surprise. Reluctantly, he lowered his blade. And a moment later it was wrenched from his grasp by one of the intruders.

Vidar felt hands on his arms, his wrists. As Angrum was taken from him, he made sure he knew which of his captors had taken it.

Something hit him in the back of the head. Hard.

The next thing he knew, he was being held up only by his captors. And there was blood in his mouth.

"That will teach you to blindside me," said a voice from behind him. He would have liked to see who'd spoken, but his arms were twisted up behind him, and he couldn't turn around.

It was only after his surge of anger had subsided, a moment later, that he realized what kind of trouble he'd bought.

That hadn't been a familiar accent he'd heard. And these warriors weren't Vali's.

Snow fell. He looked past it at his friends, now as helpless as he was. And wondered what to do next.

Then there was a thrashing at the other side of the little clearing, and one of the swordsmen dragged Tofa out from among the trees.

"Look what I found," he said. "A female."

He laughed as he threw her down at his feet. A few others laughed too.

"Can anyone think what to do with such a morsel?" He howled like a wolf, and Vidar didn't like the sound of it. He tried to pull free, but to no avail. They held him fast.

Too late he realized it had been a mistake to surrender.

The swordsman leaned over Tofa, with his hands on his knees. "What do you say?" he asked her. "Will you do for us what you did for them?"

She spat in his face.

He snarled, dragged her up by her arms. But no sooner had he lifted her than she'd planted a knee in his groin. And as he doubled over with a strangled cry, releasing her, she somehow managed to slip his blade free of its sheath.

There was a murmuring, and the intruders around her drew back. Even the one with her spittle on his face, hobbled as he was. For she wove a web of iron about her, wielding the blade with the skill of a master swordsman.

"Dogs," she said. "Is this how the *hjalamar* treat one of their own kind?"

And with that, she ripped aside her cloak, exposing the black and silver of her tunic.

More murmuring, louder than before. A single figure came forward, knelt on the snowy ground before Tofa.

"My lady," he said. His voice was threaded through with regret. "We did not know."

My lady? Vidar wondered at that.

Tofa glared at the kneeling one, then all about her. And her eyes were that hard, steely blue that Vidar had seen on the ledge.

"Didn't know?" she echoed. She grunted, spat again. Eyed the one who'd dragged her into the clearing. "Need you have known me to treat me like a prisoner—at least— and not like some field you'd like to plow?"

"My lady," whispered the kneeling one. "What . . . what can I say?"

She scowled at him. When she spoke, her voice was perhaps a trifle less harsh. "Release my friends," she said. "At once. And then we will discuss what you can say."

He rose, made a cutting motion with his hand.

"Release them," he said. And Vidar felt his arms come free. As he brought them forward, then rubbed his wrists to get the circulation back into them, he fixed his gaze on the one who held Angrum.

"My sword," he said.

Grudgingly, the *thrund*—for Vidar noticed the angular features and the copper skin beneath the helm now—returned Frey's blade to him.

"These companions of mine," said Tofa, "saved my life." She looked around. "Treat them as you would treat me."

Suddenly she seemed to slump, leaning on her sword for support.

"My lady," said the one who'd knelt. "Are you all right?"

"Aye," she said. "Fine." But Vidar saw how she trembled. This little display had cost her most of her strength.

Ullir came up to her, took her arm. For a moment, he and the *thrund* exchanged glances. Then the *thrund* stepped aside as Ullir helped Tofa to a more sheltered place.

"All right," said the warrior—apparently, the one in command of this group. He looked around him at his troops. "Comb the woods. Look for any sign of the demons, any sign at all."

The soldiers scattered. And Vidar heard only a little grumbling as they fanned out among the trees.

When the last of them had gone off, the commander approached Tofa. Removing his helm, he shook loose his thick, straw-colored hair. He had a broad, likable face, Vidar saw, though a white scar ran across his face from nose to jawline. And his mustache would have put a walrus to shame.

"Again," he said, "my apologies, Lady Tofa." He looked at Vidar and the others. "To all of you. We thought we had caught some of the riffraff that seems to cling to the demons." He frowned, shrugged. "We were too eager."

Tofa nodded. "Aye," she said. "Too eager indeed." She

regarded the *thrund*. "And some of you for more than blood."

She turned to Vidar.

"This is Half," she said. "One of Jalk's captains."

The *thrund* extended his hand, and Odin's son took it.

"I hope you are not hurt," he said.

"Only my pride," said Vidar.

"Good," said Half. "That should heal easily enough."

"My friend's name is Vidar," said Tofa. "He's from beyond the mountains. And you should count yourself lucky he surrendered so quickly. I've seen him cut down a *tarsas* with a single blow."

Then she took the time to introduce Ullir, Eric, and N'arri, one by one. "N'arri," she said, "does not speak."

As Half's attention fell on him, the elf averted his eyes. And like Tofa, Half seemed not to notice anything amiss.

"From beyond the mountains, eh?" asked the *thrund*. "I've heard the winters are pretty fierce out there."

"One gets used to them," said Vidar.

Half grunted. "Aye," he said. "I suppose one would have to."

He seemed to remember something then, and his features hardened. He turned to Tofa.

"You were guarding the gate, last I heard."

"Aye," she said. "We were attacked. That's where I got the wounds that hobble me now."

Half nodded. "And the others?"

Tofa's silence was the only answer she gave. But it was all that was needed.

Half's jaw fell. "All of them?" he asked.

"All of them," said Tofa.

Half just stared at her. "Jalk," he said finally, "must know of this."

Tofa agreed. "That's why we were headed for Erithain. To tell him."

Half said that he would provide them with an escort, then went to see to it.

Vidar and his companions were left alone with Tofa. In

the east there was an edge of molten light fusing with the darkness.

Vidar only verbalized what must have occurred to the others as well.

"Half called you 'my lady,'" he said.

Tofa looked at him, and something seemed to stiffen in her.

"So he did."

"Something tells me," he said, "that you're not just another of Jalk's warriors."

She looked at the others, shrugged.

"Perhaps not."

But that was all the information she seemed willing to offer.

XI

THEY followed the river, surrounded by ten of Half's soldiers like a hand in a glove. Soon the forest receded. They saw farmlands off to either side of them. The water became sluggish—the mark of a deeper channel—and there were no boulders left for it to froth over. The ground too became flatter and almost featureless, allowing them to spur their horses into a canter.

By day's end they came in sight of Erithain.

It was a great city—bigger by far than Skatalund or Indilthrar. For that matter, Vidar noted, bigger than Asgard.

The walls of Erithain were red—the color of rust. Such stones, Tofa explained, could only be found far to the south.

A legendary queen had brought them to this place ages ago, to defend her court against her enemies.

"Nor have the stones ever failed us," she added, sitting behind Vidar as before. "Not even when the cursed pale-of-flesh descended on us from the other world. Not even then."

Vidar saw why. The true virtue of the barrier was not in the character of the stones, but in the height to which they'd been piled. The wall soared a good hundred and fifty feet, seeming to crowd the gray, brooding heavens.

The gates, too, were massive. Made of oak, Vidar judged, and reinforced with bands of hammered iron. At present they were open only wide enough to allow a thin stream of *thrund* in either direction.

Most of those who passed through the gates were farmers, with wains full of grain, or merchants. But all heads turned as Vidar's entourage went by. And there were whispers, pointed fingers.

It was Tofa they seemed to be whispering about.

"They all appear to know you," commented Vidar.

"Well they might," said Tofa. But again she offered no further explanation.

There were two guards in Jalk's livery stopping people at the gate, checking the contents of their wagons.

"There have been rumors," explained Tofa, "that outlaws and reavers have allied themselves with the demons. We are making sure they do not sneak them into Erithain."

"Outlaws and reavers?" asked Vidar. "Would they be the riff raff that Half mentioned last night?"

She nodded. "The same."

Vidar hadn't made the connection then—he'd been too busy wondering about Tofa. But now it all came together.

Could these supposed outlaws have been Vali's Aesirmen and mortals—glimpsed in the company of his marauding thursar?

It seemed a good bet.

When the guards saw Tofa's group approaching, they had just completed their examination of a wagon full of pelts.

"Well met," said one, older than the other *hjalamar* Vidar

had seen. He had a squarish face, accentuated by a harsh, closely cropped beard.

"Aye," said the other guard, a good deal younger. His was a smooth face, with wide, innocent eyes. "What news from upriver?"

On Vidar's flank, a few of Half's black-and-silvers mumbled something to one another, then glanced at Tofa. In time the youth's eyes were drawn to her too.

And as he recognized her, his expression changed. The eagerness vanished, to be replaced by something awful—the face of a man who's just felt a cold blade in his bowels.

"Tofa," said the youth. There was a great echoing emptiness behind that sound.

Vidar felt her loosen her grip around him, slide down from their horse. She walked forward between two other beasts and the *thrund* that sat them, until she stood before the guard.

"My sister," he said as he held back tears.

She took hold of his arms. Squeezed them.

"Be brave," she said. "As brave as she was."

His temples worked. "The demons?"

"The demons," she confirmed. She held his gaze. "When Half returns, you might speak to him. He might have a place for you on the next patrol out."

The youth nodded. "Aye, my lady. Thank you."

Vidar considered him, marking his sorrow, knowing what it was like to lose one's kin.

Half had seen Tofa and suspected trouble at the gate. This youth had known it for a certainty.

Among the *thrund* too, then, blood was thicker.

Tofa let her hands fall, turned to the other guard. "And now, I must see Jalk. Is he still on the practice field? Or have they finished for the day?"

"Neither, my lady. He is gone."

"Gone?" asked Tofa. "Where?"

The guard glanced at Vidar's party, and at the wagon drivers waiting behind it. "I cannot say, my lady. Not out here, where it may be heard by reaver spies. But it's common enough knowledge *why* he went—to chase down a rumor. A demon sighting."

"And he led the investigation himself?"

"Aye," said the guard. He shrugged.

Apparently it was unusual for Jalk to follow such leads in person. So why know—unless it was more than a rumor he chased? Possibly, it occurred to Vidar, Jalk had found the demons' main camp. *Vali's* main camp.

Vidar wanted to know more. But he wasn't likely to find it out here. Tofa didn't look as if she'd press the point.

She muttered something beneath her breath. "Then I will have to take my report elsewhere." She looked to one of the mounted soldiers. "Egil—see my friends to the Inn of Four Winds. And arrange for their accommodations."

"Aye," said the figure in black and silver.

Tofa turned to regard Vidar. "You'll be comfortable there. And I'll look in on you in a few days."

Vidar inclined his head. "Thank you," he said, "my lady."

Under other circumstances she might have smiled. She looked at all four of them. "No," she said. "It's you who deserve thanks."

And with that, she got up behind another of the *hjalamar*, and a moment later they'd started forward.

The one called Egil swiveled in his saddle. "Come," he told Vidar. Before he'd turned forward again, his steed had begun to move.

The guards stepped aside, and Vidar tried not to look at the younger one as he passed. It was enough to bear the pain without being stared at by strangers.

Patting his horse's neck to keep it calm, Vidar rode into the shadow of the gates. As they loomed on either side, it occurred to him that he'd accomplished what Vali could not —and with considerably less effort.

He'd become the first Aesirman to enter Erithain.

The gates opened upon a square awash with *thrund*—choked with wagons and ringed with peddlers. Visible everywhere among the masses were Jalk's people—evidence of his standing here.

But when it saw Tofa, the entire crowd parted—as naturally, Vidar noted, as the Red Sea had parted for Charlton Heston. A couple of Half's soldiers split off from their group to follow her—more as a gesture, it seemed, than out of any real need to protect her.

Egil, meanwhile, led them in another direction. The crowd parted for them, too, though not quite as quickly. And there was some grumbling, Vidar thought.

Egil gestured toward one of the streets—the narrowest, it appeared. "This way," he called back.

He rode that way and they followed—in single file, because there was no room to do otherwise. The passage was cold and dank, saturated with an early tinge of night, and Vidar's horse was tentative on the cobblestones.

But they soon came to the end of it, and Egil brought them out onto a somewhat wider street. Here they could see two mighty towers that prodded the sky. There were smells of food in the air—real food, not journeybread. Strangely, it brought to mind a little Hungarian restaurant Vidar had once liked—a restaurant worlds away. He couldn't remember the name of it.

Vidar noticed symbols carved into some of the doors, and he asked Egil about it. It seemed like the sort of question a wayfarer from beyond the mountains might ask.

Egil laughed. "They mark the inns," he said, "so that travelers like you can tell one from another. You see the ravening beast carved there? That's the Inn of the Red Wolf. Very popular with trappers during the spring market. And there—the wheel? That's the Guesting House of Gar the Great, usually filled with trinket merchants. Though no one remembers now why Gar should have deserved such an honorific."

They turned one corner and then another, and suddenly Egil stopped. It was only then that Vidar noticed the picture carved into the door. A face with puffed cheeks, blowing with all its might. Not unlike the image of the Greek god Aeolus found on ancient European maps. In contrast to the other inn symbols, it was small and unobtrusive. The mark of more comfortable accommodations, he guessed, if Erith-ain had anything in common with Earth.

As Egil went in to see to their rooms, leaving his reins in the hands of one of the other soldiers, Vidar's companions rode up beside him.

Eric surveyed the exterior of the place. He grunted, and not with displeasure. "It sure beats sleeping out in the snow," he said. "Just who was it that said this journey would be a hardship?"

N'arri, of course, was silent. But Vidar could tell by his posture alone that he didn't appreciate their accommodations as much as Eric did. To one who'd lived in caverns all his life, a bed and a roof were hard things to get used to.

Not to mention walls that pushed against the sky.

Their room wasn't exactly sumptuous, but it more than met their needs. The fireplace blazed with heat, the floor was clean enough, and there was a sturdy, fair-sized bed for each of them. Also, a pleasant view of a small square with a fountain at the center of it, although it was too cold for the fountain to be working at the moment.

Ullir plunked himself down on one of the beds, prodding the feather mattress with his fingers. "Ah," he said. "A good meal—none of those barley cakes for now—and a soft bed. What more could one ask for?"

"Don't get too comfortable," said Vidar, leaning against the windowsill. That got the attention of Eric and N'arri, who'd been warming their hands by the fire. "I want to know where this Jalk character went. And what he proposed to do once he got there. Unless I miss my guess, his trail may lead us right to Vali."

Ullir nodded glumly. "I was afraid you'd say that." With an effort, he got up again.

"Where do we start?" asked Eric. "With the taverns?"

"Sounds reasonable," said Vidar. "Especially if they're frequented by Jalk's soldiers." He gestured toward the window with a tilt of his head. "Like the one on the other side of this square. I've seen more than a couple of the black and silver go through that door in the last five minutes alone."

"You know," said Ullir, "it might not be so wise for us all to go in there at once. We're all strange faces." He glanced at N'arri, who'd taken his hood down for the first time since they entered M'thrund. "And some stranger than others."

The elf pretended to be hurt.

"He's right," said Eric. "In a large group, we're more likely to be noticed. And those we meet may be wary of us."

"Then we'll split up," said Vidar. "You and Ullir take the tavern down there. N'arri and I will wander around until we find another one."

Eric agreed. "And the first pair to return with what we seek," he said, "gets the beds nearest the fire."

Vidar chuckled. "Done," he said.

The tavern was dark, sour with the smell of spilled mead, crowded. More than a few of the *hjalamar* graced the place with their presence. They leaned across tables and laughed together, or sat in shadowy corners with their feet propped up and their eyes closed. In the center of the room, four or five of them were engaged in some sort of game.

But wherever they were, the serving maids seemed to attend to them first, and everyone else afterward.

N'arri glanced at Vidar from beneath his hood, clasped his arm briefly, and melted into the shadows. It was amazing how easily he did that, thought Vidar, considering the dearth of anything vaguely like a tavern in under-G'walin. But then, he supposed, dark places were dark places.

"Can I help you, friend?"

Vidar turned and saw a *thrund* in an apron. He was a portly one, bald, with a cascade of a beard and a mouth made for laughing. Judging from his demeanor, he was either the steward of this tavern or the owner.

"I could do with some mead," said Vidar.

"Aye," said the *thrund,* turning toward a wall full of wooden kegs. He approached one that already had a tap in it, opened the tap, and held a tin mug beneath it. When the foam started to rise, he held it out to his guest.

"My very best," proclaimed the portly one, though Vidar

saw that every keg on the wall looked the same. Vidar dug a silver coin out of a pouch on his belt and tossed it to the *thrund*.

It seemed to be enough. Without even glancing at the coin, the *thrund* slipped it into a pocket of his apron.

And even if he had inspected it, would he have known how old the coin was? Or that it had been a souvenir of Vali's first foray into M'thrund, taken from a *thrund* corpse and left with Magni for safekeeping?

If Vali had won here, Vidar mused, he would have taken his spoils back to Asgard with him. But having lost, he'd not have wanted any mementos too close to hand.

As the *thrund* looked on approvingly, Vidar lifted the tin and let the tawny liquid flow. Nor was it half bad. Vidar made a satisfied sound and wiped his mouth with the back of his other hand.

"Ahh," he said, "we don't have mead like this back home."

The *thrund*'s eyes twinkled. "Not unless your home is in Mog, down on the coast. That's where we get all our mead." He leaned a bit closer. "Unlike some taverns in the city, which do not go to such trouble—and their empty benches show it."

"Quality goods," said Vidar, "will always draw a crowd."

The portly one smiled contentedly. "Kind of you to say so."

Vidar assumed a look of concern then. "But what will you do," he asked, "now that Jalk has cut off the roads to Mog?"

The *thrund*'s brows met. "Cut off the . . . to Mog? Are you sure?" He looked about, as if to make sure that none of the soldiers were listening. "I'd heard that Jalk was on his way to Gnipa. To root out a nest of demons."

Gnipa. Vidar filed the name away.

"But . . . why Mog?" asked the *thrund*. "There have been no reports of demons down there. At least, none that I've . . ."

But Vidar never heard the rest. Something crashed to the floor behind him, and someone else shouted—and as he whirled about instinctively, he saw N'arri facing off with a pair of Jalk's stalwarts.

One was big—very big. In fact, he would have given a thursar a run for his money.

But it wasn't the bruiser that worried Vidar so much. It was the lean, almost gaunt one that stood at his side. Fingering a dagger, or something similar, beneath the folds of his cloak. Vidar could tell by the look in his eyes that he wouldn't hesitate to use it. Worse, he'd probably enjoy it.

The crowd had withdrawn to the corners of the room. The *hjalamar* too—although they looked ready enough to join in if the opportunity presented itself.

The big one kicked a half-shattered chair out of the way and took another step toward N'arri. The elf took a step back. But to his credit, he didn't draw his sword. And wouldn't, Vidar guessed, until his antagonists did.

"Who were you cheating for?" thundered the soldier, his blue eyes smoldering in his dark and ruddy face. "Answer me, damn you, or I'll twist your hands off your thieving wrists!"

"Aye," said his companion, the wolfish one. "And down on your knees as you tell us. Or it will be the last handful of wager stones you ever peek at." He smiled, thin-lipped, and Vidar kept a careful eye on the hand by the dagger.

N'arri was silent. What else could he be?

"Well?" roared the big one. "No answer?"

"He can't," said Vidar, standing at the edge of the crowd. "He's got no tongue." And as he'd hoped, their attention was drawn to him now.

The bruiser approached Vidar, stood over him. He poked a massive finger into Vidar's chest, left it there.

"Is that so? And who are you? His mother?"

"We travel together," said Vidar.

"Travel together," said the *thrund*. His eyes narrowed as he grinned. "And is that all you do together?"

Vidar held himself in check.

"That's all."

"Are you sure?"

The big one's face was close enough for Vidar to smell the mead on his breath.

"Aye," he said. "I'm sure."

The giant grunted. He turned, as if to walk away.

And drew his sword.

"Then here's your chance," bellowed the *thrund*, "to die together."

As the blade came for his head, Vidar rolled to one side, found himself underneath a table.

"Come out of there!" roared the *thrund*. Vidar could see the bruiser's boots shuffling around the table, trying to anticipate his exit.

But he didn't exit at all. Instead, he lifted the table and heaved it in his opponent's direction. Tin mugs clattered against the floor. Shadows danced as a candle went flying.

And taken by surprise, the *thrund* lost his footing. Fell, with the table on top of him.

As Vidar got to his feet and drew Angrum, he had a moment to check up on N'arri. He watched the elf batter the wolfish one's blade, try to launch an attack of his own.

Then the giant had flung the table aside, and he was advancing on Vidar. His face was a mask of fury.

The last thing Vidar wanted to do was murder one of Jalk's *hjalamar* with half a dozen others looking on. It was the wrong move for a stranger in town.

So when the *thrund* swung at him, he swung back with all his strength—hoping that the impact would wrench the blade from the giant's grasp.

But he miscalculated. Instead of hitting the blade straight on, he dealt it a glancing blow. Too late, he felt it sear the flesh of his shoulder, cutting his tunic open.

Quickly, Vidar clutched at his wound. Not because of the pain that he was only beginning to feel there, but because he hadn't treated his shoulder with berry juice—and anyone who looked closely enough might have wondered about the pallor of his skin.

"He's marked!" someone cried out—probably a soldier.

"Aye, Meili—you've got him now!"

Vidar set his teeth. Perhaps Meili did have him. And perhaps not.

He circled to his left, jockeying for position—and holding on to his shoulder.

A smile spread over the giant's face as his eyes followed Angrum. "Pretty blade you've got there. I'll be glad to take care of it when you're dead."

Then Meili advanced again, holding his own sword high. But Vidar didn't watch the weapon. As Heimdall had taught him long ago, he watched his adversary's eyes.

And the *thrund*'s eyes gave him away. When he lunged, Vidar was ready. His point caught the giant just below the wrist.

Crying out in pain, Meili couldn't help but let go of his sword. And before he could make another move, Vidar's blade was at his throat.

"Don't move," said Vidar. "Unless you want a second mouth as big as the one you have now."

Meili's mouth twisted. But he didn't move. Blood trickled between his fingers where he held his wounded forearm, and it reminded Vidar of his own wound. With a little flourish, he pulled his cloak around to cover it.

He dared to glance in the direction where he'd last seen N'arri. The elf was unharmed, but he'd been pressed against the wall. At the moment the wolfish one's attention was focused on Vidar.

"Better leave that dagger where it is," said Odin's son. "Or your friend here will regret it before I will."

The wolfish one laughed. "My dagger is the least of your worries. Did you really expect to get out of here alive? Don't you see that you're surrounded by black and silver?"

That's when Vidar remembered his ace in the hole.

He scanned the faces of Jalk's soldiers. There were at least a dozen of them in the crowd. And if their comrade's ongoing existence hadn't depended on their restraint, they'd have been on top of him long ago.

"Would you kill us then?" asked Vidar. "My companion

and I—who saved the lady Tofa's life not long ago? Would you risk her wrath by murdering her friends?"

That got them mumbling among themselves.

"A fine tale," said the wolfish one. "But will we believe it?"

More mumbling.

Vidar decided to take a chance. He removed his point from Meili's throat, half expecting to be mobbed by soldiers.

But no one attacked him. Not even Meili himself. The giant glared, but that's all he did.

"Are we just going to let them leave?" asked the wolfish one. "After the shambles they made here? After they spilled a *hjalamar*'s blood?" He spat. "Anyone can see it—they're lying through their teeth."

"No," said one of the soldiers. "I rode into Erithain with the lady Tofa just this afternoon. And I heard it from her own lips. They're her friends all right."

Vidar didn't recognize the *thrund* who'd come forward. But he was grateful that he had.

Slowly, carefully, he put his blade away. Then he walked the width of the tavern to join N'arri.

And together, they left, feeling very lucky.

Eric stood up when he saw them open the door.

"Finally," he said, obviously relieved. "We thought something had happened to you."

Vidar grimaced. "Something did." He pulled his cloak aside to reveal the wound.

Ullir's eyes narrowed. "Is it deep?"

Vidar shook his head. "No. Just a nuisance. But I'll need a new shirt, I'm afraid."

Ullir turned to the elf. "And you?"

N'arri raised his arms to show that he was whole.

The Aesirman chuckled. "Praise Vali for small favors."

"So?" asked Eric. "Need we drag it out of you?"

Vidar shrugged. "One of Jalk's people thought N'arri was peeking over his shoulder while he played some game. It snowballed. And I had to invoke Tofa's name to get us out of there." He paused. "Did you find out about Gnipa?"

"Aye," said Eric. "But you can take my place by the fire. You may need your wits about you tomorrow."

Vidar regarded him. "On the road to Gnipa?"

"No," said the boy. "Right here in Erithain."

"There was a messenger here shortly after we got back," said Ullir. "A messenger from the Queen. And she requested your presence tomorrow morning—in her chambers."

"The Queen?" echoed Vidar. "But why? And why only me?"

Eric grunted. "Why indeed."

XII

"I will deck you with flowers," said Freya of the Vanir, "for I know the secret places where they grow in bright profusion. I will feed you sweet berries and bathe you in cool grottoes, if you'll come to Asgard and be my true love."

"But Odin will show me secret places as well, where I'll die at the hands of his enemies. I'll eat their blades and choke on my own dark blood, and my bones will lie forever in midnight streams."

Ottar the King shook his head from side to side.

"It is here I will stay, and live my life long."

"I will ride with you," said Freya, "to the wild-deer wood, and show you fields of black sky where the stars cavort. And when the moon comes out, I'll press my mouth against yours, and make you forget the cares of men."

"But Odin will send me riding as well, through iron hills where the wind howls and ravens. And there I'll know the bite of death, from which no man can recover."

Ottar the King shook his head from side to side.

"It is here I will stay, and live my life long."

"Then you will never again know the softness of my skin, the sweetness of my lips, the caress of my voice. You will never know again the whiteness of my breast, the glamour in my eyes, the warmth of my thighs."

As if in pain, he cried out.

"I cannot live without the softness of your skin, the sweetness of your lips, the caress of your voice. I cannot take leave of the whiteness of your breast, the glamour in your eyes, the warmth of your thighs."

"Then you will come with me to Asgard?"

"Aye," said Ottar the King. "I will come with you to Asgard."

"And be my true love?"

"And be your true love."

"Good," said Freya. "My heart bursts with joy. But don't forget to bring plenty of your warriors with you, for Valhalla is a lover too, and in need of men to make her rafters ring."

Sin Skolding
Bolmsö, 465A.D.

XIII

THE Queen's hall was smaller, less impressive than Vidar might have imagined. No bigger than a chieftain's hall in Asgard.

But as he approached it with his escort of soldiers, he saw how much older it was than the buildings around it. It had a certain stateliness, a dignity that more than made up for its lack of size.

Once inside the courtyard, they dismounted. Grooms took Vidar's horse and those of the *hjalamar* as well. Other servants moved to open the doors to the keep. And with his escort intact, Vidar went inside.

The place smelled of age and mildew. They followed a short hallway, past faded tapestries and arrangements of crossed swords, to the threshold of a large enough chamber. It was stark and undecorated, but lit well by three tall windows in the southern wall.

A throne stood at the far end, caught in a splash of light. It was an ornate, wooden seat, embellished with uncut rubies and emeralds and a variety of yellow stones that Vidar did not recognize.

The slender figure on that barbarous seat could only have been the Queen. Vidar waited at the entrance, out of courtesy. When she beckoned, he approached, and this time the *hjalamar* stayed behind.

As he drew closer to the Queen, he began to understand how Tofa came by her status here. It was hard not to notice the family resemblance.

The same piercing blue eyes, though a few faint lines of age surrounded them. The same high, strong cheekbones, the same copper-colored skin. And the same pale, golden hair, radiant in the morning light, though the Queen's was plaited about her head.

She wore a long gown of simple weave, as fair as her hair. And no crown of any sort—nothing to mark her royal blood but the way she held herself.

"You are Vidar?" asked the Queen as soon as he'd come to a stop.

"Aye, my lady." He tried to affect a little nervousness— for how often were wayfarers from beyond the mountains invited to speak with their distant ruler?

"Be welcome then, Vidar." She regarded the *hjalamar*, still standing by the doorway. With a gesture she dismissed them.

They hesitated.

"It's all right," she said. "Go."

They left.

The Queen turned back toward Vidar, smiled. "Some privacy," she said, "at last." She pointed to a chair by the wall. "Bring that over here," she told him, "and you won't have to stand as we speak."

He went and got the chair, placed it near hers.

"That's better," said the Queen. She looked at him. "Do you know why I asked you here, Vidar?"

He shrugged. "It must have something to do with the lady Tofa. You and she look much alike."

She smiled again. "So I have been told. But thank you for telling me again." She paused. "I asked you here to tell you how grateful I am—to you, and to your companions—for finding my daughter. And for bringing her back to Erithain." Her brow wrinkled for a moment. "Tofa means a great deal to me. She is my only child, and my main source of joy since the death of the royal consort."

"I'm glad we were able to serve you," said Vidar. "But once we saw her, we could hardly have left her there."

The Queen chuckled, and the light glistened in her hair. "I

should have known you'd say something like that. It's the way they talk in the lands beyond the mountains—isn't it?"

For a moment Vidar believed that she had seen through his disguise. That she was giving him enough rope to hang himself.

But he'd gone too far to stop now.

"Aye," he said. "Perhaps it is." He met her gaze. "Have you ever been to our lands, my lady?"

She shook her head. "Myself, no. But my grandmother made the journey, years ago. And we still tell stories of what she found there."

"Well," said Vidar, "should you yourself wish to visit, you'll find a warm welcome among us."

She laughed. "Aye," she said. "I've no doubt of it."

So far, so good, he told himself.

"You know," said the Queen, "Tofa was quite impressed with you. And she is not easily impressed. She spoke of the way you conquered that *tarsas* in terms she usually reserves for Jalk himself."

"The lady Tofa might have exaggerated," said Vidar. "It was a lucky blow, born of desperation."

The Queen looked at him askance. "I think not. If there is one matter in which Tofa is expert, it's swordsmanship." She frowned almost imperceptibly—but enough for Vidar to see that the Queen disapproved of Tofa's soldiering.

He recalled the way Tofa had bristled when he'd first suggested that she was no common *hjalamar*. Now he thought he understood.

Like many children of royalty, she'd decided to go out and *earn* the people's respect. In this case, as one of Jalk's warriors.

And that, apparently, did not sit well with her mother.

A moment later, however, the Queen's frown vanished. "But come," she said. "Tell me some news, what you've heard on the road. About the demons, I mean. Jalk tells me so little, I must discover my own sources of information."

Vidar shrugged. "We heard a different description of the

demons from every mouth that could hold a tale. It is difficult now, my lady, to separate one from another."

The Queen nodded, her eyes narrowing a little. She leaned forward. "Did any of these mouths call the demons pale-of-flesh?"

Vidar regarded her. "Like the ones who came to conquer us long ago?"

"Yes," she said. "Like those."

Again he had to wonder if she were toying with him. "No, my lady," he said after a while. "I do not believe so."

She sighed. As she leaned back again into her throne, she looked disappointed.

"I'm sorry," said Vidar. "I wish I could provide what you seek."

The Queen shook her head. "No, don't be sorry. It may be that there's nothing there. Perhaps the *hjalamar* were jesting when I heard them speak of it."

She fashioned a smile. "And even if the pale-of-flesh have returned, what need is there to worry? Jalk rid us of them before—and he will do it again."

Vidar wondered at her choice of words. "*Jalk* rid you of them?"

"Of course. Don't they tell that story anymore beyond the mountains? Of how Jalk turned back the invader?"

"But that was ages ago," said Vidar, as calmly as possible.

"Of course it was."

Then how . . . ?

Was *jalk* a title, then, handed down from chief councillor to chief councillor? Or . . .

The possibilities flooded his brain in quick succession.

Odin—newly emerged from his stay in Niflheim. Sowing the first of his seeds here in M'thrund.

Vali, his son—representing all that he had come to hate —trying to conquer this place just as Odin was rising to power here. Trying to build his empire as Odin had done, unaware that the Valfather had become chief councillor to Erithain's queen.

The chance—for Odin to strike his first blow at Asgard. To open the first chink in Vali's armor—without giving himself away at the same time.

The result—Vali's defeat, the only one he would ever suffer. Odin's affirmation as the most powerful councillor at court. The beginning of Jalk's domination of Erithain—and a base from which he might go about sowing his other seeds.

"You seem troubled," said the Queen. He looked at her, gazed into the depths of those dark, blue eyes. "Is it something I said?"

Vidar shook his head. "No, my lady. It . . . is only that I am a commoner, unused to such surroundings."

The Queen looked around, shrugged. "To me it has always seemed a plain place. Then again, I have lived in it all my life." She regarded Vidar. "But you did not come to Erithain, I know, to sit in a queen's hall. Leave me now. Enjoy yourself. And remember that you have my gratitude."

Vidar rose, inclined his head. "I'll go," he told her. "But of all I'll see or hear in Erithain, I will remember best my meeting with the Queen."

It seemed the kind of thing a country boy might say.

The Queen laughed. "Don't be too sure of that, Vidar. By the time you leave, you might think differently.

When Vidar returned to the room, it was empty. Perhaps, he mused, the others had gotten hungry waiting for him.

He stretched out on his bed and considered the ceiling beams.

Had he been wrong?

Was Odin in M'thrund after all—at court, as they'd first suspected? Not as a new influence, but as an old one—a very old one?

The lack of a discernible trap for Vali had thrown him off. Perhaps Odin had set one, and something had gone wrong. Or perhaps there had been no time to prepare one.

Odin. Here.

He had no proof yet, of course. But if Jalk *were* the Valfather, it meant that there was a chance of ending it in M'thrund—the long, tortuous trail they'd followed in pursuit of him, the wars, the slow-fast shuffle toward the Ginnungagap.

All they'd have to do is return to Alfheim, gather their forces, and try to accomplish what Vali could not. Far from easy. But if they'd truly tracked Odin to his lair, it would be a different kind of war now—a stand-fast-and-fight kind of war, not a battle with shadows. And when it came to the former, Vidar had some confidence they could win.

The creak of a door jolted him out of his reverie. He sat halfway up, wary until he saw Ullir poke his head in.

"Vidar? Ah, you're back."

Eric and N'arri came in behind the Aesirman. The elf shut the door.

"We've got news," said Ullir. "But little of it good, I'm afraid."

Vidar sat up the rest of the way, swinging his legs over the side of the bed. "Why? What happened?"

"We were down at the market square," said Eric. "Loitering about, to see what else we could learn. And as we were pretending to inspect all the peddlers' wares, a messenger came riding through the gate. A messenger from Jalk."

"Aye," said Ullir, sitting down on the bed opposite Vidar's. "It seems that Jalk was successful in Gnipa—damn him. And according to the messenger, he's on his way back, with a handful of the demons as captives."

"But if there are captives," said Eric, "perhaps we can get close to them. Close enough to find out where the remainder of Vali's armies are."

"Aye," said Vidar. "We could try that. But there's a more pressing matter at hand now."

And he told them about Jalk.

For a moment no one spoke. Then Ullir broke the silence.

"This does seem to put a new face on matters," said the Aesirman.

"If it's true," said Eric. He glanced at Vidar. "Forgive me, my lord. But after all this time, it's hard to know what to believe." He looked to the others. "Still, I suppose we'll know for certain soon enough."

Ullir nodded, turned to Vidar. "Aye. The messenger said that Jalk was only a half day's ride from Erithain. If we return to the square this afternoon, we ought to at least catch a glimpse of him."

N'arri grunted. He pointed to one of his eyes, then made a cutting motion with his head.

"He's right," said Vidar. "A glimpse is all we'll need."

The day grew dismal quickly, and by midafternoon there was snow falling. But that didn't seem to dissuade the *thrund* from gathering in the market square.

Word, it seemed, had gotten out.

Vidar grew cold waiting for Jalk, and after a while he almost welcomed the bodies that came to press against him. The fabric of the day grew threadbare, the light thinned, and they could feel darkness coming on.

But in the end they weren't disappointed. Just before dusk, Vidar glimpsed a ruddy light through the open gates. And as it got closer, he could see a torch. Many torches. A mounted contingent of the black and silver, the flames reflected in their mailshirts and in their helms.

Though it seemed that the square was as packed as it could get, a path opened for the conquering heroes. The *thrund* before him were pushed back, and Vidar had to give ground as well. But being a little taller than most of them, he still had a pretty good view.

Behind the first wave of soldiers came a second, and a third. There was a torch in every gauntleted hand, rippling like a blood-red banner in the frigid wind.

Nor was the spectacle lost on the crowd. Vidar looked around, saw the firelight dancing in their eyes. There was a hush of admiration, devoid of the grumbling he'd heard here the day before.

Into that hush, a sound. A squeaking, as of wagon wheels. And soon after, the wain itself trundled through the gates. Vidar squinted to see past the torches. There were two white horses pulling the wagon, a pair of soldiers seated behind them. And in the back, where a farmer might have loaded his grain, something huddled.

Something big and pale, something naked and shivering. Something bound with thick, black chains.

A thursar.

The wagon moved forward, and the crowd buzzed like a hive of angry bees. Someone up front threw something, just missing the giant. He raised his head and Vidar saw the black eyes, the jutting brow, the graven-stone face that was incapable of expression.

But there must have been fear there, a slow panic writhing in the thursar's gut. And shame—at his nakedness, at his being paraded in chains before a sea of strange faces.

Nor could the thursar know that among all those faces, there were four it might have recognized. Welcomed.

Someone else threw something, and it glanced off the giant's head. He roared with pain, rose as far as the chains would let him—which wasn't far at all. Roared again, trying to lash out at something, anything. But he was bound too well.

There were jeers from the *thrund,* laughter even. Vidar had an urge to stifle that sound, to shove the laughter back down someone's throat. But he couldn't have if he'd tried. Pressed on all sides by the crowd, he was fettered as surely as the giant was.

A second wagon followed the first. Another naked thursar. More hooting, more taunts and thrown things. But this captive didn't react as the first one had. He just seemed to cower, peering out at the *thrund* from the shelter of his shackles.

And as he went by, Vidar saw why. The giant's side was all covered with blood—some of it caked, some of it fresh.

Nor was he the only one who saw. He heard an undercurrent of dismay rise amid the jeers. A few whispered protests that there was a limit to cruelty—even cruelty to one's enemies.

But before long, the jeering had drowned them out.

A single rank of soldiers followed, none of them carrying torches. Each held his horse's reins in one hand, and his other hand rested on his hilt. They had the air of a personal guard about them.

Those in the front of the crowd began to pass the word back. *Jalk. It is Jalk.* Vidar felt a tightness in his throat.

A moment later Jalk rode through the gates, flanked on either side by a pair of warriors. And Vidar knew it was *him*.

The bearing and the build were familiar—not unlike his own, in fact. But that wasn't what sent a shiver of recognition through Vidar, what made him giddy suddenly.

It was the mask. Not the same one, of course, that he'd worn in Utgard when he'd gone by the name of Ygg. That one had been left in a cave in Asaheim.

The mask he wore now was flat, featureless. If anything, more terrifying than the Ygg visage. Nearly as terrifying as the ruined countenance it concealed.

All around Vidar, the *thrund* spoke his name. *Jalk. See him? It is the lord Jalk.*

The masked head turned, surveying the crowd. Jalk made no sign, said nothing. That slitted gaze was all he favored them with.

A number of things went through Vidar's mind—things that had nothing to do with bringing this knowledge back to Alfheim.

First—that without Odin to stir it up, there'd be no more war. Not with the *thrund* or anyone else.

Second—that he could probably cut Odin down before the *hjalamar* could move to stop him.

Third—that if he were quick enough, he might even slip away in the confusion.

And fourth—that he might never again get a chance like this one.

There was no time to consider the price of failure. Only time enough to act.

He made his way forward through the crowd. Nor did anyone think to protest as he jostled them, for all eyes were on Jalk. Soon, as the masked one came forward, Vidar reached the second rank—close enough, for he did not want to be recognized.

His fingers closed on the sword. It was growing warm, hot, almost painful to the touch. As if it sensed what Vidar had in mind.

Odin passed him, his flankers a half step behind. Vidar steeled himself, waiting for them to move up just a little, waiting for the opening he needed.

The last thing he expected was that someone would beat him to the punch. But before he could make his move, a hooded figure had darted out of the crowd to his left.

N'arri.

Who'd lost his tongue to Odin in the dungeons of Indilthrar.

Who'd seen a way to even the score.

As the elf slipped in behind Odin's guards, there was a cry of warning, the hiss of blades leaving leather sheaths.

Vidar shoved a couple of *thrund* out of the way and broke through into the open. At the same time, he heard the clash of swords, and another cry—this time, one of rage. Horses wheeled, bellowing, unable to escape the close quarters.

Angrum was out before he knew it. But there was no reaching the elf, hidden as he was behind a wall of horses and the warriors who straddled them. And a moment later there was no time to even look, for a *hjalamar* had pegged him for a second assassin—and was leaning out of his saddle to take Vidar's head off.

Vidar ducked. The blade missed. As the *thrund* completed his swing, Vidar grabbed him by the cloak and dragged him down. A quick jab, and he made no effort to rise up again.

The riderless horse retreated, effectively blocking off some of the other *hjalamar* as they tried to get to Vidar. Behind him there was more confusion, for in trying to control their horses, the riders had become entangled with the crowd. And off to one side, Vidar caught sight of Eric, laying about him in order to keep the soldiers at bay.

Suddenly one mounted figure loomed out of the chaos. Its masked head swiveled and its gaze fell on Vidar.

Their eyes met, locked.

Odin dug his heels into his animal's flanks. It leaped ahead, and Vidar had to shuffle to one side to avoid it.

Then Odin's blade was descending upon him, as if from a great height.

He fended it off, felt the shock travel through his arm up to the shoulder. Vidar staggered, recovered. But he was at a tactical disadvantage, he knew, as long as Odin sat his horse.

A second time the masked one brought his blade down— and a second time Vidar battered it aside. Sparks leaped, a glint of blue fire. But before Vidar could get in a counter-stroke, Odin had put the horse between them. Without warning, the beast reared, pawing at the air with savage hooves. Vidar gave ground to avoid being hit, circled to his left.

And Odin was on him again. Vidar flung Angrum up just in time, heard the screech of blade upon blade.

Your horse is a weapon too. Use it.

He'd heard those words a long time ago. And it was Odin who'd uttered them.

But what can I do, Father, when it's my enemy who's mounted? And I stand on the ground?

Wait, Odin had told him, *until he makes a mistake. And if you can wait long enough, he will.*

Again Vidar drove off the attack from above.

And again. And again.

And the next time, suddenly, he saw his chance. He braced himself, met Odin's backhand with equal fury— turned it so that the blade was thrown wide and high. For a moment Odin's breast lay exposed—Odin himself off-bal-ance, too surprised to do anything about it.

As Vidar brought Angrum back, he saw the eyes in that mask. Saw the shock in them. Felt the smallest pang of remorse for what he was about to do, hesitated for the slightest fraction of a second.

Forgive me, Father.

Then there was a flash of light, and thunder, and afterward came the darkness.

XIV

VOICES. The sound of metal scraping against metal. A sudden light, then gone again.

All these things he noted as if they were happening elsewhere, to someone else. As if they were only parts of a dream. Then he saw something slither by, close to his face, its claws ticking against the cold stone floor. He flinched, repulsed, rolling away as quickly as he could.

When he looked back, the thing had disappeared. He surveyed the place in which he found himself.

Four wet, shiny walls, no windows. A heavy, iron-bound door with a slot cut in the bottom. Before the slot, a tray with half a loaf of bread and an old jug. Both looked dirty.

On the floor, scattered straw, illuminated by what little light managed to filter in around the door. A threadbare sleeping mat in one corner, a hole for his waste in another. And a few smaller holes between them, in the wall facing the exit—through one of which the clawed thing had come and gone.

It was no dream.

He felt the back of his head. It hurt at his touch. And when he took his fingers away, there was an ooze of blood on them.

Apparently, one of the *hjalamar* had gotten to him before he could get to Jalk. *Damn*. So close, so close . . .

If he hadn't hesitated at the crucial moment, it might have worked. *If*.

He tried to put that from his mind. There was no profit in lamenting lost chances. Not even chances as critical as this one.

It was more important now to find a way out of this dungeon. To get back to Alfheim with all he knew—as they had originally planned.

They. He felt an emptiness in the pit of his stomach.

Were they imprisoned as he was? Had they been that fortunate? Or had he lost them in that sudden, desperate battle?

Vidar crawled over to the slot in the door. Called out their names, heard them resound in the corridor outside.

But there was no answer. Only the sound of muted laughter. Guards—of course. To make sure that Vidar didn't gradually pound the door off its hinges. Given time, there was no door he couldn't batter down—though it had been awhile since he'd seen one as sturdy looking as this one.

Still, there was more than one way to skin a cat. Or to remove an obstacle like a door.

That is, if his guards might be subject to a little mind bending. Granted, he was no *baleyg*—but he'd used the talent to free himself from similar situations.

Vidar concentrated, casting his power out like a fishing line. After a time, he brushed against a *thrund* consciousness. Sensed its alien texture. Tried to put a hook into it.

But it was no use. Like the minds of the elves, the *thrund*'s offered him no purchase. No opening.

Then again, that was no surprise. Odin would have known he'd try to influence the guards—and if it had been a possibility, he'd have taken precautions against it.

The Valfather left nothing to chance.

Vidar sighed, moved away from the slot, sat back against one of the walls. It wasn't long before he realized how hungry he was. How long had he been here, he wondered, before he'd woken up?

He considered the tray, pulled it to him. Picked up the bread, turned it in the gray light. When he'd located the least dirty part, he tore a chunk out of it. It didn't come away easily, of course, being stiff and stale. He forced himself to take a bite, then chewed as quickly as it allowed him to.

It was only then that he realized his other loss. His hand strayed to his sheath, found it empty.

It figured. He'd fought the sword's presence since he'd first agreed to carry it. And now that it was gone, he wished he had it back.

Would Odin think to look at it? There's no question that he'd recognize it for what it was.

And what couldn't he do with Angrum in his hands?

Vidar whispered a curse. He found himself chewing harder, the anger rising in him like bile.

Suddenly there were sounds from outside. Voices again. And they were getting closer.

When they were right outside, he heard a bolt move. Another. A creaking as the door worked its ponderous way open.

Vidar had to shade his eyes against the light from the corridor, though it couldn't have been much. There was a torch flaming on the far wall, and that was about it.

Someone moved into the doorway. He recognized the black and silver garb, the broad shoulders—and the mask. There were two others behind him—*thrund*, but not *hjalamar*. Only dungeon guards.

"What a surprise," said Vidar.

One of the guards growled a warning, but Vidar ignored him. He was watching the one in the mask.

But Odin didn't say a thing. And with his back to the light, his eye slits were dark, eerily vacant.

When one of the *thrund* placed a stool in the corner of the cell, the masked one entered. Sat. The *thrund* withdrew and the door closed. Then Vidar heard the footfalls of the departing guards.

The door, he realized, was unbolted.

He glanced at the sword in Odin's belt, calculated his best chance of beating him to it.

"Don't even think about it," said his visitor. His voice was toneless, muffled by the mask. But the meaning was clear enough.

"Just admiring the workmanship," said Vidar.

"Of course. Just as you were admiring my parade this afternoon."

"Did you have to strip them naked?" he asked.

The masked one shrugged. "They've been too effective. The people were in terror of them. I had to make it plain that the demons could be beaten—humbled."

"And that Jalk was still invincible," suggested Vidar.

Odin shrugged again. "If you prefer, yes."

Vidar wished he could see his captor's eyes. There was something disconcerting about talking to empty slits.

"So this was your base of operations all along," he said. "And you were the one who led the *thrund* against Vali—who enabled them to turn him back."

"Aye," said the masked one. "And this time I'll crush him for good." He paused. "But first I need to know his strategies. His troop strengths."

"I don't know," said Vidar. "I've had no contact with him. But if I did know, I wouldn't tell you."

The masked one shook his head. "You're making this difficult. For both of us." Silence, punctuated only by a scurrying behind the wall. "And for your companions as well."

It was the wrong thing to say.

Vidar started for his throat, but Odin was quicker. And he waited until Vidar sat down again before he put the sword away.

"You seem to care a great deal about them," observed the masked one. "I'll have to remember that."

"Where are they?" asked Vidar.

"Safe enough. I should have taken their heads off, after they slew three of my *hjalamar* and maimed a fourth. But I decided to wait until I'd seen you."

"So you could use them to wring information from me."

"Of course."

Vidar regarded the empty slits. "You hurt them," he said, "and you'll regret it."

Odin leaned forward a little. "You think you're in a position to make threats?" He laughed a short, bitter laugh. "Kin or no, I'll get what I need from you. Vali must be stopped—before he does any more damage."

It was a strange way to put it, Vidar thought, under the circumstances.

"You make it sound," he said, "as if Vali were the aggressor. As if you hadn't brought him here yourself."

The masked head tilted to one side, achieving a quizzical look. "What do you mean? Do you think I invited another invasion?" He laughed again—almost a bark this time. "I feel sorry for you, Vidar. You've come to believe Vali's propaganda, it seems. Just as surely as you once believed Odin's."

Again, a strange thing to say—even though Odin had referred to himself in the third person before. Vidar got the feeling that they were somehow talking at cross-purposes.

And it made him wonder. Made him take another look at the one in the mask. Gave rise to the ice water that began to trickle down his spine.

"Damn," he said. "You're *not* Odin—are you?"

"Odin?" That barking laugh again. "Not last time I looked."

"Then who *are* you?"

The masked head cocked itself at an angle. "You mean you really don't know? Is it possible you came this far to assassinate me without knowing who I am?"

And suddenly Vidar *did* know. Even before his captor stood, lifted the mask off his head.

Nor had he changed much in more than a thousand years. The short, brown hair. The wide brow, the hawk wariness of his dark eyes. The expressive lips in a black, cropped beard.

"Do you know me now, brother?" Without the mask, his voice was as soft and deep as the sea, as inexorable as the tide.

It was Hod. Odin's son, Baldur's slayer. The brother whom Vali had hunted across nine worlds and beyond.

"Aye," said Vidar. "Now I know you. And other things as well, I think."

Hod sat down again, cradling the mask in one arm. "Such as?"

"Such as how I've been duped. Again. And you too."

"Duped?" echoed Hod, his dark eyes flashing. "By whom?"

"By Odin."

Hod's eyes narrowed. "Of course. And I'm a thursar's grandmother."

Vidar shook his head. "No. I mean it. He's alive and he's out to tear down all he built up. Asgard, Utgard—the works."

Hod frowned. "Save your deceptions, Vidar. I haven't been out of circulation as long as you think. I walked Vigrid Plain, not so long after the battle. I saw the pyres. Later I dared to enter Asaheim itself. Nowhere near Asgard, where I might be recognized—but near enough to hear about what had happened. I know how Odin perished, consumed by Loki's fire. So if you want to deceive me, Jawbreaker, you'll have to come up with something better than that."

"It's no deception," said Vidar. "Odin didn't die at Ragnarok. We all thought so back then, but he saved himself. Fashioned a gate at the last moment. Escaped through it to Niflheim."

He saw Hod's brow furrow at the mention of that place.

"That's right," said Vidar. "You were there once, weren't you? That's where Vali lost track of you."

"I was there," said the dark one. "Go on."

"Is my lie getting more interesting?"

Hod shrugged. "Too early to say. Just go on."

"Odin said they taught him to hate there. To despise all he'd built. To obliterate it."

Hod seemed to ponder that for a moment. "And?"

"There was an uprising in Utgard. The thursar nomads, led by someone called Ygg—with a mask. I wonder now if he knew that you wore one. And he flew your colors—the red eagle on a field of black. Everyone believed he was you—especially Vali."

Hod grunted at that.

"Until we found out the truth. I saw him, brother. He's nuttier than a fruitcake. His face was destroyed in Loki's fire, and it sent him over the brink."

The dark one nodded approvingly. "Nice touch."

"The truth always is." Vidar met his half-brother's gaze. "There was a battle. We thought we had him, but he escaped. We followed him. First to Asaheim, and then to Alfheim—where he'd managed to fire up a civil war. By that time, of course, he'd gotten Magni to join him. And Hoenir as well—though he has since died for it."

"Hoenir is dead?"

"I burned his body myself. But he told us of M'thrund while he still could. Tipped us off that Vali might be here, along with his armies. That's why we came to M'thrund—to search for them." He paused. "Though we expected to find them imprisoned, not roaming the countryside."

Hod stared at him for a time. As if trying to peel away the layers of seeming, to find the rotten core of deceit.

"Then you would tell me," he said, "that this plague of thursar was sent here against its will?"

"Aye," said Vidar. "Along with the others."

Hod's brow knotted. "What others?"

"The Aesirmen," said Vidar. "The Vanirmen, the *dwarvin*..." Vidar saw the look on his face, stopped. "Wait a minute. That's all you found in Gnipa—giants?"

Hod hesitated before answering. "Aye. That's all I found. I assumed it was Vali's way of creating fear and confusion —before he launched his real invasion. But you are no doubt going to tell me otherwise."

Vidar thought about it. *Thursar, but no one else.* Could the gate have been selective somehow? He didn't think so. Nor could he come up with a reason for making it selective.

Then why? Why only thursar?

And then it came to him.

"Aye," said Vidar. "I'll tell you otherwise, all right. And believe it or not, Vali may have had nothing to do with it."

"No? Then where did these thursar come from?"

"From Utgard," said Vidar. "But they're not the thursar who followed Vali, if I'm guessing right. They're the ones who followed Ygg. The nomads, the priests. Somehow, perhaps long before his defeat in Utgard, he sent them through. But it would have to have been another gate, one we never found. Otherwise, half of them would have wound up in Asaheim, as we did."

"But why?" asked Hod. "If he had a quarrel with Asaheim, or with Alfheim, why stir up trouble here?"

"Because," said Vidar, thinking out loud, "he wanted you to think just what you've been thinking. That Vali is responsible for these demons. To perhaps launch a counterattack against Alfheim, and ultimately against Asgard. And in the process, to weaken yourself. So that he could wipe out M'thrund as well—at his leisure."

Hod scowled, and for a while he just went on scowling. Then, without a word, he put the mask back on. And stood.

"Where are you going?" asked Vidar as he too got to his feet.

"Somewhere else," said the masked one.

"All I've told you is the truth, brother. Don't let your feelings for Vali blind you to it. There's too much at stake."

Hod made a sound behind the mask. "Thank you," he said. "I'll try to remember all that."

He pounded once on the door, twice.

"Incidentally," said Hod, "you may have guessed why I wear this mask. And you may think you can undermine me by telling the guards what I am—by playing on their hatred of the pale-of-flesh."

Vidar heard the guards making their way down the corridor.

"But there's no rumor about me that hasn't lived and died a hundred times. So unless you can show them my face, once and for all, your stories will fall on deaf ears."

Then the door opened, and Hod slipped through it.

A moment later a guard retrieved the stool.

Time passed slowly in the cell, with no ebb and flow of daylight to mark it. Vidar was brought food again, eventually. It was the same as before—bread and water. But this time, Hod had been thoughtful. The bread was almost fresh and the water jug was clean.

When he grew tired, he slept. And he dreamed of Baldur.

He was standing on the deck of Baldur's funeral ship, trying to wake him as the flames leaped all about them. Past the fire, he could see the distant towers of Asgard, wavering in the smoke.

"Get up," he said.

Baldur's eyes opened. But they were not the laughing eyes that Vidar remembered. They were dull, like slate. Like death itself.

"Let me sleep," said Baldur.

"No," said Vidar. "We need you. Let us leave this ship."

"Go," said Baldur. "I can be your light no longer. Find someone else."

"How can we live without you?" insisted Vidar as the smoke seared his throat.

"You cannot," whispered Baldur, and his mouth filled with serpents, and his eye sockets filled with blood.

"No!" cried Vidar . . .

. . . and woke like a drowning man clawing for air. He took in great mouthfuls of it, until the sight of Baldur was gone, gone, finally gone.

Then there was a guard outside, pounding at the door. "Quiet in there," yelled the *thrund*, "or I'll come in there and shut you up myself."

"Try it," said Vidar, loud enough for the guard to hear him through the door.

But the guard must have thought better of it. Vidar heard his slow retreat down the corridor.

Too bad.

It was only after he'd lain back against the straw that he felt the pain in his forearm. Holding it up in the meager light, he saw where he'd been bitten. The wound was small but nasty.

He listened, but there was no sound of the creature's passage behind the wall. Of course not. The filthy little thing had had its dinner already.

Vidar shuddered at the thought of it.

Then again, perhaps it had been a fair exchange. A little flesh was a small price to pay for being woken out of that dream.

The sound of footsteps roused him. Not one set, but many.

Had the guard, stung by Vidar's taunt, decided to round up some friends to help him?

The Aesirman scrambled to his feet. He didn't care how many of them were out there, or how well they were armed. As long as they opened the door.

The bolts grated as they moved. Vidar brushed the straw aside for better footing, braced himself.

The door moved, swung open. Squinting, he counted five of them out in the corridor. But it was another moment before he realized that one of them was Tofa.

She stepped into the cell. With a gesture, she got the guards to close the door behind her.

Her eyes told him that he wasn't her favorite person these days.

But she'd admired him once. The Queen had said so. If he could convince anyone of the truth here in Erithain, it would be her.

"Jalk told me who you were," she said. "But I wanted to hear it from your own lips."

"It's not the way it appears," said Vidar.

"Are you saying you didn't lie to me?"

"I did," he admitted. "Obviously, I'm no *thrund*. Nor are my companions—if they're still alive."

"They are," she said. Nothing more.

"But you have to understand—we didn't come here to

hurt you. Or to aid in any conquest. We came in search of friends of ours. And to stop someone called Odin."

Tofa smiled, but it was all bitterness. "Aye," she said. "Jalk told us the story. Of how you claim to hunt your own father."

"Did he tell you," asked Vidar, "that it was his father too?"

Her brow wrinkled, but only for a moment.

"Another lie," she said. "They come easily to you."

"Believe what you will," he told her. "Beneath that mask, Jalk is as pale as I am. Or as I will be, once this berry juice wears off." He paused. "Why do you think he wears the mask in the first place?"

Again, the slightest wrinkle of doubt. But not enough. He tried a different tack.

"Did Jalk send you here?"

"No," she said. "Of course not." She straightened. "In fact, he forbade it."

"Then why did you come? Just to hear me confess?"

She glared at him. "To ask you why."

"Why what?"

"Why you brought me down from that ledge. You couldn't have known who I was—how I might have been of use to you. Why not just let me die?"

He shrugged. "If you won't believe the rest of it, my lady, you probably wouldn't believe that part either."

Anger leaped into her eyes.

"You mock me," she said.

"No," he told her. "You mock yourself. For once in your life, look past Jalk's truths. Open your eyes."

He could almost hear her teeth grating together. Her eyes were hard, deadly. And he noticed that her hand was on her hilt.

"Would you rather kill me," he asked, "than ask yourself if Jalk could be wrong?"

Her nostrils flared, but she didn't draw the sword. Instead, she rapped on the door with her knuckles. The guards came a moment later.

"I have heard all I wish to'," she told them.

And like Hod before her, she left unconvinced.

For what seemed a long time afterward, he had no other visitors. It occurred to him that he might seek help from the Queen—that he might cash in somehow on all her protests of gratitude. On one occasion he even tried to talk his guards into carrying word to her.

But they only laughed. If their roles were reversed, Vidar conceded, he might have laughed too.

And so it went. Food was passed in, and he ate. Empty trays were withdrawn.

Twice more he himself was nibbled on. He began to wonder if there was such a thing as rabies in M'thrund.

And then, some number of days after he'd woken in this cell, the door opened without warning.

A group of *hjalamar*—not dungeon guards—waited without.

"Come with us," said one of the soldiers. "And don't try anything."

"Where are we going?" asked Vidar.

"You'll see when we get there."

Vidar didn't like the sound of that. Or the expressions of the *hjalamar*. Prisons this old, he knew, always had torture chambers.

Was it possible that some of the *hjalamar* had decided to have some sport with the pale-of-flesh prisoner? Sport that wouldn't leave too many marks and arouse Jalk's anger?

Or had Hod concluded that Vidar was lying after all—and that he wanted those answers he'd asked for?

No matter.

To Vidar, it was a chance to get free of his cell. And with some luck—a great deal of it—out of this place as well. With an incredible amount of good fortune, he might even be able to take his friends with him.

"All right," said Vidar. He got up slowly, approached the doorway. And as he did this, the *hjalamar* parted, so that some could walk before him and some behind.

Once out in the corridor, Vidar was surprised at the length of it. He counted five torches arranged at intervals, and that was only before the turning of the passageway.

A spearpoint prodded him in the back.

"Move," said a *thrund*.

He moved. And they moved with him.

But only until they were past the first torch, in a place where the light could have been better. Then he whirled, grabbed the spear that had prodded him, and snapped it in two.

Lashing out with one of the fragments, he caught someone across the face. Someone else took the jagged end of it.

A sword flashed in the corner of his eye, and he turned in time to catch its owner by the wrist. With an effort, he flung him into two of his fellow soldiers.

Then the way before him was clear and he was flying down the corridor. Behind him there were cries and rapid-fire curses.

He didn't know where he was going, didn't know where this passage might lead. But the *hjalamar* seemed frantic enough to stop him, so it seemed a good bet he was headed for a way out.

The corridor twisted, twisted again. He ran as fast as the twistings would allow him to, listening to the thunder of his pursuers as it echoed at his heels.

And by the time he saw the group of *hjalamar* up ahead, it was too late to stop.

So he did the next best thing. He lowered his shoulder and plowed straight ahead.

It caught them by surprise. He bowled over the first two he met. But as they fell, their feet got tangled up with his, and he hit the floor.

Before he could rise, he was peering down the length of a sword. A moment later he felt a spearpoint in his back again. And another.

Someone laughed. It was almost a cackle, and it sounded oddly familiar.

Vidar looked up and saw the face at the far end of the

blade. It was the wolfish one—the *hjalamar* he and N'arri had met in the tavern.

"What have we here?" asked the *thrund*. "An intruder in Jalk's dungeons?"

"It's the pale-of-flesh," said a voice from behind Vidar. "The one that tried to kill Jalk."

"Is he?" Another laugh—this time deep and resounding. Vidar turned just enough to see the one called Meili. "Then this is our lucky day. I never thought I'd see the bastard again—to repay him for the other night."

"Have a care," said Vidar. "I was on my way to see Jalk. I don't think he wants to be kept waiting."

The wolfish one waved his point before Vidar's eyes. "No," he said. "We wouldn't want to keep him waiting." He laid the cold iron of his sword against Vidar's cheek. "So what we do must be done quickly."

"Jalk wanted him whole," said the voice from behind Vidar.

The wolfish one shrugged. "There's whole and there's whole," he said. "And would it be reasonable to expect that an escaping prisoner could be caught without a scratch?" He turned the blade, so that the edge of it pressed against Vidar's face. "Of course not."

"Take that blade away," said Vidar, "or you'll wish you had."

The *thrund* drew the blade along Vidar's cheek, slicing into his flesh. The Aesirman could feel the warm trickle of blood.

"Will I?" asked the wolfish one.

Meili laughed again. "Too bad your friend in the hood's not here—though I'm sure we'll see him soon enough."

Vidar turned to glower at him, costing himself more pain, more blood. "Coward," he said. "If you didn't have your comrades all around you, we'd see how brave you really are."

Vidar's comment had the desired effect. Meili sputtered with rage, shouldered the wolfish one aside.

But before he could do anything else, there was a murmuring among the *hjalamar*. Heads turned.

And Vidar recognized the one called Half—the warrior captain they'd met that night on the road to Erithain. He had a couple of the black-and-silver at his back.

"What's going on here?" asked Half.

"What business is it of yours?" returned Meili. From the way he glared at Half, Vidar could tell there was no love lost between them.

"When it's Jalk's business," said Half, "it's my business. Or didn't you know that he is waiting to see this prisoner?"

"He tried to escape," said the wolfish one. "Luckily, we were coming down the corridor, and we stopped him."

Half regarded Vidar, saw the cut across his cheek.

"Aye," he said. "I see how efficient you were." He turned toward the giant, eyed him coolly. "I'll take charge of him from here on."

"As you wish," said Meili. "And if you watch him very carefully, perhaps you can keep him from running away again."

Half scowled. "Someday," he said, "I'll have to still that wagging tongue of yours."

"Someday," echoed Meili. He laughed, winking at the wolfish one.

Two of the *hjalamar* raised Vidar to his feet, and he was moving down the corridor again, surrounded by black-and-silver. The giant's laughter followed them for quite some time.

XV

WHEN they arrived at his chamber, Hod was waiting for them. He stood by a window, his mask ruddy in the torchlight.

"My lord," said Half, entering first. "The prisoner you asked for."

Hod looked at him for a moment, perhaps wondering how Half had gotten involved in this. Then he glanced at Vidar.

"Bring him in," he said finally.

Vidar came ahead before the spearpoints could prod him again. The blood on his face was beginning to dry, but it would have been difficult for Hod not to notice it.

"Was there a problem?" he asked.

Half shrugged. "He tried to escape, my lord. Sokk and some of the others stopped him."

Hod nodded once. Apparently he'd learned all he wished to know. Then, with a gesture, he dismissed the *hjalamar*.

Half didn't question the wisdom of leaving Jalk alone with the prisoner. He just left, pulling the door closed behind him.

"Sit," said Hod. He indicated a plain wooden chair next to a plainer wooden table, and Vidar saw that his tastes hadn't changed. His rooms at Gladsheim had been like this—stark and cold.

The hearth, Vidar noted, was dark. He guessed that Hod had been away—had just returned, perhaps.

He sat. Hod remained standing.

They looked at one another. As before, the mask seemed

hollow, empty. The eye slits black and mysterious. Nor did Hod take the thing off this time, perhaps anticipating a sudden interruption.

"You recall," asked the masked one, "that Odin used to be able to sniff out gates? Before he learned to make them himself?"

Vidar nodded. "Of course. In the early days, when he traveled with Hoenir and Lodur."

"Exactly." He paused. "I developed a similar talent, here in M'thrund. As a defense against Vali."

Vidar thought about that for a moment. "Because if he were to attack again, he'd have created a new gate for the purpose. One that couldn't have been guarded."

"Aye."

"Impressive," said Vidar.

"Not really. But it's enabled me to sleep a little better." He seemed lost in thought for a moment. Then he went on. "Right after I saw you, I rode out to a place called Miskur —to track down another report of demons." He grunted behind the mask. "As it turned out, there were no demons in Miskur after all. But there *was* a gate—close enough for me to feel its presence."

"A gate," said Vidar. "To where?"

Hod told him.

Vidar leaned back in his chair, pondered the information.

"I went through," said Hod. "Carefully. As it happened, there was no one on the other side. No guards at all. But I needed no further evidence. It already made perfect sense. Here was the gate Vali had used to transport his thursar to M'thrund. And as before, he'd placed a world between Asaheim and this one, to serve as a buffer."

"Or," said Vidar, "it was Odin who made the gate."

Hod made a snorting sound. "That's the next thing that occurred to me. So I'd still proven nothing. And that's the position I was in when I returned to Erithain. But when I arrived, I found that my *hjalamar* had broken the thursar— the pair we'd brought back from Gnipa. One of them had confessed that he was indeed an agent of Vali, sent to weaken us in preparation for an invasion. However, the other thursar had grown feverish from his wounds, and what he blurted out in his delirium was much to the contrary."

"He spoke of Ygg," said Vidar.

"Aye," said Hod. "And of a cold, barren place he'd had to cross in order to reach M'thrund. And of a fortress, built into the side of a mountain."

Vidar knew that fortress. Knew it only too well.

"And so," said Hod, "you see my dilemma. It is difficult to believe your story about Odin. But it is becoming more difficult to ignore it."

Vidar had some reservations of his own. If Odin was holed up in that fortress, what army was he holed up *with*? More Utgard thursar? Could there have been that many of them?

He had the feeling that there were prodigious forces moving just beneath the surface—forces he didn't understand. As if all Odin had done until now had only set the stage for what was to come.

But he didn't mention any of this to Hod. The issue was clouded enough already.

"Look," said Vidar. "Take us to this gate. Send us through. And then put a guard on it. What have you got to lose?"

Hod shrugged. "Much, I think—if you're working for Vali. First off, you've seen Erithain. Taken stock of her defenses. Second, Vali doesn't know we've found the gate—and if we let you tell him, we'd be losing the opportunity to set a trap there."

Vidar shook his head. "Damn. I wish that you'd seen what I've seen, brother. That I could show you somehow—prove that while we sit here talking, Odin is gathering kindling for the conflagration."

Hod regarded him. "Interesting that you should say that—because it's exactly what I had in mind. For you to show me that you're telling the truth."

Vidar met his eyeless gaze. "How?"

"By going through that gate with *me*. By making the journey to that fortress the thursar ranted about. That way, if your story is true, you'll have learned what you claim you need to know. And you'll be free to summon whatever aid is necessary." He paused. "And if your story's false, you'll be there to pay the penalty."

For a moment Vidar thought about Baldur, and how they'd found him floating with that arrow in his breast. He tried to put it from his mind.

"Fair enough," he said. "And my companions?"

"One will come. The Aesirman."

It was more than Vidar had hoped for.

"In case something happens to you," Hod went on, "we'll still have someone who can carry on your mission—again, allowing that you're telling the truth."

"What about the others?" he asked.

"They're unharmed, and they'll stay that way. No one touches my prisoners unless I give them leave."

Vidar ran his finger over the slice in his cheek, awakening the pain. "No one?"

Hod grunted. "Occasionally I brook exceptions. But you need not worry about Sokk and Meili."

"Why not?"

"They'll be coming with us."

They sat their horses in the courtyard of Hod's hall—actually more of a compound, walled in as it was from the rest of Erithain, crowded with *hjalamar* who glared at them from time to time.

Its practice fields, white with fresh snow, were visible through a broad archway. And while there were only a few riders out there now, clashing and disengaging and clashing again, it reminded Vidar a lot of Valhalla. Indeed, Valhalla must have been the model for this place.

"You saw them yourself?" asked Ullir.

"Aye," said Vidar. "He gave me that much."

"And? Are they well enough?"

Vidar shrugged, frowned. "Cuts and scrapes, sustained in the square. They were lucky. We all were."

Ullir nodded. "Good. The last time I saw N'arri, I thought he was done for. I'm glad I was wrong."

Vidar patted his gelding's neck. It was the same horse he'd ridden into M'thrund, recovered from the inn.

"In a way," he said, "it's good that they'll be staying here. It strikes me that they'll be safer than you or I."

Ullir regarded him. "Then you think we'll really find him this time?"

"Aye," said Vidar. "I do. I've got a feeling in my bones."

"It makes me wish they'd given us back our swords," said the blondbeard.

"Mine especially," said Odin's son. He paused. "You know, you were right. I should have attuned to it when I had the chance."

"Was I?" asked Ullir. "If you *had* attuned, we'd only have succeeded in killing your brother. And a lot of *hjalamar* to boot. And we might never have learned what we know now —about the thursar, and about the gate." He smiled a little. "Perhaps you knew it was not the right time. In your bones, as you say."

Then their attention was drawn to another, smaller archway on the other side of the main building, where there seemed to be some activity brewing. A moment later a group of mounted *hjalamar* rode through the arch.

Hod, masked as always, was at the head of them. And Vidar counted five others—a small enough group for the reconnaissance they had in mind, yet big enough in case they ran into some trouble.

He wasn't surprised to see Tofa among them. After she'd been shamed twice—once by her defeat at the gate, and again by having befriended Jalk's would-be assassin—she must have pulled every string at her disposal to become part of this mission. It was the only way she had of redeeming herself.

Meili was there too, and Sokk beside him. Just as the masked one had promised.

"Those were the two I told you about," said Vidar. "The big one, and the one who rides with him."

"I'll watch out for them," said Ullir. He surveyed the others. "The warrior on the left there—he looks familiar too, doesn't he?"

"Aye," said Vidar. "That's Half."

"Of course. The *hjalamar* we met by the river."

"And the one who interceded for me last night—or Sokk might have carved away a little more."

He knew the last figure also, though he couldn't place him at first. Then he remembered.

It was one of the warriors who'd flanked Hod as he returned to Erithain. Vidar conveyed as much to Ullir.

"He looks young," said the Aesirman.

"Perhaps. But he must be deadly as well, to have earned a spot at Hod's side."

"Why not, I wonder, bring *only* those who ride closest to him?"

Vidar shrugged. "Good bodyguards don't always make good traveling companions. I once knew a chieftain who never let his bodyguards near him when he was alone—only when he was surrounded by other people. In that way his guards protected him from the masses, and the masses protected him from his guards."

Ullir smiled. "I see. Hod decided that one guard was enough to guarantee his safety—and more may have jeopardized it."

"Something like that," said Vidar.

Then he felt it—the sudden pull, the yearning. And it must have shown in his expression, because Ullir asked him what was wrong.

"The sword," said Vidar. "It's nearby."

Ullir's brows knit. "You mean here? In the courtyard?"

"I believe so. And it seems to be getting closer."

That narrowed it down to the group who had just come through the arch. Their eyes were drawn to the sword at Hod's side.

But it wasn't Angrum that dangled there. The hilt was too long, too plain, the blade itself too broad.

And then Vidar found it. Not at Hod's side, but at Meili's.

"There it is," he said. "The giant's got it."

Ullir looked. When he spotted Angrum, his eyes narrowed.

"He admired it in the tavern," said Vidar. "When he found out who I was last night, he must have gone searching for it in Jalk's armory. And found it."

"But he can't know what he's carrying," said Ullir.

"Nor can Hod," said Vidar, "or he would have confiscated it for himself."

"Then you'll have your chance to attune to it after all."

Vidar looked at him. "You mean, while the *thrund* is carrying it?"

"Why not? It will just take a little longer, that's all."

"And when the attunement is complete, I can take it from him."

"Aye," said Ullir. "But it must be at the right moment. When we need the sword's power."

"Of course," said Vidar. "When we need it."

But once attuned, how long could he restrain himself?

It was just as Hod had said. A crevice in the rock, concealed by the bushes and young fir trees that grew up around it. Clogged with soft snow until they dug it away, and then even Vidar could sense the gaping eternity within it.

Hod went first, then Vidar.

As when he'd entered M'thrund, there was the blackness, the hum—the numbing of the senses. The feeling of walking on a bridge of air, a span of nothingness. Then they were through, sooner than Vidar had expected.

And once more, as in ages past, he looked out upon Jotunheim.

They stood on a broad ledge beneath a raw, red wound of a sun and looked out across a monstrous valley. The wind rode through it, wailing, freezing the side of Vidar's face.

Down below, at the bottom of a long escarpment, there was a river. It writhed its way among cruel, sheer surfaces, where the ground seemed to have risen up and split apart—

twisted and torn into shapes never seen on other worlds. Where it pooled, the river looked like blood.

Beyond the valley he saw the true mountains of Jotunheim. Gnarled formations that made these hills look orderly, and the least of them would have dwarfed Earth's Everest. Covered with a glaze of snow, they looked pink in the glare of Jotunheim's sun.

Nor, as Hod had attested, were there sentinels at this gate. No one to warn Odin of their approach.

But then, Odin—ignorant of Hod's talent—would never have expected them to find this gate in the first place.

"Strange," said Hod, "is it not? To be in this place again?"

"Strange indeed," said Vidar. And though he tried not to remember his last visit to Jotunheim, he could smell the funeral pyres as if they burned even now.

Hod pointed. "You know that river? I followed it when I was fleeing Vali." He paused, scanning the broken hills. "There's a keep not far from here—I think."

None of it looked immediately familiar to Vidar. If he'd ever come through this area on one of Odin's raids, he'd managed to forget about it.

"All right," he said. "Then you lead."

A moment later Meili came through the gate, looking a little shaken by the experience. Sokk came next, then Ullir, Half, and the guard—whose name, they'd discovered, was Lami. Tofa came last.

"This way," said Hod, before his *thrund* had a chance to be daunted by the forbidding terrain. "And be careful. If you break your legs, we'll have to leave you where you lie."

So saying, he half crawled, half slid down the escarpment. Vidar slid after him, shielding his eyes from the wind-driven gravel that rasped across the slope.

Hod had been right, of course, to leave the horses in M'thrund. They would have been useless here.

At the bottom of the escarpment, there was a bank. It was treacherous with loose stones—the detritus that had been shorn from the frozen mountainsides over thousands of years. Maybe more like millions.

And beyond the bank the river plunged and roared.

Hod turned toward the bloody sun, already on its descent. The river ran in that direction, thundering, throwing up sheets of spray.

Hod shouted something.

Vidar could barely hear him over the crashing of the water. They were standing in a spot where it cascaded, hammering the rocks below.

"What?" roared Meili.

"West," bellowed Sokk, who'd been right beside the masked one. "West with the river."

They started along the bank. The sun angled before them, giving off a ruddy light, but precious little warmth. High above, the wind shrilled like a banshee, finding secret places in the stone.

Then the sun grew indistinct, vague, and finally vanished altogether. It began to sleet.

The ground underfoot became slippery, slowing them down. And the river geysered up from the rocks, drenching their cloaks until they stiffened and grew heavy with ice.

From beneath his hood, Vidar peered up at the gray cliffs. He could almost see the ghosts of Odin's heroes riding there —silhouetted against the colorless sky, ready to stoop with fire and iron on the keep of some giant who'd grown too proud.

He spat.

In the end they'd all grown too proud, hadn't they? And even Odin's keep had fallen to fire and iron.

Beside him Ullir grunted. "Nice weather we're having."

"Aye," said Vidar. "Delightful."

"It's like carrying a bear on your shoulders," said the Aesirman. Even with his hood drawn down, his beard had rimed over.

"Hod mentioned a keep," said Vidar. "With any luck it's not far off."

But as the sun vanished behind the jut of the mountains, and the sky in the east purpled like an angry bruise, there was still no sign of the keep. And it was growing harder and harder to see where they were going.

Where's that keep, brother?

Hod heard the words in his brain, responded.

Up ahead, as I said before. Unless you'd like to lay your cloak out here, Jawbreaker.

No thanks. I have every confidence in you.

I'm touched.

The shadows fell and the temperature fell with them. The wind sliced at them with the skill of a surgeon, and the *thrund* shrugged down deeper into their cloaks, never having felt such cold before.

It was one thing to know winter, another to know Jotunheim by day. But the vast and deadly night of this world was an entirely different experience.

And then, in the last bleak, gray light, they spied it. A stone house, halfway up a slope streaked with white-ice gullies.

As they started up, Vidar made contact again.

You know, I just had a thought.

What's that? asked Hod, not even bothering to look back at him.

If Odin wanted to keep an eye on his back door, but not be too obvious about it, he might have used this keep—as an outpost. The river passage may be the only one through these hills, and the keep so conveniently overlooks it.

Interesting idea, said Hod. *But welcome mat or no, I'm not going to freeze out here tonight.*

I just wanted you to be ready. You're the one with the sword.

But when they reached the keep, the doorway was empty. Open to the wind.

As it turned out, the rest of the place was empty too. Or at least there was nothing alive in there.

But there were bones aplenty. Huge skeletons with splintered ribs and caved-in skulls. And a couple of smaller skeletons as well—Aesir, Vanir, or human, it was hard to tell which.

Apparently the hrimthursar hadn't yielded this place without a fight.

Fortunately there were still some logs piled up near the hearth, and kindling, and when Half struck his flint the room flooded with light.

They took some of the bigger logs and piled them by the doorless entrance to block out the wind. For the most part it worked.

Unwrapping whatever food they'd brought along, they ate. Few words were exchanged, for the weather had robbed them of their strength. When they were done, they pulled themselves as close to the fire as they dared, eager for every caress of warmth it could give them.

Vidar waited until the others were asleep. Then he crept closer to Meili. Closer to the sword.

Finally, finally, he opened himself up to it. He concentrated, seeking the very thing he'd been avoiding all this time—the pool of bright fury that lay at Angrum's heart.

At first there was nothing. Then gradually a trickle of energy, a greater trickle, a flow.

He let it fill him like a fiery wine, felt himself flush with only a hint of its power. And before the tide of force could subside in him, he gave it something of himself—sent his own being flooding into Angrum. Greedily the sword accepted it, drank it as a vampire bat leeches blood.

Moments later the feeling was gone, as if it had never happened. But Vidar knew better.

The attunement had begun.

XVI

THE hrimthursar raided Asgard once again, and once again the two-hundred-foot-high walls were too much for them. Then the Aesir rushed forth from the city's mighty gates and routed the invaders. Their swords whistled and their shields glinted in the sun, and when the dust had cleared, there were only nine hrimthursar left standing.

"Spare us," said one of the giants, "for we are nine brothers, and surely our father Hymir will pay our ransom."

"What ransom can tempt the Lord of Asgard?" asked Odin. His speartip was red with giants' blood, and his hands were sticky with it.

"A caldron," said the hrimthursar. "A great caldron made of black iron. Whenever mead is brewed in this caldron, it comes out as sweet as honey."

"Very well then," said Odin. "Go back to your father. Tell him that Odin will accept his caldron as ransom. But every day that I am kept waiting, I will lop off the head of one of your brothers. And if I wait nine days, then you must return and give me your head as well."

The giant, whose name was Skavid, had little choice but to agree. Right then and there, he set off for Jotunheim and his father's keep. When he reached that place, high in the gray, hard mountains, he told the hrimthursar Hymir all that had happened.

"And for every day that Odin waits, he will lop off one of

my brothers' heads. So let us be quick, Father, and bring him the caldron before sunset."

Hymir heard this story and shook his head.

"My great iron pot," he said in misery. "How can I live without it? When the winds come cutting and the trees lose their leaves, the honey-sweet mead is my only joy."

"But, Father . . ." said the giant.

Hymir held up his huge hand. "Silence," he said. "I shall ponder this."

And so a day went by, and a night, and the next day Skavid came to Hymir again.

"I have already lost a brother," he said. "Was the caldron worth his head? Now let us be quick, Father, and bring Odin the caldron before sunset."

Once more Hymir shook his head.

"My great iron pot," he moaned. "How can I live without it? When the winds come cutting and the cattle grow thin, the honey-sweet mead is my only joy."

"But, Father . . ." said Skavid.

Hymir rolled his tiny black eyes. "Quiet," he said. "I shall ponder this."

A second day went by, and a second night, and with the dawn Skavid came to see his father again.

"Two brothers gone," he said. "Is the caldron so dear to you? Let us be quick this time, and bring Odin the caldron before sunset."

A third time Hymir shook his shaggy head.

"My wondrous kettle," he cried. "How can I live without it? When the winds come cutting and the rivers freeze, the honey-sweet mead is my only joy."

Skavid tried to protest, but Hymir growled at him. "Peace," he said. "I shall ponder this."

Hymir gave the matter much thought, but that was all he gave. Altogether, eight days and nights passed, and on the ninth day Skavid came to stand before him.

"Eight days have passed, and eight brothers with them. Now," said Skavid, "I must return to Asaheim, as I swore I would. Is the caldron worth my head too, Father? If I'm quick, I can bring Odin the pot before sunset."

Hymir heard his son's words and looked upon him. Skavid, the pride of his house. Of all those who had gone raiding in Asaheim, only this one remained—the tallest, the broadest, and the most skilled with sword and ax. His last son, his only son, the strength that would guard him in his old age.

All these things Hymir took into account.

But in the end he shook his head.

"My great iron pot," he said. "How can I live without it? For when the winds come cutting and the wolves circle the keep, the honey-sweet mead is my only joy."

Sin Skolding
Samsey, 419 A.D.

XVII

THEY woke shivering and stiff, their fire having died down to embers. But they could see through a chink in the stones, near the roof, that it was morning.

Hod barked some orders, got them moving. Half and Lami went outside to get a chunk of ice, and Meili brought some more wood over, while Sokk set a blackened, iron pot on a tripod. And soon they had brewed a drink of hot water to wash their food down with.

"Not much of a taste," said Ullir, "but welcome nonetheless."

"Indeed," said Vidar, passing the cup back to the blond-beard, for they hadn't found enough cups to go around.

"And how did you sleep?" asked Ullir, not inquiring about sleep at all.

Vidar shrugged. "Like a sword in its sheath."

Ullir smiled a little, nodded.

After breakfast they returned the keep to its ghosts. The wind assailed them out of a gray, trundling sky, piercing their cloaks, gnawing at their flesh and bones.

They followed the river again, until it pitched over a cliff and eluded them. Then Hod led them south, since it presented the easiest path. And because it was the way he'd taken before, although he didn't tell his *hjalamar* that.

As the ground rose sharply on their right, they got some protection from the wind. But soon after, it fell away on their left, exposing them to a smooth slope of eighty feet or so. And at the bottom of it, a field of jagged rocks.

For some time they went on like that, hugging what grew to be a sheer rock wall on one flank, careful to stay away from the slope on the other.

Then, sometime around what would have been noon, Lami spotted them. Gray hunters, white-masked. A dozen of them, sleek and big-boned, slinking among those cruel formations at the bottom of the slope.

The wolves of Jotunheim.

Vidar watched them, remembering how they'd ranged over Vigrid Plain. He recalled the fierce, yellow eyes, the jaws slavering with Aesir blood . . . the gobbets of furred flesh that flew before his sword . . . the howls of rage and pain . . . .

One of them started up the slope, its tongue lolling in its mouth. Another started up after it.

But they slid back down again.

Again they tried, but to no avail. The slope was just too icy.

"Filthy beasts." Meili sneered.

"Aye," said Sokk. "I wish I'd thought to bring a bow."

"Forget them," said Hod. "If they cannot reach us, we've nothing to worry about."

"Aye," said Tofa. "It's too cold to stand here gaping."

So they went on. But the wolves paced them, weaving in and out of the rocks. And whenever Vidar glanced down, he found them looking up at him.

He began to wonder. If Loki had learned to make wolves his allies on Vigrid, and Hoenir had done the same in the mountains of Alfheim . . . then why not Odin?

Was that why he needed no one to guard the gate—because his sentinels went on four legs?

He expressed the thought to Hod, up ahead.

Mentally his half-brother shrugged. *And if they were under Odin's power? What could I do about it?*

Nothing much right now, of course. But I don't want you to say I didn't warn you.

Thanks, said Hod, *for the warning.*

Don't mention it.

The wolves made them all nervous, but it was Meili they seemed to bother most. He couldn't take his eyes off them. And every time they tried to scrabble their way up the slope, his hand darted to Angrum's hilt.

Finally he couldn't take it anymore. When they came to some loose boulders that had dislodged from above, Hod and those just behind him—Tofa and Lami—made their way between them. But Meili saw his chance.

"Furry bastards," said the *thrund*. "I'll teach you to nip at our heels."

Putting his considerable weight behind the largest of the boulders, he got it to rock a little. But it wouldn't roll.

Below them the wolves stopped to watch.

They all did. Even Hod, though he said nothing.

"What are you doing?" called Half, last in line.

"What does it look like?" asked Sokk. "He's removing a danger from our flank."

"And starting a rockslide," said Half, "if he's not careful."

Sokk's eyes slitted. "Perhaps," he said, "you'd like to stop him."

Half spat. "Perhaps I will." And with that, he made his way past Ullir.

But it was too late. Meili had already propped one foot against the sheer rock face. And as Half came forward, the giant pushed with all his strength.

For a moment it looked as if the boulder wouldn't budge. Then, abruptly, it tipped over and came crashing down the slope.

But as hard as Meili had pushed, he couldn't stop himself. When the boulder lurched forward, so did he.

And before anyone could stop him, he went sliding down the escarpment, bellowing as he fell toward the wolves below.

Along with the sword.

Vidar's first impulse was to slide down after him, try to stop him somehow. But he knew it would do no good. They'd only tumble down together.

"Spread yourself out!" cried Sokk. "Use your hands—your feet!"

Meili must have heard him, for he did just that. And miraculously he ground to a halt—his boots not twenty feet from where the wolves were regrouping.

A bolt of gray fur shot up the slope, snarling. Fell just short of Meili's heels and slid down again.

Another wolf leaped, failed. And another.

Each time Meili cried out in alarm.

And each time Vidar feared the sword lost.

But in the end the giant didn't panic. He remained motionless, clinging to the slope.

And before long the wolves learned patience. They ceased their efforts, content to pad silently along the base of the slope. The beasts seemed to know that their prey would have to move—eventually. And when he did, they'd have him.

"Are you all right?" yelled Half.

Meili turned his head slowly, dared to look up. And they

saw what the stopping had cost him. His face had been scored by the rock, bloodied. But at least he was alive.

"We've got to get him," said Tofa. "Somehow."

Hod shrugged. "I told him to ignore the beasts. He's gotten no more than he deserves."

The *hjalamar* looked at Hod, and none of them dared speak against him. Not even Sokk, though he seemed about to explode.

You can't let him die, said Vidar. *Not for disobeying a casual order like that one.*

Hod's answer was sharp, curt. *This is none of your business, brother.*

True. But Angrum was his business, even if he couldn't say so.

Vidar tried another approach. *He must be of value to you —to us—or you wouldn't have brought him along.*

That seemed to sway Hod a little. But not enough.

You know nothing of these people. They only follow me because they fear me.

Down the slope Meili grunted with pain, and the wolves snapped to attention.

Don't you think you've made your point already? Give the damned fool a break.

Behind his mask Hod regarded him. *Interesting talk, coming from someone who has reason to hate this damned fool.*

Because if he dies, I'll never have a chance to pay him back.

Hod seemed to accept that. It was characteristic of the Vidar he'd known.

Very well, he said. *Have you got a plan?*

Vidar glanced downslope. Meili had pressed his face into the stone again and was muttering curses. He didn't think the *thrund* could hold out much longer.

The wolves must have come to the same conclusion, for they'd begun to growl softly, their teeth bared in anticipation. They seemed to be laughing at Meili's predicament.

Aye, said Vidar. *I've got a plan.* And he described it quickly to Hod.

The masked one considered it. Considered Vidar. Finally he nodded.

"All right," he announced. "We've let him dangle there long enough."

There was a collective sigh of relief from the *hjalamar.* And from Ullir as well.

Hod surveyed the rocky path they'd come along, found what he was looking for. Then he pulled out his sword and, with both hands, drove it deep into a small crevice.

He tested it. It held.

"We'll form a chain," he said, "until we reach Meili." He knelt, taking hold of the sword. "I'll be the anchor."

No one argued. Lami was the first to move, grabbing Hod's middle and lowering himself down the escarpment, until he stretched full length.

Half came next. He edged down the slope beside Lami, hanging on to the youth as he descended. When he reached his feet, Half stopped, and got a good grip on Lami's ankles.

Then came Ullir. The blondbeard slithered down alongside the others, without waiting to be asked.

"He's a pale-of-flesh," complained Sokk. "He'll kick us free as soon as we get down there."

"Then he'll be dropping his companion as well," said Hod. "Now, move—and quickly."

Tight-lipped, Sokk made his way down the chain. And Tofa followed him.

Then it was Vidar's turn.

Hurry, said Hod. *I can't hold this weight all day.*

I'm hurrying, said Vidar.

His elbows and knees scraping against the rock, he lowered himself along the living ladder. He'd gotten as far as Tofa when he heard Meili's strangled cry, turned, and saw what had happened.

Meili must have lost his grip, slipped, and regained it again. But it left him lying even farther down the slope.

It stirred the wolves to a frenzy. Vidar saw them barrel up

the escarpment, jaws snapping. And they were coming a lot closer than before.

He descended more quickly than prudence dictated, reached Tofa's ankles, and swung his legs out as far as they would go.

"Can you reach me?" Vidar cried.

"Almost," yelled Meili. "Come a little closer."

But it was as far as Vidar could stretch.

He heard the clawing of the wolves, the rumbling deep within their throats. The barking as they fell earthward again.

"Please!" screamed the *thrund*. "They're tearing at my feet!"

That's when Vidar noticed the flower, growing out of a tiny crevice in the stone.

Rimebrother, the hrimthursar used to call it. Not only for its pale blue color, but for its tenacity in the face of wind and frost.

Vidar let go of Tofa's foot with one hand, gripped the flower's stem, tugged on it. It *seemed* sturdy enough.

And if he waited too long thinking about it, Meili would be wolf food.

Letting go of Tofa with his other hand, he dropped himself down another couple of feet, allowing all his weight to depend from the flower.

Above him Tofa cried out, believing that he'd lost his grip and fallen.

Below, a huge hand took hold of his foot. He felt his shoulders strain with the additional weight on them. And then Meili was dragging himself up with what strength he had left, clambering over Vidar like a drowning man clutching at a raft.

Vidar suffered the fingers that caught in his hair, the boot that tried to find a foothold in his neck. It only lasted a little while, and then Meili was gone.

The wolves leaped and growled, realizing that they'd been cheated of their prey somehow. They threw themselves at the slope and Vidar watched them for a moment, knowing a little of the fear Meili had felt.

Then, with the help of the flower, he pulled himself up enough to grab one of Tofa's feet. Releasing the stem, he grabbed for the other one, found it. And careful not to let go of her, clambered up alongside her.

Their eyes met, and the look in hers was the same look he'd seen after he slew the *tarsas*.

But only for a moment. Then Tofa turned her sweat-streaked face away from him, as if to deny what he'd seen.

He reached up and took hold of Sokk's foot, his hand just above hers. "Go first," he told her.

She turned back to him, but her face was set now. Stern. "No," she told him. "You."

"All right," said Vidar, beginning to climb again. "Suit yourself."

Getting back up was harder than going down. And slower, for it was difficult to find hand- and footholds.

But in time he got there. And Tofa came soon after.

It went quickly after that, much to the wolves' loud chagrin. Sokk was next, declining a helping hand from either Vidar or Tofa. After Sokk came Ullir, Half, and Lami—the reverse of the order in which they'd descended. Finally Hod was able to rise from his crouch. With some difficulty he drew his sword out of the crack, sheathed it.

Then he whirled and grabbed Meili by the front of his tunic, shoved him hard against the stone wall. The giant looked down uneasily into those narrow eye slits, still breathing hard from his ordeal, his face bruised and bloody.

"Count yourself lucky," said the masked one, in a voice that was even, almost placid. "The next time you choose to disobey me, I'll throw you to the wolves myself."

Suddenly Hod turned to look at the sky. As if he'd heard something more than the clamor of the wolves, or the distant skirl of the winds.

What is it? asked Vidar.

"Storm." He said it out loud. "From the north—and soon."

Vidar knew what that meant. He'd seen storms in Jotunheim before. And the northerlies were the worst of the lot.

He looked at the part of the sky that Hod was facing, even as the others did. And he saw nothing ominous. But he knew better than to argue weather with a *stromrad*.

Especially a *stromrad* like Hod. Of all Odin's sons, none had mastered the elements as well as he.

Without another word he released Meili and resumed his trek. But this time he moved with a sense of urgency.

Nor did anyone question him. Lami fell into line, then Half and Tofa.

Down below, the wolves started to move too. Obviously they weren't about to give up.

Vidar turned to follow Hod, felt a hand close on his arm. He looked up into Meili's lacerated face.

"It's because of you," breathed the *thrund*, "that I've fallen from favor. The time'll come when you'll pay for that." His lip twisted. "You hear me, pale-of-flesh?"

There was a retort in Vidar's mouth, but he swallowed it. Words would only lead to violence, and he didn't want to risk something happening to the sword. Nor was the time ripe for claiming it.

So he said nothing.

And after a moment the giant relinquished his grip on him, though his baleful eyes continued to burn.

"Let's go," said Sokk, giving Ullir a push from behind.

The Aesirman wheeled, but Vidar restrained him—just in time.

"There's no time for this," said Odin's son. He felt the tension in Ullir's muscles, noted that even peacemakers have their limits.

Sokk just smiled, his hand on his hilt.

"Look at them," he said. "Two of a kind."

Meili chuckled, spat at Vidar's feet. "Aye," he agreed.

"Come on," said Vidar, taking the blondbeard in tow. And reluctantly Ullir came along.

The Aesirman glanced back at their tormentors, scowled.

"You would think," he said, "that after we saved his comrade's life . . ." He shook his head, cursed softly.

"Aye," said Vidar. "There's gratitude for you."

Somewhere in the distance, there was a rumble of thunder.

Vidar contacted Hod. *We need shelter, brother.*

No kidding.

Got something in mind?

Aye. Just hope that we can reach it in time.

Again the thunder. A little louder than before. A smudge of darkness, barely discernible on the horizon.

The way widened abruptly, allowing them to move more quickly. At the bottom of the slope, the wolves kept pace, weaving among the sharp-edged rocks in their path.

The smudge widened, deepened. Vidar saw the far-off glint of lightning, heard the thunder too soon after.

"Damn," said Ullir. "That *is* coming quickly."

Vidar grunted.

Without warning, the wind assaulted them. It was like a giant hand trying to crush them against the mountainside. Up ahead, Tofa stumbled, too light to withstand it, and Half helped steady her.

There was no way to make progress against that wind, so they lowered their heads and waited. In time it died down, and they scuttled forward.

Then it came at them again—with redoubled fury. Vidar felt himself buffeted, spun about and thrown against the stone wall beside him. There were cries from ahead and behind, cries of startlement and pain.

But that wind abated too, and when it did, the company was still intact. They picked themselves up, went on.

In the north the sky had grown black and woolly, threaded through with lightning. Thunder droned long and loud, reverberating off the barren flank of the mountain.

As the sound faded, Vidar heard a different kind of din. He looked down, saw that the wolves had taken to trying to climb the escarpment again. And though the *hjalamar* forged ahead, the wolves would not.

There was nothing in their way, only the jagged rocks they had been negotiating all along. And yet they acted as if they'd come to some unseen barrier, some invisible boundary they would not cross.

Vidar wondered at that, but only for a moment. Their shelf of rock had begun to twist, coiling about the mountainside. And incidentally exposing them even more to the oncoming storm.

The sky, meanwhile, was filling quickly with a mass of smoky-black clouds. Lightning writhed, illuminating their fearsome underbellies. Thunder boomed, once and again.

Then the wind, already quiet for too long now, grew quieter. The air became thick, heavy with the scent of ozone.

Vidar could hear his blood pumping in his temples, the gasps of exertion coming from the others as they toiled to keep up with Hod.

It was the calm before. Vidar cursed, for he knew from experience how little time there was at this point.

Up ahead Hod disappeared around a bend in their course. He was yards ahead of Lami now.

Ah. Finally. Vidar heard the thought even as Hod formed it.

What?

The cavern system I was looking for. See it?

No. Not yet. He watched Lami negotiate the bend, followed by Tofa and then Half. A moment later it was Vidar's turn to slip around it. *I . . . yes, now I do. Once again you've justified my faith in you.*

The cave was as big as an airplane hangar. And the stone path broadened quickly to form a plateau before them, making it that much easier to reach it.

It was more than any of them might have hoped for. They pelted toward the opening for all they were worth, for the very air seemed to be quivering in anticipation of the next blow.

It fell like a sledgehammer just as Vidar ducked inside.

Lightning flashed, blindingly close. Thunder shook the mountains, rattling the bones in their heads.

Then they were all inside, panting in the welcome darkness.

Safe.

XVIII

OUTSIDE, the storm raged. Winds shrieked and lightning flared, filling the cave opening. Each time, the thunder seemed to be louder than the time before.

Vidar sat with his back against a red-veined stalagmite and chewed the dried meat that Hod had supplied them with. Beside him, Ullir drank from his waterbag, set it down. When the lightning was dormant, Vidar could barely see the Aesirman's face—much less those of the others as they huddled on the other side of the cave.

"Penny for your thoughts?" asked Vidar.

Ullir looked at him. "What?"

"It's an expression in Midgard. I just wondered what you were thinking about."

The blondbeard shrugged. "My sons." He took a deep breath, let it out. "The older one, Leif, is about the same age as that Lami. Yet the *thrund* carries himself like a seasoned warrior—someone who has been hardened in the heat of battle."

"Perhaps," said Vidar, "he is, and he has."

Ullir nodded. "I suppose so."

Then, as if he'd overheard their conversation, the one called Lami turned to peer at them. Lightning illuminated the cave, throwing all of them into sharp relief. Gloom fell again, punctuated by the most deafening of thunderclaps. And still he regarded them.

Vidar marked it, but said nothing. The *thrund* was entitled to his curiosity, wasn't he?

Then Lami rose and came over to them.

From where he sat in the deepest part of the cave, Meili observed this and remarked on it. Sokk, sitting beside him, nodded. There was a muted chuckling between them.

But Lami didn't seem to notice. Or if he did, he ignored it. When he reached the Aesirmen, he stopped, frowned. For a moment, he seemed uncertain. Then, as if he'd made his decision, he got down on his haunches. Taking out his own provisions, he began to eat.

Mostly he averted his eyes, keeping them trained on the floor. Only now and then did he look up at them.

"I'm glad you decided to join us," said Vidar. "Though I can't help but wonder why you'd want to. None of the others seems to be seeking out our company."

The youth raised his eyes to meet Vidar's. They were narrow and hard above proud, high cheekbones.

"I just wanted you to know," Lami said, "that I saw what you did. How you let go of Tofa to get Meili—to bring him back up." He glanced at Ullir, then again at Vidar. "And you didn't do it for a friend—you did it for someone who hates you, when you could just as easily have let him die."

"We pale-of-flesh," said Vidar, "are like that sometimes."

Lami nodded. "The stories would have it otherwise, but I believe it now that I have seen it." He spoke low enough so that only the Aesirmen could hear him. "And if that is so, then perhaps you're telling the truth about the demons—that they're your enemies as well as ours." He regarded them. "If I thought that the demons were your allies, I'd kill you here and now. For what they did to our people on the roads, and for what they did to my comrades at Gnipa—for they did not go down easily. But I believe you. And I think you will lead us to the source of the demons, even as you claim."

"Thanks," said Vidar, "for the vote of confidence."

The *thrund* almost smiled. Wrapping up the rest of his food, he put it away in the pouch he carried. Then he got up and crossed the cave again.

The others looked up, but no one said anything. Not even Meili.

"Well," said the blondbeard, "we've made a friend. I think."

Vidar chuckled. "Perhaps we have at that."

Lightning flashed, and Ullir shielded his eyes.

"How long do you think this will last, my lord?"

"Not long," said Vidar. "A couple of hours at most. In fact, the worse they are, the quicker they pass. And this one's about as raucous as they get."

As if to underscore his judgment, the thunder made the mountain shudder. It seemed to go on for a long time.

And then, as it died, they heard another sound.

A hissing.

Vidar knew what it was. As he turned to peer into the dark recesses of the cave, his heart started pounding.

Ullir followed his gaze, his brow knitting. "What is it?" he asked.

Vidar still couldn't see it, but it was there nonetheless.

"Serpent," he said, breathing the word.

And as he spoke its name, the monster showed itself. Not all at once, but little by little. First the huge, horned head, black with streaks of blood red. The slitted, yellow eyes, the darting tongue. Then its sleek, scaly coils, unwinding along the cavern floor.

It was the one living thing that even Odin had backed down from. And they had taken shelter in its lair.

On the other side of the cave, the *hjalamar* scrambled to their feet. Their sheaths whispered as they drew their swords.

Nice choice of cave, he told Hod.

I didn't hear you complaining before, brother.

It's not too late to find another.

Yes it is. There aren't any—none close enough, anyway.

So we stay and fight?

Aye. We stay. And fight. A pause. *Besides, it's only a youngling.*

The serpent eyed them, blinking, its gaze shifting from one to the other. Then it seemed to fix its stare on the Aesirmen—perhaps because they were the closest.

The massive head rose, loomed. The red-streaked maw opened, revealing rows of long, sharp teeth.

It's got a bead on you, said Hod. *If you can keep it occupied for a moment, I think I can kill it.*

You mean stand here?

Aye.

Give me your sword, said Vidar. *Then you can stand here while I kill it.*

But Hod had already started to advance on the serpent—from the side, where he might not be noticed. The *hjalamar* made as if to follow, but at Hod's signal they hung back.

Nor was the masked one wrong. This was best done by those with some experience in it.

"Go," he told Ullir.

The Aesirman hesitated. "You can't face this thing alone," he said. "You haven't even got a weapon."

"And a lot of good it'll do either of us if you stay. Now get out of here," said Vidar.

Reluctantly the blondbeard moved back toward a cluster of stalagmites.

Vidar had expected the monster's gaze to stay fixed on him, since he was more accessible. But instead, its cruel head turned and its eyes followed Ullir.

Suddenly the long, pink tongue flicked out from between its jaws. And Vidar knew he only had a moment or two.

He hit Ullir square in the back just as the worm spewed its load of venom. Both of them went sprawling, finally brought up short by one of the stalagmites.

The venom—a brownish-green liquid—splashed and sizzled as it struck the spot where Ullir had been.

Vidar looked up from behind the stalagmite, saw Hod inching closer to the serpent. He was just below and behind its eye now.

"Thanks," said Ullir, glancing at the pool of venom.

But the creature seemed to have found them again. A second time its maw opened, and a second time its tongue darted out.

"Don't thank me yet," said Vidar. He shoved the Aesirman before him. "Let's move."

And move they did. Each took two steps and dove for cover, just as the serpent released another load. Vidar heard it spatter just behind him, and suddenly there was the smell of something burning.

It took another moment before Vidar realized what it was. The worm's poison had eaten three large holes in one of his boots.

"Are you all right?" asked Ullir, careful not to raise his head up.

Vidar nodded. "Fine." And as he peered around the stalagmite, he saw that Hod was just about to strike. Nor had the serpent taken notice of him yet.

But just as Hod would have plunged his sword into the monster's eye—the quickest route to its brain—it must have caught a glimpse of him. For its head turned, lizard-quick, and spoiled his aim.

The sword was driven into the corner of its eye instead of the center, lodged there. There was a terrible hissing as the serpent felt it, and its head snapped up like an out-of-control elevator car.

With one passenger—Hod, still hanging on to his sword.

Vidar linked with him. *Drop, damn it!*

But there was no response. Either Hod had been taken by surprise and judged that he had too far to fall now—or he thought he had a chance to push the sword in deeper.

Whatever his thinking, the serpent would have no part of it. It whipped its head about in quick, spasmodic jerks, trying to dislodge its tormentor. Thin, red slime oozed from the corner of its eye.

For a moment it looked as though Hod might have had a chance. He managed to hook his leg around one of the scaly horns that projected from the creature's head and, with a mighty effort, pluck his sword loose. The huge black head tossed and shuddered, but he held on.

And gripped his blade in both hands.

And raised it.

And cried out in triumph.

But before he could deliver the deathstroke, the serpent's head struck a low-hanging stalactite. The entire formation cracked off, smashed against the cavern floor. The scaly head recoiled from the unexpected impact, and Hod was thrown loose.

He hit the ground hard and lay there, motionless.

It took a moment for the worm to realize that it was free of its burden. A moment before it stopped thrashing and saw the morsel before it.

Vidar didn't hesitate. He darted out from concealment, headed for the slumped form in the mask.

But as he did so, he slipped on the serpent's venom. He tried to keep his feet, but to no avail, managing only to clear the pool of deadly secretion before he fell.

As he rose again, lightning struck, bathing the cave in a sudden, shattering light. And in that light he saw the others pelting toward Hod, a swarm of figures in black and resplendent silver.

Lami reached him first. He skidded to a halt, straddling his fallen chieftain—just as the serpent began to understand the situation.

This time it didn't bother to spew its venom. With heart-sinking speed, it catapulted forward and snatched Lami up in its jaws.

His screams filled the cavern as the other *hjalamar* hit the snake at a run, slashing at its thick, scaly hide with their blades. But the worm hardly seemed to feel it, so intent was it on trying to swallow Lami whole.

There were two swords lying on the ground now—Hod's and Lami's. Ullir picked one of them up, started for the monster. And Vidar was about to pick up the other when he saw something even deadlier lying just beyond Hod.

The stalactite that the serpent had dislodged. It lay more or less intact, with a long, thin point that could pierce deeper than any sword.

More screaming, drowned out by the maddening doombeat of thunder. Spurred by it, Vidar lunged for the stalactite.

But before he could reach it, the worm's tail came sweeping toward him out of the depths of the cavern. He leaped as it whipped along the ground, narrowly avoiding it. But Half and Tofa sprawled, blindsided by the thing.

A few more steps and the stalactite was in his grasp. He embraced it as if it were a lance. And as he looked up, he saw Sokk go flying too, swept aside by the serpent's tail.

One heartbeat, two, as the tail snapped back. Then Vidar pounded across the cavern floor, his weapon cradled in his arms.

The worm never saw him coming. He aimed for the spot where the red streak that began at its maw came to an end.

There was a tremendous *thunk*, and then sheer, unbridled chaos. Vidar was flung, came up hard against a cavern wall. When his head cleared, he looked up.

The serpent, he saw, was writhing like a thing possessed —a thing in agony. The stalactite had bitten so deep that only the blunt end of it stuck out. Like a boiling, black sea, the worm hissed and spat.

Meili and Tofa had managed to drag Hod out of harm's way, lest he be crushed by the monster's spasms. And the others covered their retreat, undaunted by the destructive force of the snake.

Vidar knew, however, that their labors weren't finished. As much as he'd annoyed the serpent, it would work the stalactite out eventually. And return its attention to Lami, who seemed to have fallen from its maw, though he couldn't be located at a glance.

In the blinding glare of the lightning flash that followed,

he spotted the other sword. It lay in an open area, unguarded by the monster's coils.

The opening wouldn't last long. As the thunder cascaded down the mountain, Vidar dashed out after it. And out of the corner of his eye, he saw the serpent's head jerk in his direction.

He dove, closed his fingers about the hilt, rolled—just as its huge black head came crashing down at him. For a moment, Vidar had a glimpse of that great, dripping maw. Then the red-streaked jaws bit down on nothing but air, and Vidar found himself only a few precious feet from his goal.

That massive yellow eye slid back in its socket, drawn by the motion as he scrambled to his feet. As the worm whipped its head about, Vidar thrust for all he was worth.

In the end it was the creature's own force that drove the point home.

Vidar felt the weapon torn from his grasp, so quickly he thought his wrists had been broken. The monster coiled in on itself, became a ball of seething, black scales—as if it were trying to tie itself into a knot.

Its tail whipped once, twice. The second time it almost crushed him.

And then the worm lay still.

Lightning scorched the cave entrance, and the thunder hammered at their brains.

Vidar leaned against the cavern wall and rubbed his aching wrists. One by one his companions approached the snake—even Hod, though he limped a little.

Only one was missing.

"Where's Lami?" asked Tofa.

They peered into the depths of the cave.

"He's not in the worm's maw," said Ullir. "He must have been thrown clear."

"No!" cried Half. "Look!"

And he clambered up onto the carcass just behind a mighty lump in the monster's body.

Vidar's gorge rose, but it didn't keep him from climbing up after Half, who'd drawn his sword.

"Give me that," said Vidar, wresting the blade from the *thrund*. "He could still be alive in there." Nor did Half protest as the Aesirman dug into the serpent, prying away raw flesh and scales.

A moment later Hod was digging at his side. And Tofa as well, though she hadn't the strength for it.

Soon they were covered to the elbows in brown-red slime.

This is useless, said Hod. *He'll have suffocated by now.*

Then why are you working so hard at it? asked Vidar.

The masked one glanced at him through those empty eye slits.

Why are you?

Finally they found what looked to be Lami. Vidar pulled at him while the others tried to wrench chunks of flesh away. It seemed a long time before his legs slid free, and then the rest of him.

He looked like a newborn, running with the serpent's blood. And he wasn't breathing.

Right there, among the monster's coils, Vidar pumped at the *thund*'s chest and tried to breathe air into his lungs. Just as they'd taught him at the fire house back in Woodstock.

When that didn't work, he tried what he'd learned in Asgard. He poured himself into Lami with all the strength he could muster, taking back the ruin in return. He searched through Lami's being for a spark of life, something he could nurture. . . .

"Vidar?"

It was a voice, very far away.

"Vidar? It's over, my lord. Come away."

He recognized the voice. Looked up, and saw Ullir.

The Aesirman clasped him by the shoulder. "It's no use," he said. "He's finished."

With Ullir's help he rose and got down off the snake. Gingerly the others lowered Lami to the ground.

Outside, the lightning raked the heavens, and for a moment the *hjalamar*'s corpse was caught in its glare. Then it became dark again, and the thunder groaned.

XIX

"HE was a gem, my Aurvandil was. A fire to warm one's hands at, a light to drive away the darkness. When he jested, no one could keep from laughing; when he sang, he could wring tears from a stone.

"Only Baldur shone brighter in the mead hall, so golden was my Aurvandil. Now he is dead, and nothing can bring him back. But should the giants who slew him walk when he cannot? Should they breathe when he can breathe no longer, see what he cannot?"

She fell to her knees before Odin.

"It was in your name, my lord, that my husband raided the hall of the giant Skrymir—for it was said that this hall held treasures beyond telling. Will Aurvandil now go unavenged?"

"No," said Odin. "He will not. A brave warrior is more valuable to me than all else I possess."

"Let me see to it," said Vali, Odin's son. "I will visit Skrymir's hall, and see that Aurvandil's death is answered in kind."

And so Vali made the long trek to Jotunheim, and after much searching he found Skrymir's house. But when he got there, he saw that it was well guarded. Three huge hrimthursar stood before the door, and when they saw him, they hefted their spears.

"Who goes there?" asked the biggest one. "An Aesirman, come to have his bones cracked like those of his friends?"

"Then you do not deny," said Vali, "that you slew Aurvandil."

"Why should we deny it?" asked the hrimthursar. "We ran him through like the other Aesirmen he traveled with." He took something out of his pocket. "See? I kept his toe bone for good luck. And now we'll do the same to you, for none may lay hands on Skrymir's treasure."

But before they could all fall on him together, Vali held up his hand. "Wait," he said. "What kind of sport is this—three against one, and each of you a full head taller than I am? Are you so afraid of a lone Aesirman that you must gang up to protect yourselves?"

"All right," said the biggest giant. "Have it your way. But you'll find that even one of us is more than a match for you."

But as the hrimthursar charged, spear in hand, Vali took out his sword. And before the giant knew what was happening, Vali's blade was buried to the hilt in his gut. A moment later he fell to his knees and died.

"A lucky stroke," said the second giant. "But you will not live long to gloat over it." Having said that, he came at Odin's son like a bull. But Vali sidestepped his rush and took his head off, so that he fell on the ground next to the other corpse.

Finally it was the third giant's turn to face the intruder. But by now he'd guessed the truth.

"We should have surrounded you when we had the chance," said the hrimthursar. "For you are one of Odin's sons, and no giant in the world can hope to beat you. Now I stand here alone, trying to do what greater warriors could not."

"You are right," said the Aesirman. "I am indeed Odin's blood. And I have come to make you sorry that you ever saw Aurvandil."

Before the giant could say anything else, Vali opened his throat, and he died on the spot.

Stepping over the bodies, Vali entered Skrymir's hall. Inside he found Skrymir himself, gnawing on the shank of an ox. When he saw Vali standing there with fresh blood on his sword, Skrymir put the shank aside and wiped his mouth.

"And who are you?" he asked. "Who comes to my hall and slays my guards, all by himself?"

"None else but Vali, Odin's son. And I've come to exact revenge for the warrior called Aurvandil."

"Have you?" asked Skrymir, who'd grown shrewd over the long, cold years. "Or have you come instead to carry off my treasure?"

Vali shrugged. "It has been a long journey, and a difficult one. While I am here, I might as well take your treasure too."

"You're much too sure of yourself," said Skrymir. "Perhaps you will find that some giants are stronger than others."

With that, Skrymir took a huge, two-headed ax off the wall and swung it in Vali's direction.

No sooner had Vali turned the first blow aside than he saw the truth of Skrymir's words. Never had he faced an enemy so big and so powerful.

From the time the sun set until it rose again, Vali strove with the hrimthursar. And only when morning came, blinding the giant's eyes, was Vali able to reave him of his life.

But after Skrymir had breathed his last and the house was quiet but for the wind in the cracks, Vali heard a scratching.

"It must be mice," he told himself, "scratching among Skrymir's treasures."

So he followed the sound to a trapdoor and lowered himself into a great cellar below the house. A cellar with three big baskets in it.

Vali opened the first basket, and there he found rings of silver—such as Odin gave to the warriors who pleased him the most.

He opened the second basket, and there he found armbands made out of gold—such as only the wealthiest lords might wear.

But the scratching sound went on. And when Vali opened

the third basket, he found neither rings of silver nor arm bands of gold.

Instead, he found Aurvandil.

Sin Skolding
Saeverstod, 525 A.D.

XX

DARKNESS fell before the storm abated, and Hod suggested that they sleep among the serpent's coils—to take advantage of whatever warmth the carcass still provided.

This they did, and it kept them from freezing that night. As before, Vidar stayed awake longer than the others, attuning to Angrum while Meili slept.

But he'd been weakened by his attempts to save Lami. As he opened himself to the exchange of energies, he got more than he'd bargained for. He found himself jerked suddenly from this existence into another—a smoky place that reeked of blood and fire. He felt his flesh seared by the flames in which Angrum had been bathed, felt his bones shudder beneath the pummeling of the hammer, felt the cruel grip of the tongs. And when it was all over, he tasted the blood in which the sword was left to cool, heard the hissing as it worked its way into the iron.

Then the sword's memories faded, and his own came unbidden . . .

. . . apples turned to gold by the sunset, swaying in a singing wind . . .

. . . bodies bursting from black tents, twitching to the
music of death . . .

. . . wild, white horses climbing gray crags to the horizon . . .

. . . a red Volkswagen swinging out into the mist-choked
street, tires squealing, headlights stabbing the darkness . . .

. . . a mountain of coins glittering in the moonlight, its tiny
eyes burning like coals . . .

. . . the face of a beggar boy, peering at him from an alley-
way . . .

. . . a flaming ship against a dark confusion of sky . . .

. . . the fall of a red velvet dress, pale arms reaching out to
embrace him . . .

. . . a sea of wolves with devil's-fire eyes . . .

. . . a flock of carrion eaters taking to the air like
smoke . . .

. . . Stim . . .

. . . M'rann . . .

. . . Ar'on . . .

. . . Buri . . .

. . . Lami . . .

He shrank from those ghosts, from the way they stared at
him with empty eyes, blaming him with their silence. But he
could not banish them without shutting out the attunement.

For a time he endured them. Gazed into their eyes, saw
their final agonies. Then it was more than he could take.

He broke off the exchange.

Afterward he felt the sweat drying cold on his face and
opened his eyes. But when he looked around, afraid that he
might have cried out and woken someone, he saw that his
fears were unfounded. His companions still slept like babies,
nestled against the scaly body of the snake.

Nestling likewise, he drowsed off.

With the dawn, they left the cave—and Lami—and resumed their trek along the ledge, which narrowed again

quickly. The field of jagged rocks ended abruptly in a steep drop, and they looked out upon a deep, broad valley. It was as twisted and scarred as the rest of Jotunheim, but somehow it looked more inviting through the haze of distance.

Up above, the sky showed blue in patches, the storm having dragged the worst of the clouds along with it. It was cold, but the wind had no bite to it, and the sun was less livid than usual.

They might almost have imagined that they were someplace other than Jotunheim.

At first they walked single file, strung out along the stone shelf. Then Vidar found Tofa walking beside him.

She peered at him from beneath her hood, blue eyes glinting in that copper-colored face.

He met her gaze, said nothing. For it seemed there was something on her mind, and she was only searching for words to dress it in.

Finally she seemed to find them.

"You did something to me," she said. "Back at the gate, when you found me lying there with the others. The same thing you tried to do to Lami."

Vidar saw that she was waiting for his answer. "Aye," he told her. "I healed you. And later, so did Ullir. It's a talent that some of us pale-of-flesh possess."

She nodded, grimly.

"Then I was hurt worse than you led me to believe?"

He confirmed the truth of that.

"And if not for this healing of yours, I would have died as my comrades did?"

"Most likely," said Vidar.

Tofa grunted, turned away from him.

"You are a puzzlement," she said stiffly.

"Unless I'm telling the truth," he offered. "Then it all falls into place, doesn't it?"

But she didn't answer. She only stared straight ahead. And after a while, when the ledge narrowed again, she fell back and walked behind him.

As the day wore on, their shelf became narrower still, and

finally they had to leave it altogether. Fortunately the slope below it had become less treacherous by then, and they found the beginnings of a ravine at the bottom of it.

At one time a river might have run there. Now it was clogged with misshapen trees and rocks and ice.

But it was a way down, and it led west, so they took it.

"We'll never get to Hlymgard at this rate," said Ullir, after a while. He avoided a root that seemed to reach out for him.

"Count your blessings," said Vidar. "At least we're out of the wind."

Indeed, the wind had grown fierce again, and the clouds thick and gray. They promised sleet, and perhaps more than that.

Twilight came on quickly. The air grew frigid, reaving feeling from their fingers and toes. Before long it hurt just to breathe.

When the sleet fell, it completed their misery.

Not much farther.

Vidar started, unprepared for Hod's message.

That's good to know, he said. *Another cave?*

No. Another keep.

Even better. But privately he wondered why Hod had offered him the information.

The masked one answered as if he'd read Vidar's mind—which, of course, was impossible.

This time I decided not to wait until you asked.

Thanks for being so damned considerate.

But Hod didn't respond to the jibe. Something else had taken hold of his attention just then, churning up his consciousness.

Vidar looked past him, through the twisted trees. And saw something moving there.

Instinctively his hand went to his hip, reaching for the sword that wasn't there.

Then he realized what it was he'd seen, and he relaxed.

A river. Just a river.

He communicated as much to Hod.

Aye, said his half-brother. *But do you see what's beyond it?*

Vidar strained to see through the fir branches. After a while he made it out. There was the keep, halfway up the craggy slope.

I see, said Vidar. *We've got to cross the river to get to it.*

Exactly.

Vidar recalled how they'd swum such rivers in their youth. On a dare. But then they'd brought plenty of bear fat to rub themselves down with, and now they had no such insulation.

Nor would the *thrund* make it across, even if they did. The iciness of the water would stop their hearts first.

You and I might survive a crossing, he told Hod. *But not the others.*

I know, came the reply. *I know.*

As they got closer, the others spied the river too. Behind Vidar, Meili and Sokk started muttering—complaining about the cold and the descending darkness, and wondering what they'd do when they reached the water. When the trees thinned out and the wind began to cut into them, they muttered about that too.

Then the ravine opened up and deposited them almost on the riverbank, and it didn't take Heimdall's eyes to discern the keep on the other side. Abruptly the muttering stopped.

The river flowed slowly before them, crawled almost, hardly raising a collar of foam around the occasional rock. Nor did it look to be very deep. But it was broad—quite broad. Perhaps the length of a football field, at this point.

They stood and watched it. And peered up at the keep. And shivered terribly in the cold.

How did you cross it last time? asked Vidar.

Last time it was frozen.

Oh.

And then it came to him. He glanced back at the ravine, at the trees within it.

You look like you've got an idea, observed Hod.

I do, returned Vidar. *The trees. If we can hack one down, we can use it to float the others across.*

Hod didn't answer. He just made his way back up into the ravine, drew out his sword, and started cutting at a tall fir tree.

A moment later Meili joined him, positioning himself on the other side. The rest of them could only watch and wait.

Spurred by the increasing cold, the pair worked quickly. It was almost full dark when they finished, the giant red-faced and grimacing, his fingers curled into nerveless claws. As Hod gave it one last nudge, the tree fell with a resounding crack.

Then Hod sheathed his somewhat blunted sword, and Meili put Angrum away—though with some difficulty.

"Well," said Hod, "don't just stand there. Help me get this thing down into the water."

It proved harder than they might have thought, for the tree was heavier than it looked, and its branches offered stiff resistance as they dragged along on the ground. But in time they got the top of the tree into the water, and the rest came easier after that.

Without hesitation Hod waded into the cold, black flood, and made his way to the treetop.

How's the water? asked Vidar.

The masked one ignored him, shouted out commands. "You—Aesirman, the one called Vidar. Take hold of the lower boughs and keep them steady. The rest of you find a place among the branches—one where you won't fall out so quickly."

Vidar waded in as Hod had before him, feeling his muscles clench in the water's icy grip. But as he reached for a bough, he heard a sloshing behind him.

It was Ullir, entering the river in his wake.

Vidar went back to stop him.

"What are you doing?" he asked.

"Helping," said the Aesirman. "I'm not going to ride a tree while you do all the work."

"You'll never make it," said Vidar.

Ullir grinned. "Won't I? There's more of Odin's blood in me than you might think. Now come—there's no time to argue."

He was right about that at least. Vidar could feel his calves starting to cramp where the water had sopped through his boots.

He frowned. "All right. Let's go then."

And together they steadied the tree as the others climbed along its length.

It took only a few moments. Then Vidar felt Hod tugging on the top of the fir, and he pushed. On the other side of the trunk, Ullir did the same.

And after a moment, the tree slid out into the current.

The farther out they went, the deeper the water got. First it clamped around Vidar's knees, then his thighs. Before long he felt his testicles retract. But when it reached his waist, and he could feel his stomach muscles spasm at its touch, it stopped and went no further.

After a while, Vidar couldn't feel his feet anymore. They were senseless lumps at the ends of his legs, dead weight as they plodded along the rocky river bottom.

Once or twice he stumbled, drenching his upper body as well. But he had the tree to hang on to, and he was able to right himself.

"We're almost halfway," called Hod over the whirring of the wind. But he bit off the end of each word, as if he were shivering too badly to complete it.

The crossing seemed to go on forever. Vidar's limbs grew lethargic, weak, their strength draining away with the current. Soon his brain began to fuzz over as well.

At one point he caught a glimpse of Ullir through the branches. His skin was as pale as ivory, like the skin of a corpse. His lips, too, were as blue as death. Nor did he notice Vidar's scrutiny, for his eyes were glazed, trained on something Vidar couldn't see.

Vidar's own eyes began to burn, and he thought that strange. Burning was the last thing he'd expected.

The water shooshed softly past, inviting him to lie down,

to sleep. To let go of life, of effort and travail, to become another rock in its bed. But he pressed on through the endless dark, muscle and bone moving as if of their own accord—fueled by their own separate resolve.

He shut his eyes and pushed.

Then, somehow, the river was falling away from him, releasing him with the reluctance of a lover. It receded to his thighs, to his knees.

Something jolted him, and he fell. Water filled his mouth, rocks pressed into his cheek. But he didn't have the strength left to turn his head, much less lift it.

He felt a clutching at him, a tugging at his sodden garb. But it was a moment before he realized that he'd been dragged free of the water. And even longer before he knew he was being carried up to the keep.

XXI

WHEN Vidar's head cleared, there was a fire going, and his bare feet were warming at it. There was some pain as feeling returned to them.

He looked around. He saw their boots off to one side, drying in the heat from the flames. He saw the pile of wood, even greater than the supply they'd found in the last place.

Ullir was lying next to him—barefoot also, and asleep beneath his cloak. Past the Aesirman, Hod sat with his arms wrapped about his knees and dozed.

As if he felt Vidar's gaze upon him, his head came up. The mask turned around to face him, and Vidar could see glints of fire reflected in its eye slits.

Any more river crossings? he asked.

Hod grunted aloud. *Not as I recall.*

It seemed warmer in here than in the other keep. Vidar propped himself up on one elbow and looked in the direction of the entrance.

As he'd suspected, there was a door. The hinges had all but rusted off, but the *hjalamar* had wedged it into place with some splinters of firewood. Half and Meili were just driving in the last of them, using the pommels of their swords as hammers.

When he turned back toward the hearth, he caught a glimpse of Tofa. One arm was full of iron cups; the other hugged a cooking pot. For a moment their eyes met. Then she looked away, frowning.

Sokk came out of a side entrance to the room, spat.

"Empty," he announced. "Not even any bones this time."

Vidar found that strange. But then, the males who'd lived here might have gone off to defend Hlymgard—perhaps even been part of the raid on Asaheim that started it all. And it was not so unusual to find a keep without females, for a great many of them had died in childbirth.

They filled the pot with water from their own skins, knowing that they could refill them at the river in the morning. And once again they had something hot to drink with their meal. Nor did they have to pass cups from one to another, for this time there were enough to go around.

Vidar made sure that Ullir woke up to take some food and water. He accepted it gratefully, mumbled something, and was asleep again within moments.

Following his example, the *thrund* drew their cloaks about them and clustered as close to the hearth as they might—without displacing either their leader or the Aesirmen.

As luck would have it, Meili settled down right next to Vidar, for it was the only spot left directly in front of the fire—and the giant had moved more quickly than any of the others to claim it.

Vidar saw Angrum's hilt protruding from Meili's sheath.

He felt the sword's presence, recognized his chance to further the attunement. And as before, he reached out.

But the struggle with the river had hollowed him out, claimed too much of him. There was nothing left to set before Angrum.

A flicker of energy passed from him to the sword and back again, but that was all.

Vidar sighed, turned his face to the rafters. Closed his eyes. There was time, he told himself, to strengthen his bond with Frey's blade. Nor did he mull over his failure for long, for soon he felt himself drowsing, falling into the dark spaces between his bones . . . drawn down into the pit of sleep.

Something wrenched him upright, something so loud that it seemed to echo inside his skull. Without thinking, he tore his cloak aside and whirled, gathering his feet beneath him —just in time to see Meili flung across the room like a rag doll.

The *thrund* hit a wall—hard. And when he fell to the floor, his head lay at an impossible angle.

The wind blew cold into the keep, aswarm with ice crystals. Two creatures stood just inside the threshold. They were angular, bony, leather-skinned in the dancing firelight. With heads like pterodactyls and eyes like red-burning coals.

And they were big—much bigger than Meili. Bigger even than the hulking hrimthursar, for they dwarfed the doorway.

One of them made a crackling sound—something akin to laughter. It indicated Vidar and his companions with the business end of a truncheon.

"Aesssir," it hissed. It was only partly right, of course, but Vidar didn't see how it would have helped to correct the error.

In one long moment the pieces fell into place. Nightmare warriors. A distaste for Aesirmen. And an affinity for Jotunheim's frigid climate.

Odin must have gone far afield to find such specimens.

In the next moment things started happening. The *hjala-*

mar drew their blades, stepping clear of the cloaks strewn before the hearth. Sokk drifted over to Meili's side. And brandishing their truncheons, the intruders advanced.

"Ich'bod'nod'dee!"

The cry was Hod's, and it stopped everyone dead in their tracks.

Even the creatures. Their heads swiveled toward the masked one and their eyes slitted.

"Ral'crak'bak'bal!" spat the foremost.

You know them? asked Vidar.

I thought I did, said Hod.

"L'asss'fa'dul!" croaked the other creature.

"K'roosh'dag'dam!" argued Hod.

The leather-skins seemed to hesitate, their eyes glittering like rubies. They muttered something, one to the other.

But before Hod could press his case, whatever it was, Sokk shouted a curse. The pterodactyl heads turned his way.

"You killed him," rasped the *thrund*. His lips were drawn back over his teeth. "Damn you, you'll pay for that."

"Sokk!" hissed Hod. "Wait!"

But Sokk wasn't listening anymore. Suddenly there was a dagger in his other hand. And before anyone could stop him, he'd attacked.

The *thrund* was quick, much quicker than Vidar might have guessed. But not as quick as the leather-skin. The truncheon came across and down, met Sokk's rush with terrible force. There was a sickening sound, a splintering sound, and the *thrund* was swept aside.

Suddenly Hod seemed to have changed his mind about diplomacy. With a cry he rushed the creatures, Tofa and Half close on his heels.

Vidar reached into the woodpile at the same time as Ullir. The clubs they found there were sturdy enough—not as thick as the intruders', but they'd have to do.

As they crossed the room, Half took a glancing blow to the head and crumpled. Immediately, before the creature could come forward to finish him off, Vidar filled the breach.

But not for long. Though he managed to turn aside the creature's first jolting blow, the second shattered his club.

A moment later the thing caught him by the throat in one clawlike hand. Vidar felt his breath cut off, and suddenly he was raised up off the floor.

He tore at the creature's wrist with both hands, but it was no use. The thing's tendons were like steel.

Darkness began to close down on him. He lashed out with his foot, found its ribs, but the creature didn't even seem to feel it. As his limbs lost their strength, the pterodactyl face seemed to swim up at him.

"Aesssir," it spat as it looked into his eyes.

He wished he had the breath to spit back.

"Die," it told him. The word rattled around in its throat for a while. Everything started to go black.

Then something happened—something loud and fierce—and Vidar found himself on the floor, gasping for breath in great, wheezing mouthfuls.

When he looked up, he saw that his companions had come to his aid. Hod was somehow keeping the other creature tied up while Tofa and Ullir hacked at this one.

Right about then, Hod's adversary got hold of him and swung him into the wall. Again. And again.

Vidar felt the anger rise into his face. That was his *brother*. And as he looked about for a weapon, he realized that Meili's corpse was right behind him.

He glimpsed the wide-staring eyes, the rivulet of blood that ran from his gaping mouth. And tried to forget them as he searched for the sword. But when he followed Meili's arms to his hands, they were empty. Nor was Angrum lying on the stones nearby.

Then where?

Hod bellowed in pain—a sign that he couldn't take much more.

And in that moment Vidar realized where the sword might be. Scrambling to his feet, he dragged Meili up by the front of his tunic—and found Angrum on the floor beneath him.

Another cry of pain, worse than before.

Thrusting the corpse from him, Vidar knelt, wrapped his fingers around the skillfully carved hilt.

But before he could move to help, he heard something more like a growl than a battle cry—and Sokk came shambling out of nowhere, a sword in his hand.

The intruder was too busy grinding Hod to a fine paste to notice him. He came in low and struck at the place where its hamstring ought to have been.

The creature made a sound like a thousand fingernails raking a thousand blackboards. Clutching at the back of its leg, it dropped to one knee.

Mercifully Hod dropped too.

The thing eyed Sokk, hissed—and rounded on him, useless leg and all. Vidar tried to intervene, but he was too far away.

Sokk half stumbled, half ducked, and the truncheon missed his head by mere inches. In his awkwardness—for one arm dangled uselessly by his side—he slipped in a puddle near the hearth. And unable to stop itself, the creature tripped over him, flopped to the floor.

Vidar reached it just as it sprawled. He pounced on its back, straddling it, digging his knees into its sides. Then he raised Angrum high and thrust—into the base of the creature's neck.

The creature screamed again, shattering the air with its cries. It reached back with one arm, trying to pry Vidar loose. It raised itself off the ground and tried to stand. It spun around and flipped over, so that Vidar was underneath it, and tried to use the stones of the floor to scrape him off.

But Vidar had wrapped his legs about the monster's torso, and he wouldn't let go. Little by little, he drove the blade in deeper.

Gore spurted, hot and sticky.

Again, deeper.

The thing writhed, shuddered. And finally stopped struggling.

For a moment all Vidar could hear was the pounding of

his own blood in his ears. And then, all at once, the clamor of battle came rushing back to him.

Lodging his bare feet against the creature's back, he strove to slide Angrum free. It came loose with an awful sucking sound, and the carcass slumped over on its side.

Then he was up, sword dripping, and the battle before him.

But as the other creature caught sight of him, it must have realized it was alone now. And already hard-pressed by Hod and the others, it may have decided the odds were against it.

Whatever the reason, it suddenly changed tactics. Flailing wildly with its truncheon, it cleared a path for itself. And a moment later it bolted out the door.

Hod was the first one after it.

"No!" cried Vidar. "Not alone, damn it!"

But it was too late. Hod was already gone.

Vidar vaulted across the room, brushed past the splinters left in the doorway, and emerged into the frozen night. He spotted Hod partway down the nightmare slope, the monster further below him.

But as fast as the thing was, Hod would never catch up to it. And if this were one of Odin's warriors—a scout, perhaps—it would only be a matter of time before Odin knew they were on to him.

Frustration rose like bile in Vidar's throat. To have come so far, to have lost so many lives, only to be thwarted now —it was more than he could bear. Frustration turned to anger, and anger to rage.

Before he knew it, he'd raised Angrum shoulder high, its point trained at the creature's fleeing figure. Suddenly flame spouted from the blade, shot down the slope in the thing's direction.

It ended in an eruption, a ball of yellow flame. And within it Vidar could make out the vague, dark shape of the creature. He could hear its screaming even over the knife-sharp wind.

Nor did it stop when he lowered the blade. For once loosed, the magic would run its full course.

Tofa and Ullir watched from the doorway behind him. And after a moment Half joined them, the side of his face bruised and bloody. He muttered something about Sokk being dead, having fallen on his blade.

Meanwhile, Hod had sheathed his own weapon, and was making his way back up to the keep. His mask was badly dented, and he held his left shoulder with his right hand. And his feet were the color of ivory.

When he passed Vidar, he glanced at Angrum, but said nothing. Then he brushed by the others and went inside.

The burning went on for a long time.

XXII

THEY cleared the keep of bodies—those of the *thrund* as well as that of the creature Vidar had slain. Carrying them outside, they laid them down on the slope. And before they were done, their stomachs were churning at the sour stench of blood.

Then Vidar burned them, as he'd burned the first creature, so as not to leave any evidence of what had transpired here. As the flames leaped and the smoke rose thick and black, the valley seemed to howl with glee. But it was only the wind.

Once back inside, they piled firewood in the doorway, trying to shut out as much of the cold as they could. And in the chinks between the logs, they stuffed the cloaks of their dead comrades.

But even when that was done, and it was well into the night, no one slept. They sat before the fire and looked at one another—or at the place where the creature's gore had stained the flagstones. As if the slime itself might rise up and smash them.

"They were my enemies," said Half, breaking the silence. A log hissed and spat, and for a moment the flames leaped higher. "Yet I confess, I admire the way they died. Meili was the first one that rose to meet the monsters. And Sokk too fought bravely, though it was an accident that took his life."

He stared into the fiery caverns formed by the coals. "There are no friends of theirs here to mourn them—indeed, their only friends were each other. But someone must speak of their deaths, and their courage." He thought for a moment. "And of poor Lami's, as well. For they died as *hjalamar,* and they should not be forgotten."

Tofa nodded in agreement.

Hod looked at them, grunted. "Aye," he said. "They died as *hjalamar.*"

In the stillness that followed, Vidar made his contact.

There is much for us to talk about, brother.

Hod's head turned in response.

That there is. Such as how you came by that sword. It's Frey's, isn't it?

Aye. But first I want to know about those creatures.

The masked one regarded him, and for a moment it seemed that he'd keep silent until his own questions were answered. But instead, he continued the contact.

They're Nidhoggii, he told Vidar.

Nidhoggii . . . !

It made sense. After all, they were the ones who'd turned Odin's hand to destruction in the first place. Why not join him as he acted out their precepts?

He communicated this to Hod.

It fits with your story, returned the masked one. *I'll give you that. But these were different from the Nidhoggii I knew.*

Different? How?

These were warlike—obviously. But the ones I met in Niflheim were peaceful—almost apathetic. True, they once embraced a form of nihilism. But whatever there was to tear down in Niflheim had been torn down long ago. By the time I got there, it was unthinkable to lift a hand in violence.

Vidar mulled that over.

Then Odin, in his madness, may have twisted what the Nidhoggii taught him—reshaped it in his own mind, until it held the full measure of his bitterness.

Hod shrugged. *If you say so.*

Vidar eyed him. *The important thing here is that we've established Odin's whereabouts. And seen what kind of warriors he's assembled.* He paused. *Or do you still doubt my veracity?*

I suppose I'd be a fool to do that now, said Hod. There was only the slightest hint of irony in his tone. *Now, what about the sword?*

We found it in Alfheim, and it eventually fell to me to carry it.

Why didn't you use it in Erithain—on me, for instance?

I wasn't attuned to it then.

No? Why not? You must have had plenty of time.

That's my business.

I see. A space of silence in Vidar's mind. *And Meili carried it all this time, never suspecting what it was?*

Aye.

Very clever, Jawbreaker.

It just worked out that way.

As they measured one another, the mask's imperfections —inflicted by the Nidhogg—caught the firelight.

And now you're wondering, said Hod, *if I'll try to wrest it from you.*

The possibility did occur to me.

Hod looked away from him, into the flames.

Rest easy, he said. *I'm no lifling. It would take me too long to attune to it. And the last thing we need now is to fight among ourselves—there are too few of us left, and we haven't even reached Hlymgard yet.*

The scene flashed into Vidar's mind again—Baldur floating beneath the oak tree, Hod's arrow protruding from his breast.

As you say, agreed Vidar, *there are too few of us left.*

They woke sore and stiff and bone-tired. Even their boots were stiff, having sat too long before the fire. And their comrades' deaths hung over their morning meal like a shroud.

Nor did their spirits rise after they left the keep; for the sky was a dead, gray vault, and the path Hod took them on led up into the hills again.

Shortly after they'd started, Ullir came up beside him. Like Vidar, he now carried a blade—the one that had been Sokk's.

"That was quite a conversation you had with Hod," said the Aesirman. "It seemed to go on all night."

"Indeed," said Vidar. "I see you noticed."

"Did you learn what those monsters were?"

"Aye—Nidhoggii. The same race that taught Odin his creed of destruction."

"Interesting," said Ullir. "Then that is where he got his army. From Niflheim."

"It would seem so. But one thing bothers me. According to Hod, the Nidhoggii weren't a violent race—at least not when he was there. And he's got no reason to lie about that. So how, I wonder, did Odin turn them into warriors?"

Ullir shrugged. "That," he said, "we may never know. But as you've reminded me often enough, the All-Father is capable of anything."

The higher they climbed, the louder the wind grew, hooting at them from the ridges up above. When Vidar glanced over his shoulder, he saw that they'd left the keep far behind.

"And what about you?" asked Ullir. "Are you all right—with the sword?"

Vidar peered at him from the confines of his hood. "Aye," he said. "Well enough, considering what it did . . . what *I* did to that Nidhogg. It reminded me of what I brought down upon the thursar at Skatalund."

Ullir dropped his gaze, nodded.

"It is difficult," he said, "to see beyond such things. To a purpose."

Vidar grunted. "B'rannit said something like that."

He could see her in his mind's eye, pale face framed by dark tresses, light green eyes like forest pools in deep summer.

We dwarvin hammer swords into the world, because there will always be a need for swords. Some will use them in need. Others will use them when something else might prevail. Is it not wisdom to know one from the other?

For a while Vidar thought about that, and it comforted him—at least, a little.

They trekked over the broken terrain for hours. Gradually the sky darkened behind them, became huge and black and foreboding.

But Hod only glanced at it once, and never a second time. Apparently it was nothing to worry about—either the storm was too distant to do them any harm, or it was headed in the wrong direction.

And after another couple of hours, as they negotiated a high, humpbacked ridge, the wall of darkness began to dwindle—to sink into the horizon. Soon it faded altogether.

It was too bad that the same couldn't have been said of the wind. It swirled around the ridge, flinging grit into their faces, where it seared their eyes and dried out their throats.

Late in the frozen afternoon there were gusts of fine, sparkling snow—orphaned, it seemed, from some larger and more menacing sweep of weather. Perhaps, Vidar speculated, cut off from the storm they'd seen earlier. Nor did these silvery outriders last very long, spinning themselves into oblivion almost as soon as they came into view.

It was about then that Vidar began to have a feel for the land, as if he'd come this way before. He looked around, searching for landmarks he might recognize, memorable profiles among the dark hills—and found none. But there was something achingly familiar about it all.

He was still trying to get his bearings when they came upon the eggs. They were resting on a bed of fir branches, in a hollow among the rocks. Three of them, all pink with gray and black speckles. And each was larger than a hrimthursar's head.

"Look at them," said Half, squatting beside the nest. "What kinds of birds hatch from eggs like these?"

"Big ones," said Vidar. "Big enough to carry off a full-grown warrior."

Tofa glanced at him, then back at the eggs.

"It is difficult," she said, "to imagine a bird that big."

"Aye," said Vidar. "But I've seen it. And more than once."

"Eagles' eggs," mused Ullir. He stood beside Vidar, his face rubbed raw by the wind. "Weren't they a delicacy once in Gladsheim?"

"Aye," said Vidar. "There were eagles in Asaheim, but their eggs weren't tasty enough for Odin. So he sent out small armies to forage for the Jotunheim variety." He shook his head. "It was a mark of distinction at court if you could down one raw."

Half looked up, grimaced. "Strange place, the one you come from."

Vidar grunted.

Hod stood there like the rest of them, but said nothing. And Vidar wondered what was going on behind the mask.

Memories of Odin's hall, of feasting and fighting and brags that rang from the rafters? Memories of Odin himself, seated among his white ermine pelts on his throne of black obsidian—eyes slitted, watchful, a goblet raised to his expressive lips?

Of Bragi, who made them laugh with his baudy verses? Of blustering Thor, who laughed the loudest of all?

Or of Baldur, their gold and their good-luck charm, whose simple presence seemed to hold it all in place?

Suddenly Tofa pointed at the sky. Vidar followed her gesture, saw the V shapes at the end of it.

"Damn," he whispered.

"Let's get going," barked Hod.

But the eagles had spotted them. And though they hastened to put some distance between themselves and the eggs, they'd been recognized as a threat.

The birds swooped, headed straight for them. One screamed, gathered its great gray pinions over its head, and dropped toward Vidar—its talons extended like grappling hooks.

He threw himself to the ground, heard the bird's shriek of disappointment. Saw the flurry of smoke-dark feathers as the huge wings began to beat again.

He raised his head, caught sight of the other eagle. It seemed to have waited for the first one to make its move. Now it too plummeted, slicing through the knot of winds like a knife.

This time, however, Vidar wasn't the target. It was Hod.

The masked one ducked behind a rock, but it didn't protect him entirely. The talons fell free of the nightmare bird, opened—and found purchase in the mask.

Hod's head jerked back, and his body followed. It seemed that the eagle had him.

But as he was dragged off the ridge, he caught hold of something—an upthrust of rock. For a fraction of a second, there was that bone-wrenching tug-of-war—between Hod's grip on the crag and the eagle's momentum.

They heard the sound of twisting metal, ending in a kind of *crak*. Finally the eagle broke away with a shrill cry and a thrashing of wings. And Hod was left clinging to the rock, like a drowning man clinging to a piece of driftwood.

But his mask was gone—still enmeshed in the eagle's talons.

One pass, it seemed, was all the birds had had in mind. Graceful despite their size, they made tight circles against the thick, dark sky. And set down just before the eggs, still glaring at the intruders—as if daring them to return.

Hod pushed himself up off the rock. Slowly his head came up.

Tofa gasped, her hand flying to her mouth.

And not because of the deep cuts the mask had made when it tore off his face. Not because of the blood that ran down in rivulets.

But because she'd seen the truth—finally.

After a while, Tofa closed her mouth, and her hand fell. Half just stood there and blinked, unsure what to say or do next.

Hod spat, eyes narrowed like those of the eagles.

"Well?" he said. His dark hair fluttered about his pale, dark-bearded face. "What are you waiting for? Nothing's changed."

He allowed himself a sidelong glance at the eagles, perhaps weighing his chances of recovering the mask. But if that was his thought, he decided against it. Wiping the blood away with the back of his hand, he turned and resumed his trek along the ridge.

Half hesitated for a moment. But in the end he plunged ahead after Hod. Ullir followed, putting his shoulder into the wind.

Tofa, however, seemed dazed. As if her knees would give out at any moment.

Vidar approached her, held out his hand.

Instantly she swept it aside. When he looked into her eyes, he saw that they were red-rimmed.

Before words could pass between them, she stalked off after Hod. There was anger in the way she moved, and a carelessness born of pain.

One of the eagles cried out, spreading its mighty wings— impatient to see them gone.

Obliging it, Vidar fell into line behind the others.

XXIII

THAT night there were neither keeps nor caves for them to shelter in. The best Hod could find was a hollow, not much bigger than the one that had held the eagle eggs. But it was big enough to hold all five of them as they hunkered down out of the wind.

To stave off the cold, Vidar took out his blade and drew a ring of fire about them. And though it didn't last quite all night, it kept them from being flash-frozen.

The sun rose bloody and grotesque, from a turmoil of land into a turmoil of sky. They woke shivering, and got going as soon as they could stand—for it was the only way to thaw the ice in their joints. When their fingers uncurled, they took out food and ate, hardly breaking stride.

The ridge started to descend soon after they started out, and as it did, it grew rockfalls on either flank. After a while the rockfalls widened, stretching to fill whatever gaps there were among the hills. And as the hills twisted themselves into other ridges in the distance, the rockfalls became like seas between them. As if the rocks were wealth, and the ridges the gnarled fingers of a colossus that clawed at it.

Then a sheer wall of stone began to take shape before them, a wall whose heights were lost in the roiling clouds. And it became apparent that they'd have to trek across the stonefalls until they found a way around it.

Which way? asked Vidar. *Right or left?*

Hod didn't answer. But he turned left.

As they descended from the ridge, they seemed to leave the worst of the winds behind them. It was almost quiet as they made their way down the stonefall, so quiet that they could hear the rocks grinding together beneath their feet.

It was then that Tofa came up alongside Vidar, matching him step for step. She accidentally kicked a stone loose, and it rolled down the heap.

"I owe you an apology," she told him. "Perhaps more than one."

Vidar looked at her. "Let's see now. There was the time in the cell, back in Erithain. And . . ."

"You need not recount the times," she said. "I remember them well enough."

"It was a joke," he said. "I didn't really expect an apology. It's a difficult thing when you realize that your world is not what you thought. I know. I've been there."

Tofa grunted. "I built my life around joining the black and silver. To ride behind *him*—the champion who beat back the pale-of-flesh, in the gray ages before I was born. And now . . ."

"You see that your hero is himself a pale-of-flesh," finished Vidar. "That's the trouble with heroes. They're never what they seem. But that would have been true no matter what color Jalk's skin was."

She looked at him, her brow furrowed. "What does that mean?"

"It means you keep your eyes open—you don't let someone else do your thinking for you. No matter how big a hero he is, or how glamorous he looks on his charger. And you certainly don't die for him, without ever knowing what the hell it's about. As Lami did, for instance."

There was the slightest flash of anger in those stormy blue eyes. Then it subsided, as Tofa picked out the sense among the words.

"So I was wrong to follow Jalk—blindly." She paused. "But was I wrong to wish to guard my land against invaders? Or to come here, in the hope that we'd find the demons' lair?"

"That all depends," said Vidar.

"On what?" she asked.

"On what *you* think."

A smile spread slowly over her face, despite her.

"You are full of riddles," she told him.

"The world," he said, "is full of riddles. In fact, they all are."

For a time they walked without speaking, listening to the wind howling among the peaks. The clouds lengthened, became thick and dark as they trundled across the sky. The sun writhed in and out of them.

"You're really his brother?" she asked finally.

"Half-brother," he told her. "Different mothers, same father."

"And is it truly your father who sent the demons?"

"It looks that way."

Another silence, in which Tofa's gaze was drawn to Hod.

"What was he like?" she asked. "When *you* knew him—when he was younger?"

Vidar shrugged. "Like any of us. Brave and loyal. Cruel and deceitful."

"All at once?" she asked. "That sounds like two different people."

"We had a unique upbringing," he said.

She nodded, as if that were explanation enough.

"I wonder why he helped us," she said, "when your people came to conquer M'thrund. They were his own flesh and blood—why should he stand against them?"

"That's a long story," he told her.

"Perhaps," she said, "it will help to pass the time." And she wound her cloak more tightly about her.

So he told her—about Baldur, and his murder. About Vali, and his thirst for vengeance. And about Hod himself—how he came to know Jotunheim so well.

"Fratricide," she said, "is the ugliest of crimes. But if this Baldur was as sick as you say he was, as tormented . . ." Her voice trailed off. "Then he only helped us because he hated Vali—for having hunted him. Is that what you're saying?"

"That's at least part of it," he told her. "But there may be more. You see, Hod was one of only three whom Odin had sired on his queen. Only he, Vali, and Baldur were really heirs to Odin's throne—the rest of us being bastards. So he was used to the royal treatment, the power. He may have missed it—needed it."

"And found it," said Tofa, "at our queen's right hand."

"Something like that." Vidar watched Hod, well ahead of the rest of them now, ascending to the next ridge. His black and silver garb seemed to have lost its luster here. "Or it could have been an even simpler need."

"What's that?" she asked.

"Perhaps," said Vidar, "he was lonely. And this was an opportunity to not be lonely anymore."

Tofa pondered that for a while, her eyes narrowing. But her reverie was cut short when Hod reached the top of the ridge.

And, suddenly, flattened himself among the rocks.

Half started to climb up after him. But the dark one waved him back down again.

What is it? asked Vidar.

Nidhoggii—two of them. About halfway across the next stonefall. And they're headed this way.

Vidar saw Ullir looking back at him, awaiting the outcome of his conversation. Tofa, out of reflex, had drawn her blade—but she remained at Vidar's side, having seen Hod's gesture to Half.

Did they see you? asked Vidar.

Hod's response was quick, sharp. *No. At least they haven't given any signs of it.*

Vidar surveyed the architecture of the ridge.

There are pockets in the stone, he said, *where we can conceal ourselves until they're gone. You see any point in forcing a confrontation?*

None. We could probably take them with that sword of yours, but if they're perimeter scouts, they'll be missed. And he started to wriggle back down among the rocks.

Vidar took Tofa's arm and drew her forward.

"What's going on?" she asked.

"Hod's spotted a couple of the creatures," he explained—for Ullir's benefit as well as hers. "We're going to try hiding from them among the rocks."

"Good luck to us," muttered the Aesirman.

But in moments they'd all discovered niches in the ridge. And if they weren't comfortable, at least they were well concealed.

Then they waited.

It seemed like a long time before they heard the first sounds of the creatures' passage. A scraping, as of hard leather against rock. Now and then, a hissing.

And another sound—a moan. An almost human moan.

Finally the Nidhoggii came into view. They had passed over the same place where Hod had mounted the ridge. And as soon as they'd descended, and begun to traverse the river of stones, Vidar saw where the moaning had come from.

Bile rose into his throat, and he had to fight it back down again. He felt his hands clenching into fists.

There were two of the monsters, as there had been in the keep. But one of them had a man strapped to his back.

Or *most* of one.

Vidar's mind reeled, returned to the keep where they'd first seen the Nidhoggii. Now that he thought about it, he'd seen something strangely shaped strapped to the back of the creature he'd immolated. But he'd not gotten a good look at it, nor had he thought twice about it.

This time he had a good look. And it seemed that the creatures' victim was still alive—despite his mutilations. That meant that he could give them information.

Vidar turned and saw Hod looking at him. As if to say, *You lead this time. You're the one who carries Frey's sword.*

Vidar slipped the blade out of its sheath. The only sound it made was a leathery *snikt* that was devoured by the wind.

The others pulled out their blades too. Their faces were set in grim, straight lines.

Vidar didn't dare unleash Angrum's magic, for the creatures were too close together—and their living burden would surely perish in any flameburst.

Nor would there be any sneaking up on them, not on this open field of stones. But if they were quick, they might catch the Nidhoggii unprepared.

Vidar led them as they crept out of their hiding places. At a signal from him, they darted across the stonefall.

Luck was with them. The wind chose that moment to scour the mountainside, and the howling covered the sounds of the stones they kicked loose. They were closing in on the creatures before either of them turned its head.

And by then it was too late.

As the one without the burden whirled, Vidar went for him. The Nidhogg had just enough time to strike back-handed with its truncheon.

Vidar ducked and the thing *whooshed* above his head. Then, before the creature could recover, he sliced its throat open. Angrum's fire ate greedily at the wound. Gore oozed from it, dripped down its bony chest.

It dropped to its knees, then fell face-forward on the stones.

At the same time, Half plunged his blade into the other creature's side. The Nidhogg swiped at him, missed, staggered—and tried to pluck the blade out.

Before it could do that, Ullir hit it from the other side, cutting deep into its chest. The Nidhogg spun, flailed at him with the truncheon.

Ullir caught the blow on his blade, deflected it—though it sent him reeling. Hod saw the Aesirman's vulnerability and stepped in front of the creature, prepared to take the next stroke.

But it wasn't necessary. Tofa had come up behind the monster—and with a two-handed stroke, she tore half its scrawny neck out.

Blood geysered, turning the stones black. The creature fell on its side, writhing, scrabbling. It groaned. It hissed at them with whatever strength it had left, hissed as Vidar had never heard anything hiss before. It was the sound of pure hatred.

Then it died.

Vidar found himself standing over the other Nidhogg. He looked down and saw its blood seeping between the stones.

He spat. It had been an efficient job of butchery all right. Cleaning his blade on the carcass, he went to join the others.

Ullir had already started to unstrap the Nidhogg's burden from its back, while Hod, Half, and Tofa looked on. Vidar brushed past them and knelt, thinking to be of some help. But the Aesirman's fingers moved quickly, deftly, and in a moment all the lashings were undone.

"All right," said Ullir. "Gently now."

As carefully as they could, they rolled the mutilated one onto his back. And as they did so, Vidar saw his face.

Ice water trickled down his spine. He swallowed.

Ullir gasped. "Heart's blood! I know him..."

He pushed aside the strands of red hair that clung to the Vanirman's clammy forehead.

"Irbor," he whispered, not wanting to believe it. "Irbor."

Vidar knew him too. The eldest son of Njal, a chieftain in Asgard. And his jailer, when Vali imprisoned him in Skatalund.

Before Vidar had escaped, with Eric's help, he'd slain three of Irbor's brothers—while the Vanirman watched, helpless.

And when they'd come through the split gate at Indilthrar, Irbor had been one of those lost with Vali.

Within that tangled red beard, cracked and swollen lips twisted like earthworms.

"Water," cried Vidar.

Someone handed him a half-full waterbag, and he held it to the Vanirman's mouth. He drank, and a little more clarity came into his eyes.

The wind blew, cold and gray.

"Irbor," said Ullir. "Do you know me?"

The blue eyes focused. The skin around them moved.

"Aye," said Irbor. It was more of a croak than a word. "Aye. You are . . . Heidrek's son." He paused to lick his lips. "Ullir."

"That's right," said the Aesirman. "You're with friends now."

Irbor grunted.

Ullir winced as he inspected Irbor's body—what was left of it. "What happened?" he asked.

The redbeard shut his eyes. "Bad," he rasped. "Very bad." He licked his lips again, and Vidar held the waterbag to Irbor's mouth. He drank more eagerly now, though some of the water dribbled into his beard.

"We . . . we followed Ygg. Odin—you know he's Odin?" Irbor coughed once, then went on. "Followed him here. Into . . . a trap. The Nid . . . Nidhoggii, waiting for us. Too strong . . . too many."

The Vanirman's face contracted in pain suddenly. After a little while, it seemed to pass.

"More water?" asked Ullir.

"Aye. More water."

But when Vidar tried to give him some, it only ran out of Irbor's mouth. After a moment or two, he stopped.

"What then?" asked Ullir.

"Penned us," said the Vanirman. "Like cattle." His face contorted. "And like cattle . . . they eat us." Now tears flowed from his eyes, and his voice cracked. "Eat us, Ullir. But not . . . not all at once." He groaned. "Piece by piece."

When Ullir glanced at Vidar, his eyes were wet too—and red, though not with sorrow alone. Vidar laid a hand on his shoulder.

"Journeybread," said Hod, from somewhere behind them. "That's why they carried him. He was their journeybread."

But Vidar didn't want to think about that. Not now.

"Vali," he said. "What about Vali? Does he live?"

Irbor turned to him, as if noticing him for the first time. Recognition seemed to flicker in his eyes—but only for a moment.

"What about Vali?" repeated Ullir.

"Vali," whispered Irbor. He nodded a little. "Aye. He lives."

"And Modi?" asked Ullir.

"Modi too," said the Vanirman. "But . . ."

"But what?" asked Ullir.

Irbor's eyes glazed over for a moment.

"But what?"

Irbor shook his head. Whatever had happened, he would not—or could not—speak of it.

Then the redbeard turned to Vidar again, and this time the recognition was more than a flicker. It burned in the watery depths of those eyes, burned like sea treasure.

"I know you," said the redbeard. "The one who . . . who killed my brothers." His mouth took on a new shape.

Vidar wished he could have said something then. But there was nothing to say—nothing that might have lessened Irbor's pain—or his own guilt.

The wind muttered in a thousand voices.

"Listen," said Irbor. He glared at Vidar. "I have one brother left. Asvit . . . his name is Asvit. *You* get him out. *You*."

"Out of Hlymgard?" asked Ullir.

"Aye," said the Vanirman. "Hlymgard."

"I'll do my best," said Vidar.

"Swear," croaked Irbor. "As you . . . made me swear."

Vidar nodded. "I swear it."

The fire dimmed in Irbor's eyes then, swallowed by tears.

"Good," said the redbeard.

He coughed, and Vidar gave him more water. He drank. Then his tongue came out and flickered over his swollen lips.

"He leaves soon," whispered the Vanirman.

"Who does?" asked Ullir.

"Odin. You can do it then . . . set Asvit free. After he's gone . . ."

Ullir's brow screwed up. "Odin's leaving Hlymgard? Where is he going?"

"To Asaheim," said Irbor. "To Asgard." He shivered. There will be . . . only a few of them then. Only a few . . . to guard the gates."

"How do you know this?" asked Vidar.

Those eyes fixed on him again, terrible and bloodshot.

"Odin boasted . . . of it . . . to Vali."

And mercifully the eyes closed for a time.

Silence, made ragged by the wind. The cold began to lodge in their bones.

"What now?" asked Hod. "We can't take him with us."

"We *can*," said Vidar. "If the Nidhogg could carry him, I can too."

"No," said Irbor, straining to pick his head up. "I am . . . nothing." He grimaced, sobbed deep in his throat. "There is . . . nothing left of me."

Even Ullir knew that he was right.

"Kill me," pleaded Irbor.

They all looked at one another.

Hod spat. "Go on," he said. "I'll do it." He drew his blade out.

"No," said Ullir. "I knew him."

And somehow that seemed right.

Hod put his blade away.

After Ullir had ended the Vanirman's misery, Vidar set fire to the body. And to the carcasses of the Nidhoggii as well—to keep them from being found. Gray smoke rose in three thin streams, pulled this way and that by the winds until it dissipated altogether.

"Well," said Vidar, after the ashes had been scattered, "it appears that we have a choice."

"A choice?" asked Tofa.

"Aye," said Vidar. The wind keened among the crags. "We've accomplished what we came here for. We know for certain that Odin's in Hlymgard—and Vali as well." He turned to Hod. "Nor will you stand in my way, I think, now that you've seen Odin's warriors—and heard what the Vanirman had to say. So I can go back to Alfheim and gather my armies, then bring them to Asgard's defense. And hope that we arrive in time."

"Not possible," said Hod. "You'd have too many worlds to cross. By the time you got to Asaheim, Odin would be dug in already—and you would never dislodge him."

"So it would seem. Then he'd have the base of operations he really wants—with control over most of the known gates. If we tried to take any kind of concerted action against him—say, from Alfheim and Utgard, possibly even from M'thrund—we'd have to take the long way around from place to place. And in the end that would kill us. Of course there's always the possibility that Odin's not aiming for Asgard at all—or not yet, anyway. Then we'd be bringing our armies to the wrong point of defense."

The dark one nodded. "That would be just like him—to boast of one thing to Vali, then do something else entirely."

"All right," said Half. "What's the alternative?"

"We can go ahead," said Vidar. "To Hlymgard. And try to stop Odin before he even sets out."

"You mean," said Hod, "do what Vali—and all his warriors—could not?" He sounded intrigued more than argumentative.

"Why not?" asked Vidar. "I've got the firesword."

Hod shrugged. "Vali had the Gjallarhorn, from what you tell me. And Modi had the hammer."

"But they fell into a trap, remember? This time the element of surprise would be on our side."

Hod pondered that for a moment. "Interesting," he said.

"Then we're marching on Hlymgard?" asked Ullir, sensing that a decision had been reached. "Just the five of us?"

"Only for now," said Vidar. "If most of Vali's warriors are still alive, and we can free them somehow, the odds will be a little better."

"Aye," said Hod. "All we have to do is arrest one army

from the grasp of another." He gazed westward, past the stonefall and the next ridge. "That shouldn't be too difficult, should it?"

For an answer the wind howled high above them.

XXIV

AFTER they'd lost count of stonefalls and ridges alike, the pattern was finally broken.

It was a river—so shallow that many of the larger stones protruded from it, but a river nonetheless. And it was turned to blood by the lowering sun, from the point at which it emerged from the steeper parts of the stonefall to the point at which it vanished in distance and mist.

"So that's what I heard," said Half. "And I thought it was only the wind cutting at the rocks."

Vidar watched the intricate patterns created by the rocks and the slithering water. Patterns upon patterns, shifting before he could grasp any one of them, fix it in his mind.

Odin would have enjoyed such a place. Once.

"At least," said Tofa, "we can walk through this one."

"That won't be necessary," said Hod, shading his eyes as he looked about. "All we need do is walk alongside it."

For a while, that's what they did. They walked beside the river. And it made music for them, haunting music that was very unlike this gray and somber land.

But it didn't last long. For soon they heard the crash of falling water up ahead. Like muted thunder. And even before they could see the falls, they knew they were there.

At first Vidar thought that Hod had led them astray—finally, after all this time—and that they'd come upon a cliff in the mist, a sheer drop into dark blue depths. But he found a path after all, a rough shoulder of rock that led them back and forth beneath the waterfall. And though it was slick with spray, it wasn't steep enough to give them much trouble.

When they began their descent, the cascade was threaded through with scarlet—the legacy of the sun they'd left behind. Then the scarlet disappeared, for the sun had found some crag to die behind, and it grew dark all around them. As if they were going down into a great hole, a dripping well of despair.

But for some reason it wasn't as cold as it should have been. It was night, or nearly so. Yet their limbs were still supple. And as wet as their cloaks had gotten, there wasn't a hint of frost on them.

What kind of place is this? he asked Hod. *We ought to be freezing right about now.*

Don't know, came the reply. *But then, I don't have to in order to enjoy it.*

Not that I'm not grateful and everything, but how much longer do we go on like this? It's getting harder to see—and the others don't have our eyesight. He paused. *I don't suppose you've got another of those keeps up your sleeve somewhere?*

Vidar heard something like a chuckle in his brain.

Keeps are too dangerous for us now. But I don't think you'll be disappointed.

Hod led them to a cave much smaller than the serpent's lair, but also much better appointed. For nurtured by the mists from the waterfall, the place was carpeted over with some sort of lichen. In the dim light, it looked brownish black, though it must have been closer to red in the daylight. But it was soft and yielding to the touch, and it offered them the kind of comfort they'd not known since Erithain.

Ullir offered to take the first watch, but Vidar shook his head. "Not the way you look."

It was true. Since the incident with Irbor, the Aesirman had looked gaunt, weary. Some sleep would do him good.

"All right," said Ullir. "Then the next watch."

"It's a deal," said Vidar. But he had no intention of waking Ullir. When the time came, he told himself, he'd wake one of the *thrund,* or Hod.

That settled, they sought their beds among the lichen-covered mounds. All but Vidar, who sat by the entrance and watched the river fall through the air. It was a dark torrent against the somehow lighter-colored mist, sinuous, graceful, and slow, as if in no hurry to dash itself on the rocks below.

For a time he perched there, resting his back against the rock, feeling the mist—cold, but not icy—on his face. Then there was movement in the cave behind him, and one dark figure separated itself from the gentle curves of the lichen.

Hod sat down beside him.

"Something wrong?" asked Vidar.

Hod spat. "Can't sleep." He stared into the waterfall. "You know, those scouts will be missed—along with the pair we met at the keep. Before long Odin will know something's wrong. Perhaps he already senses it."

"I'd be surprised if he didn't," said Vidar. "Blazes—he's the one who taught *us* about such things." He surveyed his half-brother's face, its cruel contours softened somehow by this darkness. "But that's not what's kept you up—is it? You've been in tighter spots than this one."

"No," agreed Hod. "That's not what's kept me up." He turned toward Vidar. "It's you, Jawbreaker. You look the same—very much the same. But you act very differently. The first time I noticed was back in that cell in Erithain— when you seemed so concerned about your companions. None of them were your kinsmen. In fact, only one was even an Aesirman. Yet you dared threaten me—risking much pain and suffering—to prevent their being harmed."

He grunted. "Then I saw the way you went after Meili— jeopardizing your own life to save one who'd proven himself your enemy. One who'd taunted you, vowed to see you dead. Since then, of course, I've figured out that Angrum played a part in your actions. But I believe you would have gone after Meili anyway—even if he hadn't borne Frey's sword."

He frowned. "Afterward, there was Lami—and the desperation with which you tore at the snake's flesh, for a *thrund* you hardly knew. And finally this business with the Vanirman. I don't know how you came to slay his kinsmen, but what does it matter? You are Odin's son. You cannot be bound by Vanir blood debts. Yet when he asked you to swear an oath—to rescue his brother—you did so. As if he were Odin's blood, and you were the half-breed. And even now, I cannot help but wonder . . . if that oath is the reason you're leading us to Hlymgard."

Hod sighed. "That is what's kept me up, Jawbreaker. For there's only one I knew who did the things you do, and he is long dead. And I can't imagine what could have changed you so."

Vidar told him. About how he'd fled after Ragnarok, how he'd sought peace in Midgard. "I was a skald," he said. "I called myself Sin Skolding, and I earned my bread singing tales of the Aesir. And every now and then some dunghill chieftain would tell me I had the story all wrong." He chuckled at that. "But humble as it was, it was what I wanted. What I needed."

"And in all that time," asked Hod, "you never came back? Never returned to see what had become of Asaheim?"

"Aye," said Vidar. "I came back. After nearly two thousand years." And he told the dark one that story too. How Modi had called for help from the cave on Crete. How he'd been deceived by Vali, imprisoned in Skatalund. How he'd been drawn into the conflict, bit by bit.

"I see," said Hod. "At least I think I do."

"But don't compare me with Baldur. I've done things he would never have considered. I've lied, betrayed, maimed, and murdered. I've brought death to my friends, and torture, and misfortune. I've allowed innocents to perish, and brought down dooms upon my enemies that no one could deserve. Before I'm done, I'll certainly do more."

The thunder of the cascade droned in their ears, steady and unrelenting. They looked at one another. And Hod's visage became almost gentle.

"Who knows," he said, "what Baldur would have done in your place? It was a different set of circumstances then—simpler. His course was always plain. Yours, it seems, has not been."

"No," said Vidar. "We make our own courses. If his was always plain, it's because he had the vision to make it so."

Hod grunted. "Whatever you say." Time passed—just passed. Then the dark one spoke again.

"I didn't do it," he said.

"Do what?"

"Murder my brother."

Vidar looked at him. "What are you saying?"

Hod's dark eyes narrowed, and his voice grew deeper. "I didn't kill Baldur. I want you to know that."

Vidar shrugged. "Why?"

"Because," said Hod, "it's important to me. It's important that *someone* know."

Vidar watched his eyes. "All right," he said. "If you didn't kill him, who did?"

Hod tilted his head, indicating the world outside the cave.

"He did."

"Odin?"

"Aye. Odin."

"How do you know?"

"I saw it," said Hod, anger creeping into his tone. "Only I saw it too late."

Vidar searched his brother's face, etched in shadow. "Start from the beginning," he told him.

"The beginning." Hod snorted, adding his breath to that of the waterfall. "I had just returned to Asgard—from a hunting trip. On my way home I passed that place that Baldur loved so much. Where the water fell at the foot of a giant oak." He paused. "Much as it's falling here."

"I remember," said Vidar.

"And there he was," said Hod. "Paler, more wretched than he'd been the day before. I could barely see his eyes, they'd shrunken so far into his brow. I took off my bow and quiver, laid them down beside the water, stayed with him. We talked. I don't remember now what we spoke about, but it was late when we saw Odin."

He wiped the flecks of spray from his dark beard.

"Odin said that he'd been looking for Baldur. That he had something to say to him—and to him only. I left. And then, before I'd walked halfway back to hall, I remembered my bow. So I came back, even though I knew Odin would be annoyed at the interruption. It was a good bow, and it had been wrought by the *dwarvin*."

The corner of his mouth twisted, almost imperceptibly. But Vidar noticed it.

"I should have remembered it sooner. Or come back more quickly. For when I returned, there was Odin—my bow in his hands. And there was my brother, floating facedown in that pool by the waterfall. With the point of my arrow sticking out of his back."

He swallowed.

"I was dumbfounded, unable to comprehend what I saw with my own eyes. Odin whirled, struck me with the bow. I fell. Then he broke it over his knee and threw the pieces at me. 'You'll be sorry you witnessed this,' he told me. 'Now, run. For once it's known that you murdered your brother, there'll be no one in Asgard willing to save you from the gallows.'"

Hod shook his head.

"I couldn't believe my ears. I was still numb with the sight of my brother's corpse. 'But I didn't kill him,' I muttered. 'It was you.' He laughed then—laughed while his own son floated near his feet. 'And who will take your word before mine?' he asked. 'Who will believe that Odin took Baldur's life—with Hod's arrow?'

"'But why?' I asked. 'Why kill him?' My voice—it shook with my anger, my disbelief. A strange look came into Odin's face then. 'Because,' he said, 'he was weak. Too weak to be my son.'"

Hod's words seemed to fall into the space between them. And like the waterfall, to hang there for a moment, before finally plunging to earth.

"I went for him then—went for his throat with both hands. But he struck me again, for there was no strategy to my attack—only the screaming need in me to kill him as he'd killed my brother. Before I could rise a second time, he was bellowing into the night. Proclaiming my guilt. And I remembered what he'd said. Indeed, who would have believed me, when it was my arrow in Baldur's body?"

He spat.

"I fled. Had I to do it over again, I would have stayed —faced Odin, been his accuser. Even if no one recognized it as the truth. But I was confused, stricken by grief. And I fled."

Hod grimaced, as if the words themselves tasted bad.

"I went where I knew it would be difficult to find me. I came here, to Jotunheim. After a time, I saw that I was being pursued. So I lay in wait for the one who hunted me, ready to crush him with a boulder as he passed by on a lower trail. Then I saw who it was—my own brother. I almost brought the boulder down on him. Almost. But even in my bitterness and my rage, I couldn't do it. So I fled him, rather than confront him. For if I'd confronted him, I might have slain him—and I didn't want to be guilty of brother slaying. Not in truth."

Vidar nodded. "Odin is to blame," he said. "He dreamed too high, he loved too much."

Hod looked at him. "What does *that* mean?"

"Before we cut Baldur's funeral ship loose, Odin came on board and whispered something in our brother's ear. Nor would he say what it was. It became the greatest of mysteries in Asgard—a source of speculation for years and years. Or at least, until Ragnarok." He licked his lips. "That's what Odin whispered—that business about it being his fault."

"Aye," said Hod. "Then he admitted it to Baldur, finally, if to no one else." His brow furrowed. "But if it was such a mystery, how do *you* know it?"

Vidar grunted. "He carved it into my chest, back in Utgard." He stopped to think for a moment. "So we know what the 'blame' part referred to. But what did he mean about dreaming too high—and loving too much?"

Hod's temples worked beneath his black locks. "The world building. What else could it be?"

"World building?" repeated Vidar, only beginning to see.

"Of course. That's what made a scarecrow out of Baldur —he told me so himself. Once, Odin had feared none of his sons would become *gaut*—creators. Then, when he saw the talent begin to emerge in Baldur, he was too eager. He rushed it. He pushed him to shape Utgard before he was ready—created a terrain so cruel that Baldur would feel compelled to soften it. And soften it he did—as best he could. But he used up too much of himself in the process. Burned himself out trying to undo what Odin had done. And by the time he realized what this world shaping had cost him, it was too late."

"Aye," said Vidar. "That makes sense. But why would Baldur have told only you?"

"I asked him," said the dark one. "He told me that he wouldn't accuse his own father—not before Asgard. That Odin hadn't known what he was doing. And that I was good at keeping secrets."

"I wonder," said Vidar, "if Odin heard any of that. Or if he slew him too soon."

"Then you believe me?"

Vidar smiled grimly. "Let's say we believe each other."

The rumble and crash of the falls.

"Agreed," said Hod.

XXV

WHEN the light emerged on the other side of the water-fall, turning the water into ruddy wine, they left the cave—reluctantly. And it wasn't long before their stairway of stone carried them away from the cascade, where it was drier.

They found themselves on the brink of a mighty canyon, with stone walls on three sides and a wide, flat plain at the bottom. There was no seeing the end of the canyon, for it stretched out into blue-gray haze.

"Recognize it?" asked Hod.

"Aye," said Vidar. "How could I forget?"

It was Vigrid, the Iron Plain. Vidar looked to the side opposite where they stood and spied the pass through which Odin's armies had thundered. And thundered.

Down to Vigrid. And they'd ridden all night, ignoring the frigid cold and the knife-sharp winds, to come in sight of Hlymgard before dawn. For their vengeance was hot and wet, like the breath of a ravening wolf, and it would not wait.

"I hope we're not going down there," said Half, sitting on

his haunches. "There's no cover at all—no place to hide if we run into the monsters."

"As we surely will," added Tofa.

"No," said Hod, "we're not going down there." He made a sweep with his arm to indicate the cliff on which they stood, as well as those that jutted beyond it. They were thick with gnarled trees and brush. "We can get to Hlymgard this way too, though it'll take a little longer. And we'll come out above the fortress, where they're least likely to expect intruders."

It seemed like a good idea to Vidar.

As they started out along the cliffs, he laid a hand on Ullir's shoulder.

"Are you all right?" Vidar asked. "You've hardly spoken since . . . since Irbor."

Ullir looked at him. It was awhile before he answered.

"I'm glad we got to him," said the Aesirman, "when we did. Before they took any more of him."

"Aye," said Vidar, searching for words to no avail.

"That could have been me," said Ullir. "If I'd come through that split gate with Vali, instead of with you . . ." He swallowed. "Bad enough to die at all in a place like this. But to die as Irbor did, little by little . . ." He spat. "What is Odin, that he could brook such horror—that he could lead these things against his own flesh and blood?"

Vidar shook his head. "I don't know. I'm his son, and even I don't know what he is."

"A monster, Vidar. A monster." Ullir stared fiercely into the gray, billowing sky. "I had no idea, when we fought him at Indilthrar. I thought he was just a power-mad chieftain, more clever than most. And later, when you told me it was Odin we'd faced, I stood in awe of him—for who could not? And I felt a little fear, yes. But only now do I begin to see what we're up against. And I realize that I didn't fear enough. Not nearly enough."

Vidar had no answer for that, either.

Ullir took a deep breath, let it out. It froze on the air, hung there for a moment like a wraith before the wind tore it to shreds.

"Vali has been here for quite some time," he said. "How many of his warriors might have gone to feed the Nidhoggii?" His eyes narrowed. "And when we get there, will there be anything left for us to save?"

"It's better," said Vidar, "not to think of such things."

Ullir looked at him, his nostrils flaring.

"How can I help but think of them?"

How, indeed? Ullir was a healer. He could bring back life where it was ebbing. But for such as Irbor, he could do nothing—for even a *lifling* couldn't fashion new limbs.

And that, Vidar knew, was what was torturing him.

"Find a way," said Vidar. "Or they'll eat you from the inside—until there's nothing left but a sword and a bag of bones." He fixed the Aesirman on his gaze. "Think of something else—your wife, your sons. Your father and mother, your hall in shining Asgard. Think what it'll be like when you return."

The wind blew, flaying their skin right through their clothes.

"Aye," said Ullir, his anger fading. "When I return." His eyes brightened a little. "When *we* return, my lord."

After that, Ullir seemed a little better. Later, he even talked with Tofa, though about what Vidar had no idea.

Around midday they found a wreckage of stone, probably fallen from some crag up above. They took shelter within it and made a meal of their dwindling supplies.

"It's a good thing," said Half, "that our journey's almost at an end. If we went on much longer, we'd all starve."

They all chuckled at that, except Hod. He was chewing his food in silence, staring in the direction of Hlymgard. As if he could see it already, as if he stood before its walls.

A chill climbed Vidar's spine, for suddenly he remembered that look. It was the mask they'd all worn, those who came riding with Odin at Ragnarok.

After they'd eaten, they went on. The area around the

cliffs grew more jumbled, more dangerous. A purple haze seemed to rise from the plain below, obscuring it, even as the sun was frozen in the grip of steel-gray clouds. Sleet began falling from somewhere.

And it got dark sooner than they'd expected.

Don't look at me, said Hod, before Vidar could even ask. *I didn't come this way last time, as you can imagine. As soon as I saw Vigrid, I headed in the other direction.*

A little while later, however, they found a crevice in the rock—with enough nooks and crannies for all five of them to fit into. Then, as before, Vidar surrounded them with Angrum's flames.

Of course, if there were any Nidhoggii up here patrolling the cliffs, the flames would be like a beacon signaling their whereabouts. But without the fire's heat they had little chance of surviving the night.

It was shortly after he wove the circle of flame about them that Vidar decided to give it a try. It was possible that they were close enough—though the distances at which such things could be managed varied considerably from world to world, and Jotunheim had never been very cooperative in this respect.

Closing his eyes, he shut down all outside sounds, all distractions. Shut out the wailing of the wind, the tick of sleet against stone. Even the breathing of his companions.

And reached out. Into the great, gray depths . . . over the plain . . . into the dark stone of the fortress itself. . . .

Vidar? Damn it all—is that you?

Aye. It's me.

Where are . . . no, don't tell me. But you must be fairly close, or you couldn't have reached me.

Vali's mental voice sounded weak, ragged, even allowing for the distance.

Close enough, said Vidar. *I'm glad you're still alive.*

So am I. A pause. *Now.* A longer pause. *I trust you have a fair-sized army with you? You're going to need it.*

I'm not alone, said Vidar. *But I wouldn't exactly call it an army.*

What would you call it?

A handful.

If Vali was disappointed, he didn't show it.

Then forget us, he said. *Go warn Asgard. Odin's set to march on Asaheim any day now.*

Asgard's ready for him—as ready as it can be. But the bulk of our armies are in Alfheim, and they don't know what's happening. Nor can we contact them in time.

Try. You're no good to us here, as few as you are.

We might be.

A trace of anger. *Do you know what Odin's got here?*

Nidhoggii. We've met them.

And you'd still pit a handful against them?

Don't you want to be rescued?

I can think of nothing I'd like better. Again, a pause. *You've got something up your sleeve—haven't you?*

It's possible. But I don't think you want to know that either. Not yet.

No, agreed Vali. *I don't. Not with Odin's penchant for clever tortures.*

I'd better go now. You never know when he might cast about for stray thoughts. But I'll be in touch again—soon.

I'll be waiting.

And then, just before Vidar would have broken contact, Vali stopped him.

A question, said the Lord of Asgard. *How did you know they were Nidhoggii?*

You'll know that soon enough, said Vidar.

And then he *did* break contact.

As he opened his eyes, he saw Hod staring at him.

"That was unwise," said the dark one. "What if Odin has already gotten word of our exploits, and is listening for us —expecting that we'll try to contact Vali?"

"He can't be listening all the time," said Vidar. "Besides, it was necessary. If we're going to free Vali's troops, we'll need some help from inside."

"Perhaps." He frowned. "You didn't mention that I was with you."

Vidar shrugged. "I didn't see any point in it."

"But eventually, he will know. And then what will he do —try to run his prey to ground, finally?"

Vidar shrugged again.

That night, he dreamed. He saw a great stone field, enclosed on all four sides by cliffs, and oak trees growing down the middle of it in two tall rows. Great trees, thick trees, stiff as iron. The wind was a metallic voice among their brazen leaves.

From each branch hung a corpse, a pale and staring thing with a spear in its ribs and its hands bound behind its back. And he knew the names of all of them, before they'd become pale and staring things.

Knew them all, for they had been his friends and companions. Eric . . . N'arri . . . Sif . . . G'lann . . . H'limif and Heidrek, M'norr and Gilling—all twisting in the wind like ghastly ornaments, all hollow-eyed, all mouthing the empty words of death.

He walked between the rows, because it seemed as if he must.

As the oak trees grew farther and farther apart, he sensed that those who depended from them were still warm. And if he'd been here only moments before, he might have saved them. . . .

Skir'nir and Njal, Vili and Thakrad and Var'kald . . .

He began to run, thinking he saw the hanged ones thrashing up ahead, trying to shake loose the cruel shafts in their sides. But as he reached them, he saw that they were as dead as those before them. . . .

Magni . . . Alissa . . . Phil . . . Modi, though there was something different about him . . .

Vidar could hear his breath, rasping in his throat, thick with grief as he plunged ahead like a sprinter. . . .

Half, and Tofa . . . Vali . . . Hod . . .

Finally he came to the end of the oaks . . . the end of life, of existence itself . . . and there was Odin, driving his spear through B'rannit. Vidar heard the splintering of her bones as it passed through her.

He was *too late, too late* he told himself as the blood soaked her garments and the rope sang with her swinging. . . .

He woke in a cold sweat, found himself sitting upright with his hand on Angrum's hilt. But the blade was not even warm—it had had no part in his dreaming.

Vidar looked around, beyond their low circle of fire. The cliffs were dark and shapeless, indistinguishable from the cavernous sky. All around them was primal night, unbroken but for Angrum's magic.

And no sign of any oak trees.

In time his breath came more slowly. And shifting about in his cloak, he found sleep again.

The next day, the terrain grew worse. The cliffs shunted this way and that at strange angles, and there were crevices —narrow but deep—that needed crossing over. What little vegetation there had been was no more.

No Nidhoggii, either—perhaps because Hod had been right, and Odin wasn't expecting an approach along the cliffs. After all, what would it avail an army to venture here? One could hardly launch a full-scale assault on the fortress from above, for the descent would be perilous and the attackers sitting ducks.

Of course if Odin *had* set a trap, they'd most likely stumble into it closer to Hlymgard—by which time their suspicions would have been allayed.

In any case Vidar kept his eyes open.

The winds, mercifully, were calmer this day, though they seemed to be booming somewhere. The sky was taut and dark, tense, as if with anticipation.

A few hours out Vidar tried contacting Vali. But his halfbrother fended him off, suggesting that it was a bad time. Vidar didn't care to speculate as to why that might be, but he found that his mouth was suddenly dry. After all, Vali had earlier alluded to torture.

After an hour or so Vidar tried again. But he got the same

response. Of course that wasn't all bad. At least Vali was still alive.

But Vidar had the sense that something was happening, and he wanted to know what. He decided to try another channel.

The answer was sluggish, somehow. Dispirited.

And then Vidar remembered what Irbor had said—and not said.

Modi? Are you all right?

There was something like a grunt on the other end. *I'm alive, if that's what you mean.*

A chill climbed Vidar's spine.

What have they done to you, nephew?

Silence. After a while Vidar wondered if the contact had been dropped. Then Modi spoke again.

He took my hand, Vidar. The one that used to hold Mjoll-nir. So that I wouldn't be tempted to try to get it back—or so he said.

Vidar swallowed back the bitterness that filled his mouth.

And then he fed it to one of them—one of his monsters. Even as I watched.

Damn, Modi. I'm sorry.

Not half as sorry as I am, Jawbreaker. Not half. Another grunt. *Sometimes I think it's still there, Vidar. I can feel it—feel my fingers wrapped around Mjollnir's haft. And then I look down, and all I see is a stump.*

Vidar began to fit words to an answer, but he realized how hollow it would have sounded.

Where's Vali? he asked instead. *I tried to contact him, but he wouldn't answer.*

He's with Odin, said Modi. *Every now and then, the bas-tard drags him up there. To administer the truth to him—just as he did with you at Indilthrar.*

Vidar felt another, smaller shiver along his backbone. No wonder Vali had refused the contact. He'd been staring Odin in the face at the time.

Then he thought of something else. *Odin's got the ham-mer, you say. What about the horn?*

Gone, said Modi. *Destroyed. When we saw that we were overmatched, I smashed it with Mjollnir. So that it wouldn't fall into Odin's hands.* Again, that grunt. *In the end it cracked like any other horn. I expected something huge and noisy, but it just shattered. And lay there.*

As its owner did at Ragnarok. Vidar spat, clambered over a shelf of rock in his way.

Are you really going to try to free us? asked Modi. *Without an army?*

Aye, said Vidar.

Then promise me something.

What?

That you'll give me first shot at Odin. And don't tell me I won't have a chance—Tyr had but one arm, and he accounted himself well at Ragnarok.

It may not be up to me, nephew.

Insofar as it is. Promise.

All right, said Vidar. *I promise.*

That seemed to satisfy Modi. *Good*, he said.

And with that, the conversation seemed to be over. There was nothing on the other end, so Vidar closed his mind again.

XXVI

THEY came in sight of the fortress in the time just before dusk—or what would have been dusk, if there had been a sun in the sky to herald it.

"So that's it," said Ullir. "The fortress of the hrimthursar."

"The place," said Vidar, "where my brothers died."

Half chewed his mustache.

"It is . . . huge," said Tofa. "It seems to grow right out of the mountainside."

"It *is* the mountainside," said Hod, "carved out of the living rock. That's what makes it so nearly impregnable. Even Thor's hammer couldn't crack that foundation."

Vidar regarded it in the dim and dying light. He remembered the dark halls, slick with blood . . . the smell of burning flesh as his comrades were caught in Loki's fire. . . .

But it was different now. Even the descending gloom couldn't quite conceal that. There was some sort of division that hadn't been there before—as if the mountain had cracked open, splitting the fortress in two. And there were bridges, he saw, as he looked more closely—three of them, spanning the crack.

Beyond that, Vidar had a feeling that the place had grown. That there had been more carving, deeper into the rock. Nor was it intuition alone that told him this. For though he had expected to see some sort of pen for Vali's troops, there was none.

That meant that they were all somewhere inside—and even Hlymgard had never been *that* big.

"Are they all within?' asked Ullir, thinking similar thoughts. He had begun to shiver, for the temperature was plummeting again with the fall of night.

Hod looked at Vidar. His eye sockets seemed empty in the encroaching darkness. "This might be a good time," he said, "to refresh your correspondence."

Vidar tried calling Vali again.

Ah, I thought I might be hearing from you about now. Vali sounded tired.

I need some help, said Vidar. *I can see the fortress now. But where the hell are you?*

Deep within. To the northern side of the bridges, there's an entrance. See it?

No, said Vidar. *It's too dark.*

Is it? asked Vali. *Sorry. I have no conception of day and night anymore.*

How far up is this entrance?

Vali seemed to ponder that for a moment. *It should be next to the second-level bridge.*

All right, said Vidar. *I've got an idea where it would be.*

Once you're inside, it's pretty simple. The tunnel twists three times, but you stay with it. And there are two side passages, but you ignore them.

How many guards?

Too many to count.

Any idea where they've stashed your weapons?

Aye. I see the place every time Odin sends for me.

How far is it from where you are now?

Not far, said Vali. *Not far at all. In fact, it's right above us. But there's only one tunnel that leads up there, and it's a narrow one. Easily defended, I'd think.*

"Damn." Vidar said it out loud.

The others looked at him, wondering.

Anything else I should know?

Silence, while Vali mulled that one over.

Needless to say, added the Lord of Asgard finally, *the place is crawling with Nidhoggii. But there's no strict schedule whereby they change shifts at a certain time, or anything like that.* He took another moment to ponder something. *A distraction might help. Something along the lines of a storm.*

Vidar glanced at Hod, looked away again.

You've figured it out then, he told Vali.

Aye. It wasn't all that difficult.

Vidar thought about telling Vali of Hod's innocence, but decided that there wasn't enough time. Not when Odin might detect their conversation at any moment.

We're all in this together, he said instead. *That's the way it's got to be—or no deal. And I want your word on that.*

Unnecessary, Vidar. I'd already decided to suspend hostilities—at least until after we've resolved the current situation.

Your word, insisted Vidar.

All right, said Vali. *My word.*

Good. Stay ready.

Before Vali's presence had slipped away entirely, Hod spoke.

"He knows," said the dark one. "Doesn't he?"

Vidar nodded. "But he's agreed to put aside his vengeance. For the time being, anyway."

Ullir chuckled. "You must have been persuasive."

Vidar shrugged. "I held all the cards." He regarded his half-brother. "Vali suggested you work up a storm. To cover our descent."

"I was thinking about that myself," said Hod.

"How long would it take?" asked Vidar.

Hod peered at the sky from beneath his dark brows. "Not long at all. There's one on the way already. All I'll have to do is turn it a little here and there."

Half looked up at the sky also. Tofa looked at Hod.

"Do we have time to sleep," asked Ullir, "before it hits?"

Hod frowned. "Aye. Some. But we'd best be up before dawn if we're to reach Hlymgard when the storm does."

Before the darkness became complete, they were able to find crevices for each of them to squirm into. Nor could Vidar line their beds with fire as he had before—they were too close to Hlymgard now to take such a risk, even though the cliffs had reared up to conceal them.

Ullir, at his insistence, took first watch.

"The other night," he told Vidar, "you let me sleep through my turn. Did you think I'd let that happen a second time?"

But he smiled a little as he said it.

As it turned out, Ullir might as well have slept, for Vidar couldn't. He could feel the fury that was impending—the slow roiling of the heavens, the crawl of black clouds—as if he himself were a *stromrad.*

Or perhaps it was more than the storm he sensed. Perhaps it was his destiny, carried on the keening winds to the mountain fortress, where it would watch for him on the cold stone bridges and wait for him in the dark stone halls.

And then, before he'd lain there very long, he heard a scuffling outside his crevice. Instinctively his fingers closed around Angrum. And slowly he raised his head.

But when he peered out over the edge of the crack, all he saw was Tofa.

"Sorry," she said, her pale hair rippling about her face. "I hope I didn't frighten you."

Vidar chuckled, feeling the tension go out of him. "No," he said. "Only a little."

"Would you mind if . . ." Her voice trailed off. Her eyes were wide like an animal's.

Suddenly he understood.

"Of course not," he told her. "There's room enough for both of us."

She crept in, and Vidar felt her press herself against him. But not like a lover. Like a child, who's woken at night and seen the dark underbelly of the world.

"Vidar?"

"Aye?"

She looked up at him, and their eyes met. Her face was only inches from his. He could smell the perfume of her hair, of her skin.

"I don't fear dying," she told him. "I guess I never have." Her brow creased for a moment, then went smooth again. "And Ullir has told me how much this means—this thing we're doing." She licked her lips. "But if we should fail, don't let them do to me what . . . what they did to the redbeard."

Vidar swallowed. He smiled.

"Don't worry," he said. "I won't."

It seemed to make her feel better. She smiled back.

"Thank you," she said.

"Don't mention it," he told her.

But a moment later, her smile faded.

"I think . . . I think I've decided about your brother," she said.

Vidar grunted. "And?"

"He was right. Even without the mask, he's still our lord. Still the one who saved us from our enemies long ago—even if, as it turns out, he himself was one of them."

A pause. "Once he dazzled me. Now I see him for what he is—cruel sometimes, as you said. But brave as well, for he was the first one to take a crack at the serpent. Nor did he give up until the creature knocked him senseless. And the other night he would have gone after that Nidhogg by himself—had already started to, in fact—when you made it unnecessary with your flamesword."

Another pause, longer than the first. "And he has M'thrund at heart in whatever he does. I believe that." Outside their crevice the wind moaned. "So I will follow him. Not as I followed him before, for that is no longer possible. But I will follow him nonetheless."

Vidar nodded. "Good," he told her. "Now go to sleep."

"Aye," she said. "Sleep."

And soon she slept.

Vidar watched the flaring of her nostrils, the occasional flutter of her lips.

So many promises. First to Irbor. Then to Modi. And now to Tofa.

He hoped he could keep at least some of them.

"Vidar?"

He opened his eyes, saw Tofa hovering over him on the lip of the crevice. She held herself to keep from shivering.

"Something's wrong," she said.

Vidar raised himself out of the crack, witnessed the edge of fire that consumed the rim of the world. It was the sun rising in the east, wedged into the narrowest of spaces, between the unbroken clouds and the horizon.

It was still cold, cold enough to freeze the blood. Indeed,

the cliffs seemed to be covered with a slick sheen, as of frozen gore.

But there was no wind to speak of. And that was strange, because there was supposed to be a storm on the way.

Hod was hunkered down in the lee of an outcropping, far back from the cliffs. His eyes were closed and his head was thrown back.

"I found him like that when I . . ."

"I know," said Vidar, grasping her arm and pulling her toward Hod. "I know."

When they reached the dark one, they knelt down beside him.

"What happened to him?" asked Tofa.

"He's fighting the storm," said Vidar.

"But why? I thought we wanted it to come."

"We do. But it may be turning away."

It is, came Hod's thought. *And you can guess whose doing it was.*

Of course. Vidar pounded his fist against his thigh. Odin would routinely turn storms away, wouldn't he? Lest they destroy the Nidhoggii he must have positioned all along Vigrid.

"Is he still guiding it?" asked Vidar.

No, said Hod. *But he gave it a good shove. I don't know if I can bring it back on course.*

Yet there was no time to whip one up from scratch. How long could they remain up here before they were spotted?

Try, said Vidar.

You think I need you to tell me that?

Vidar frowned and shut up.

By then Ullir and Half had come up behind him. He told them all what was going on, and they stared at the *stromrad.*

Half squinted in the ruddy dawnlight. "Hard to believe," he said, "that even Jalk can command such fury."

"His name is Hod," said Tofa, without looking at her fellow *hjalamar.*

Half shrugged.

"Not to me," he said.

From time to time Vidar glanced at the sky. It was dense and gray, still as stone. Unchanged and unchanging.

He took Angrum out and made a small flame among some rocks. Then he laid his waterbag over them—to thaw it out, for its contents had gone slushy overnight.

In a little while the water was fit to drink. He took a draught from it and passed it on to Tofa. Then Ullir took some, and Half.

On Hod's brow, there were beads of sweat. One ran down the side of his face.

But the sky was still unmoving. Dark and leaden.

And then they felt it.

The wind.

Slowly Hod's eyes fluttered open.

"It's done," he said.

Indeed, the heavens had begun to stir. And the edge of fire in the east was shutting down, stripping the world of its last bit of color.

"Let's go," said Hod, picking himself up. "There's not much time."

Without further comment they started out on the last leg of their journey. They hiked their cloaks up to keep the wind from nipping at their necks, and made as much haste as the terrain would allow them.

Vidar extended himself, seeking Vali's consciousness. The link was quickly made, as if Vali had been expecting it.

Soon, Vidar told him, *you'll hear thunder. We'll be right on its heels.*

How will I know you?

That was more than an attempt at humor, Vidar knew. It was a plea for information, disguised in case Odin chose that moment to listen in.

I'll be wearing a sword, said Vidar.

The contact dissipated, vanished on the gathering winds.

XXVII

SHE was Billing's daughter, and she was the fairest mortal that Odin had yet laid eyes upon. Even in her grief. Her skin was like milk, and her hair like fire, and her eyes like the sky at dusk.

Disguised as a fisherman, he came to her on the seashore, where she mourned beside a long-prowed ship.

"What ails you," he asked, "that you weep? For eyes like yours should never be dimmed by tears."

"You are kind," said Billing's daughter, "but I truly have reason to weep. My poor father's body lies here on his ship. The pine rollers have been set before it, and the wealth of Billing heaped on its decks. Yet I have no brothers, nor are my retainers plentiful enough to launch it. So it sits in the sand, to my shame and my sorrow, while the birds pick at Billing's remains."

"Ah," said Odin, "is that all that bothers you? Then I think I can relieve you of your burden. For all the fishermen in this part of the country are my friends, and if they know anything at all, it's how to launch a ship. Together, surely, we should be able to push it out to sea."

Billing's daughter looked up at him with hope in her eyes. "For such a labor, I would indeed be grateful. Nor is there anything I would withhold as payment, were it within my power to give it."

"You are wise, said Odin, "as well as beautiful. For it is the way of the world to reward those who work for you."

"It is only what my father taught me," said Billing's daughter.

"Good," said the Lord of the Ravens. "Then we have a deal. Tonight I will launch your father's ship, sending it burning over the waves. And when that is done, you will give yourself to me, as a maiden gives herself to a man."

This took Billing's daughter by surprise. But she had wept for a long time, and the fisherman wasn't a bad-looking fellow. A little older than she might have liked, but rather handsome now that she looked at him.

"All right," she said finally, her fiery hair rippling in the wind off the sea. "Only free Billing's funeral ship, and you will have what you desire."

Satisfied, Odin took her hand and brushed his lips against it. Nor did she flinch, for they were strangely warm and pleasant on her skin.

"Tonight," he said, "keep watch from your hold by the sea. But do not come down to the water's edge, for my fisher friends are shy folk, and they'll scatter at the sight of a chieftain's child."

Billing's daughter agreed. She'd watch and wait.

With nightfall Odin returned to the ship. But he had no one with him to help him free the vessel from its place in the sand. Nor did he need anyone, for he was the All-Father, and there was magic roiling in his blood.

First Odin took out his flint and set fire to an oil-soaked brand he'd brought with him. When the torch was lit, he tossed it over the gunwale. Soon the ship had caught; and its ruddy light danced in the spaces between the waves.

Then, digging his heels in, he put his shoulder to the keel. The moon shone, baleful, and the winds murmured as he worked the ship free of the sand. Finally, with one great heave, he sent it thundering forward over the pine logs.

Waves crashed against the prow, broke, and crashed again. And before they could crash a third time, the vessel was afloat.

For a time Odin watched it drift out to sea, knowing that

Billing's daughter would be watching too. Then he turned and made his way to her keep.

But when he came to the door of that place, there were a half-dozen warriors up on the walls, waving their swords at him.

"Go away," they said, "fisherman, for Billing's daughter has changed her mind. She will not lie with you, so go away."

"Is that so?" said Odin, gazing up at the warriors. "What about our agreement? I promised to launch Billing's funeral ship, and this has been done. Is payment not due me?"

Then Billing's daughter herself appeared, and cast a leather pouch down from the walls. It landed on the soft earth at Odin's feet.

"There," she said. "That is gold enough, for you and for all your friends. But I have taken counsel with myself, and I cannot pay you what you desire."

"You are fickle," said Odin, "like much of womankind. A man cannot rely on your promises."

Odin took out his flint again, and another of the brands he carried. He looked up at Billing's daughter, and at the fiery hair that tossed on the wind. He looked at her dusky eyes and her milk-white skin.

"Fortunately," he said, "some things in this world are more constant."

And he lit the brand.

Sin Skolding
Namforsen, 538 A.D.

XXVIII

"**L**OOKS like it worked," said Ullir.

The entire eastern sky was a black, brooding mass of clouds, shot through with needles of lightning. Every now and then the wind would carry the roll of thunder to them. And there was sleet in the air as well, pricking at their faces and their hands.

"Nor can it be turned away, now that it's so close, and coming so fast." Hod spat and looked satisfied. "Not even by Odin."

"But they're still out there," said Tofa, peering down at the various levels of the fortress. The Nidhoggii were still much in evidence, on the walls and on the bridges that spanned the cut.

It was only once they'd gained this vantage point, directly above Hlymgard, that they'd seen just how deeply the fortress had split. There seemed to be no bottom to the chasm—as if it ran down to the very bowels of the earth.

"No," said Half. "See, my lady? They're withdrawing—going inside."

Indeed, the monsters were starting to retreat—if slowly —in the face of the storm. Vidar watched to see which routes they used over the mountainside, which bridges, which entrances.

The wind rose, howled, and the stormfront belched lightning. Thunder came right on its heels.

"I wish they'd hurry a little," remarked Ullir. "If the storm hits while we're still up here . . ."

He didn't have to finish. They all remembered the violence they'd seen in the mountains.

One by one the Nidhoggii clambered over the dark stone. Found a way in, disappeared. They looked like gray spiders crawling over a cracked and sun-blackened carcass.

The wind screeched, threatening to drag them down from their perch. But they flattened themselves against the rock and hung on.

Getting closer, lightning carved patterns into a sky the color of slate. Thunder bawled, angry and mournful at the same time.

Vidar let his hand come to rest on Angrum's hilt. Like him, it had been here before.

But then, it had been used like an ordinary sword. For Frey had fought in quarters too close to unleash its power— or he'd have burned his own Vanirmen to cinders.

Loki, on the other hand, had been bound by no such restraints. He'd cast his flame about him like a net, happy to catch some hrimthursar in it—as long as he also snared Odin and his kin.

The walls grew bare, empty of defenders. As the Nidhoggii converged on the bridges, they jostled one another, and once or twice a fight broke out. But they didn't seem to last long. In fact, for all their bloodthirstiness, the creatures were more disciplined than Vidar had imagined.

But the storm was coming on faster and faster. The sky seemed to boil with it. Lightning sizzled in its great, dark maw and the thunder hammered at their skulls. Sleet hissed and swirled all about them.

"Come on," said Ullir, urging the Nidhoggii to greater haste. "Move, you laggards."

Eventually the last few Nidhoggii were consumed by the fortress. By then the wind was awful, and the heavens were tearing themselves apart. Lightning seared their vision and thunder roared.

"All right," Vidar bellowed over the cacophony of the storm. "For God and country." And before the words were out of his mouth, he'd begun to pick a path down from the cliff.

The sleet made the stone slippery, but Vidar found enough hand- and footholds to keep from falling. Just as a reminder, the chasm yawned on the far side of the three bridges.

Between lightnings he saw the topmost bridge loom closer. A wraith of sleet swept over it, and then it was visible again.

The wind shrieked, wrenching at his sleet-caked cloak. Reluctantly, with fingers turned to claws by the cold, he ripped open the clasp at his neck. The cloak kited out over Hlymgard, then dipped and plummeted.

Above him he saw other cloaks fly, and hoped there'd be a time when they might mourn the loss of them. He lowered himself another length, another.

And a moment later he dropped down onto the bridge.

Just as Vidar looked up to help one of his companions, he caught a glimpse of something gray and gangling. Whirling, he saw the niche in the rock he hadn't counted on—and the three or four Nidhoggii that had just emerged from it.

They came loping across the span, truncheons raised, rasping curses. Their eyes gleamed, red as rubies, red as blood.

Vidar knew he had to end this quickly, before anyone else spotted them. Pulling Angrum free, he trained it on the leatherskins. Fire erupted from the point of the blade. It shot across the bridge until it reached the Nidhoggii, and then it enveloped them.

Suddenly the creatures were writhing on the ground, trying to put themselves out. But the sword wouldn't let up. It poured out its flame at them without stint. All around the blade, the sleet hissed and was vaporized.

Screaming, one of the creatures threw himself off the bridge, a falling ember in the great gloom of the oncoming storm. Another tried to fling himself at Vidar, but fell far short.

In moments they were black and wizened things, shriveling at the center of the flames. Gray smoke rose, was flattened against Hlymgard by the winds.

"Vidar—come on! It's enough, damn it!"

It was Hod, tearing at his arm.

Vidar willed it, and Angrum stopped. The stench of burning thick in his nostrils, he followed the dark one to the other end of the bridge.

There was a black iron door there, but it did not open as they passed. Just beyond it was a stair, cut into the side of the mountain. They followed it down.

Lightning struck somewhere above Vigrid, blinding them. Thunder crashed against the cliffs.

The storm was almost on top of them.

Down one step, then the next. Clutching at the rock for purchase, Vidar kept Hod before him. His foot slid out from under him, but he caught himself.

Below, the second bridge emerged from a flood of driven sleet. The door they wanted was to the left of it—and that's where the stone stairway was leading them, more or less.

Silently Vidar praised the hrimthursar for their foresight.

Down and down, twisting, reaching, until they came to a flat stone shelf at the base of the stair. There was the door, as forbidding as the one above it—and just where Vali had said it would be.

But Vali hadn't told them how to get inside it.

Half dropped down beside Vidar. Tofa next, and finally Ullir.

Lightning shattered the sky, erupting like fireworks as it struck the mountain. The stone shivered beneath their feet, and the sound that came after was a roaring, raving madness.

Of course, there was a good chance that it wasn't locked. The Nidhoggii wouldn't have been expecting visitors in this weather.

"Ullir," yelled Vidar, pulling the Aesirman's face close to his, striving to be heard over the storm. "Get over by the door. When I tell you, swing it open."

The blondbeard nodded, his hair whipping savagely about his raw, red visage. But as he made his way to the entrance-way, the wind picked up, and the sleet grew suddenly thicker.

For a moment Vidar could see almost nothing. Then there was a break in the whiteness, and he spotted Ullir. He signaled—a quick slash with his left hand.

The black door swung aside, and he had a brief look at the monsters within. They gaped at him out of their pterodactyl heads, scarcely able to believe what they saw.

Then they came pouring out. And again Vidar unleashed the sword's fire.

Some of the Nidhoggii fell, beating at themselves, burning like living torches. The others retreated before the fiery death that suddenly confronted them, withdrawing deeper into the embrace of the mountain.

Vidar followed them in, holding Angrum before him, filling the corridor with flame. He had a sense of the others behind him, crowding between the stone walls he'd scorched and blackened.

Abruptly there was a burst of light even the fire couldn't account for. A half second later the corridor shook with the force of it.

The storm had hit Hlymgard.

But there was a storm inside the mountain as well, a fire-storm that scoured it, purging it of life. The Nidhoggii fled that unholy inferno, though the corridor was too narrow for all to flee. Beyond the wall of flame Vidar heard snarling, ragged cries torn from alien throats. He smelled burning, and kept coming. And as the fire pressed ahead, the dying twisted free of it—like fish left writhing after the tide had gone out.

Somehow one of the creatures came through standing—if barely. But Hod intervened before he could come after Vidar. There was a strangled cry and something slapped against the ground at Vidar's feet. He stepped over it.

Flame danced and feasted, curling it on itself where it touched the stone. The heat made the skin of Vidar's face crawl, shriveled the hairs on the backs of his hands. He felt sweat running down his face and gathering in his beard.

The screaming was getting louder now, echoing, becoming more frantic. The blackened forms of the dying jerked and smoked on the floor of the corridor, the fire still eating at them.

Vidar did his best to neither see nor hear, but there was no helping it. There was no escape for him, no more than for the Nidhoggii themselves.

Or was there?

Who was the master—him or the sword?

Suddenly he cut the barrage short. The wall of fury thinned, whispered into nothingness.

"What's wrong?" asked Hod.

"This is," said Vidar.

There were small fires everywhere, as Angrum's flame finished its work. Smoke filled the corridor, stinging their eyes. And somewhere beyond, there was a snarling, a shuffling as of many feet.

"What do you mean?" asked Hod. "Does it work or doesn't it?" He coughed, grimacing.

"We don't need it anymore," said Vidar, fighting the stench. "We've got them on the run."

They listened. The sounds of the Nidhoggii were growing fainter by the heartbeat.

Hod's eyes met his. They were red-rimmed beneath dark brows.

"All right," he said. "But watch the side passages."

They went on, through the thick, acrid smoke, through the garden of corpses that lit a path for them in the darkness.

But that only lasted for a while. Then they were past the places that the flame had reached. The air was better, the floor clear and the walls unscarred. And Vidar had to use Angrum once more, containing its fury so that it only burned like a common torch.

Thunder rumbled, shaking the mountain to its roots.

When the rumbling faded, Vidar heard another sound—not unlike cheering. And it came from human throats, a great chorus of them.

"Hear them?" asked Ullir, at his right hand.

"Aye," said Vidar.

They passed a connecting tunnel, and he heeded Hod's advice. But it was dark, empty.

So was the next one.

Their own tunnel turned abruptly, once and again.

The cheering grew louder.

A third time the tunnel turned. It widened, deepened.

Vidar raised Angrum so they could see better. Their shadows leaped like mountain goats.

"A door," said Hod.

It was a door, all right. A great iron door set deep into the stone, with huge, black bolts holding it in place. At one time it must have been well guarded.

The cheering was coming from the other side of it.

Hod gripped Half's shoulder.

"Watch our backs," he told him. He looked at Tofa. "And you as well—my lady."

The *thrund* moved to block the corridor while Vidar and the others approached the door, sheathing their blades. Temporarily Angrum's light was lost, and it was in near-complete darkness that each set his shoulder to a bolt.

Hod's moved first, with a resounding *clang*. Vidar's shot to a moment later, creaking horribly. Ullir's came last—first halfway, and then the rest.

Groaning on its hinges, the mammoth door swung open —but just a crack. There was shouting, and the cheering died suddenly.

That is you, isn't it?

It was Vali.

Aye, said Vidar. *It's me*.

The door swung the rest of the way, to the accompaniment of metal screeching against metal. A crowd of dim shapes gathered at the entrance.

Vidar brought Angrum out and coaxed another flame forth. In the firelight, he could see their faces. They were gaunt and pale, sunken-cheeked, Aesir and Vanir no less than men and *dwarvin*. Even the towering thursar were painfully thin.

One figure stepped forth, and Vidar winced when he saw him. Though he'd come through better than the others, he still bore the scars of starvation.

The eyes in that hawkish face flickered at Vidar, and Vali smiled. "Well met, brother." He glanced at Angrum. "Now I see why you were so confident."

There were shouts from a couple of Asgardians who recognized Ullir, for he was standing at Vidar's side, illuminated by Angrum's flame. And then other shouts, tinged with venom, for there were those who knew Hod from his likenesses in the tapestries. Even in the shadows they knew him.

In answer to their cries Hod stepped closer to the light. Yet the shadows still seemed to cling to him, to mold his visage into something dark and cruel.

Vali's eyes were drawn to him—and in turn, Hod's to Vali. For what seemed like a long time, they gazed upon one another.

Then Vali's voice rang out, and it was not the voice of a scarecrow, but a king.

"No one is to touch this one, or to hurt him. When this is all over, he will be mine. I claim him."

Hod laughed. "If you can, Vali. You were ever the one to make empty boasts."

Vali's features hardened at that. But he restained himself, keeping his word to Vidar.

"This time," he said, "you won't shake me off your trail, brother." He fashioned a smile. "You should never have come here."

"That's enough," said Vidar, before things could heat up even more. "We haven't got so much time we can waste it."

Vali turned away from Hod. "Aye," he said. "There are still others to be liberated."

"Which way?" asked Vidar.

Vali pointed it out, and they went in that direction. As before, Angrum lit the way, if only for those in Vidar's vicinity. Somewhere behind him the occupants of the prison chamber spilled out into the corridor.

There was no more cheering among Vali's warriors—only a buzzing, like that of angry bees swarming through a stone hive.

Suddenly a glimpse of ruby eyes, deep in darkness. The long, angular forms of the Nidhoggii, charging at them. Ignorant, perhaps, of what had befallen their brethren.

Gritting his teeth, Vidar raised the blade. Once again the flames jetted forth, devouring the first rank of the enemy. They screamed and fell, confounding those just behind them.

There was confusion, a trampling of leathery bodies as those behind still pushed ahead and those in the fore struggled to retreat. But in the end it didn't matter. The fire reared up and consumed them all, filling their mouths with fire, stirring their limbs into a frenzy.

After a few moments Vidar called back the inferno, hoping that it had been enough. But as soon as the fire abated, they gathered again in the darkness beyond, glaring at him with eyes full of hate. Thinking perhaps that the devil flame was spent, they came on with renewed purpose.

Nor was there any way around the creatures—not if they were to reach the others that Odin had imprisoned.

So Vidar unleashed Angrum once more, and the flames spurted, and the Nidhoggii burned. In clumps they burned, all tangled together, so that one could not say where one corpse ended and the next began. The smell was unbearable, stomach wrenching, worse than that of any charnel house.

By the time they reached the next prison chamber, Vidar's hands and face were black with smoke. His eyes felt like hot coals in their sockets and his throat was dry as dust.

The door was blocked with still-smoldering carcasses. But no one hesitated, not Aesirman or elf or graven-faced thursar. Ignoring the flames, they flung the blackened bonebags out of the way.

The bolts shot to, and the door swung wide, and a red-bearded bear lurched out ahead of the others. Like Vali, he'd grown too lean, and his right hand ended at the wrist in a livid stump.

"He's coming," bellowed Modi, his face as red as his beard in Angrum's light. "Just now he taunted me. Warned me that he was on his way—to crush us."

He spat, eyes narrowing—just as Thor's used to.

"I told him to sit on the sharpest blade he had."

They looked at one another. Vali had a sneer on his face. Hod looked grim.

"Some of us must continue down the passageway," said Vali, "and free those others on this side of the bridge."

"While the rest of us go on to the arsenal," finished Modi.

"No," said Hod. "Not all of us. If we're to meet him, it must be out in the open. Where he can't outmaneuver us. Or press us so close together that Vidar can't use the sword."

"Out on the bridges," said Vidar.

"Aye," said the dark one.

Vali nodded. "Then go out to the bridges and wait for him—by now the storm will have abated enough to allow that. Pit the sword against his hammer for as long as you can. I will see to the freeing of the others. And Modi will lead the assault on the arsenal."

Vidar had to admit it, if only to himself. Vali was good at giving orders.

"Just one question," said Vidar.

"Which is?" asked the Lord of Asgard.

"What's the quickest route?"

Vali showed him.

XXIX

IT was as before. Vidar led the way through the corridor, Hod and Ullir just behind him, Tofa and Half close on their heels.

But now they had a company of *dwarvin* in tow, armed with splinters of the truncheons they'd found among the corpses. The dark elves had sworn their loyalty to Vidar outside the walls of Indilthrar—and they'd not forgotten their vow.

Thunder reverberated throughout the tunnels. Since they'd parted company with Vali, they'd met with no resistance. But Vidar was still careful each time he entered a turning, lest he find Nidhoggii lying in wait for him.

Another round of thunder, a heavy pulse in the stones of Hlymgard. It was louder than before—a good sign that Vali's directions had been accurate, and they were getting closer to the surface.

Two more turnings, two more empty tunnels. Providence? Or a trap?

Vidar felt the movement of air across his face, smelled the odor of burnt flesh on it. Yes. Definitely closer.

Just then something brushed against his consciousness. An attempted contact, a word.

Vidar.

He didn't respond. It would have distracted him, slowed him down, and that was just what the caller wanted.

Again, that touch, like a dry and shriveled leaf.

I'm glad you've come, boy. Glad indeed.

Vidar tightened his grip on Angrum and concentrated that much harder. The stench grew worse as he advanced. And there were traces of smoke in the air.

Finally they found the passage by which they'd entered Hlymgard, littered with velvety black bones. Nor were the fires finished, for they would continue to feed as long as there was anything left to feed on.

Something popped and sizzled as Vidar entered the tunnel. Thin streams of carbon rose on either side of him, like the beginnings of an exotic forest. The air shivered where flames still danced.

He wished he had his cloak still, to cover his face, to keep the stench out of his nostrils. But he made do with a tattered sleeve, ripped somewhere along the way.

He tried to avoid the bones, but they were everywhere. Skulls seemed to look up at him, glaring with eyeless sockets. Limbs splintered beneath his feet.

The passage was longer than he remembered. An eternity longer.

Ashes stirred, flew into his face. They stuck to his skin, mingled with his beard. He could taste them in his mouth.

And then it came to them—a wind, a true wind. Dispelling the stink of death, shivering the tendrils of smoke, and scattering the weightless skeletons. It was cold, deadly cold, but it felt good for all of that.

Somewhere up ahead there was a flash of light. And a moment later the roller coaster roar of thunder.

Vidar hastened, despite himself. He couldn't help it. He longed for the fresh air, even if it was driven by the lash of the storm.

Angrum's torchlight flickered and flagged, shredded by the wind. But they no longer needed it. Gray light filled the corridor now.

Suddenly there was the door, and beyond it a sliver of dark, purple clouds. Vidar headed for that, burst out into the full fury of the elements.

And just in time. For at the far end of the stone bridge,

there was a gang of Nidhoggii starting to make its way across.

Lightning slithered and thunder bawled. As Vidar came forward to take a position on the bridge, the winds tried to tear him off, send him hurtling into the abyss below. But he stayed low and held his ground.

The Nidhoggii scarcely seemed to feel the buffeting of the storm. They bore down on him like the predators they were, their long limbs eating the span that separated them in great gulps.

And then, when they were almost upon him, he turned Angrum loose. Flame geysered from the blade, fighting the winds that clawed at it. Nidhoggii fell, embroiled in balls of yellow fury.

A couple got through, but might have wished they hadn't. Vidar's companions, far outnumbering them, dispatched the creatures in short order.

For a time, nothing. No Nidhoggii emerging from Hlymgard's other flank. No one on the bridge below, and no sounds from the bridge above.

Lightning carved a blood-eagle into the blue-black clouds. Thunder wrenched at the mountain. Winds swirled, howling.

Vidar shivered, even with Angrum flaming in his hands. He shivered and watched.

Finally there was movement at the far end of the bridge. Lots of it, in fact. But these Nidhoggii seemed less eager than the others. They waited for their numbers to swell before they advanced. Finally, when they did come forward, there was another form among them—that of the one who brought them here, to hone them into his instrument of destruction.

His hair, long and white, rippled in the wind—having grown some since Vidar last saw him in Indilthrar. There were scraps of a beard as well, as much as would sprout from that ruined countenance.

He was well wrapped in furs—wolves' pelts, by the look of them. And in his hand he held Thor's hammer.

This time, when Odin reached out, Vidar accepted the contact. Why not? What harm could it do now?

I see, said the Valfather, *that you've brought me the sword. You have served me well, Vidar—even as I knew you would.*

No, said Vidar. *Even you couldn't have planned it this way. You didn't want us to find you here—at least not before you took Asgard.*

Even at a distance he could see Odin's expression change. The twisted mouth twisted even more. But he didn't break his stride.

All your plans are in disarray now. It's over, Father.

Odin seemed to find humor in that. *You've a lot to learn, princeling. And so little time in which to learn it.* His mouth twisted again, this time into a monstrous grin. *A pity, really.*

"Damn," said Hod, on Vidar's left flank. "It's really him. And look at—" The wind snatched the rest of his words away.

Until now Odin seemed not to have noticed his other son. But when Hod spoke, it drew his attention.

I must thank you too, he told the dark one as Vidar listened in. *For saving me the trouble of seeking you out. I have a place for you in my plans, Hod. You are not like the others—why pretend to be? They hate you. They have always hated you.*

Vidar watched his brother's face. It was a mask of loathing.

Perhaps, said Hod. *But not nearly as much as I have hated you.*

Odin's grin only widened.

So be it, he said.

And with a cry that could be heard even over the wind, Odin came for them. The Nidhoggii were right behind him.

Vidar cursed, realizing only then that he'd let them get too close. He'd been so preoccupied with his father's offer to Hod, he'd become careless.

Still, there was time to stop a good many of them. Raising the sword, he trained it on the center of the mob—on Odin. But just before Angrum spewed forth its flame, the Lord of the Ravens dropped back, allowing his warriors to shield him from the blade's power.

They caught the stream of fire as if grateful for it, staggered forward as far as they could. When they fell, more monsters leaped into the breach, flinging themselves into the inferno.

Vidar saw what was happening. The Valfather was sacrificing his creatures in waves—knowing that the closer he pressed, the less useful the sword would be.

A third rank sprang up after the second had collapsed, but this time Vidar couldn't get them all—for the wind had torn a ragged hole in the wall of flame. Growling and spitting, the survivors rushed him.

For he was the prize, the wielder of the demon flame. Once he was crushed, the others could not stand.

Vidar would have held out longer, would have taken out more of the enemy while he had the chance. But on either side of him, his companions moved to protect him. And for fear of hitting them, he had to quench the fire.

Hod was one of those who met the first attack. Ducking a truncheon blow, he slashed a leatherskin's side open.

Ullir confronted another one, deflecting its weapon and impaling it on his blade.

But the elves were not so fortunate. Without true weapons they could only slow the Nidhoggii down. One fell with his skull caved in, another clutching his arm.

A monster loomed before Vidar, intent upon driving him into the ground. Just in time the Aesirman skipped to one side and the bludgeon shivered against the surface of the bridge. Vidar was about to skewer the Nidhogg on his smoking blade when another creature followed it through. Before it could bring its club into play, Vidar lunged forward and cut at its knee. Blood sprayed and the leatherskin toppled.

Then the rest of the Nidhoggii were on them, like dogs on

raw meat, forcing Vidar's company back across the span. There were the dull, sickening sounds of truncheons pulverizing flesh and bone, the cries of the elves as they faltered beneath that pounding.

But sometimes, too, the Nidhoggii fell, clawing at shivers of wood that protruded from between their ribs, scrabbling at splinters that had been driven into their throats. Nor did the other creatures stop to help them. They trampled them as if they were weeds growing in the stone.

Vidar gave up ground slowly, reluctantly. And all the while, he searched the sea of lumbering, gray warriors for Odin's nightmare visage.

A cut, a thrust, a gout of blood. A blow caught on his blade, turned, but enough to make his bones quiver. A close inspection of a pterodactyl head with its burning-coal eyes, its rotting-flesh breath, before he buried Angrum in the monster's bowels. A bubbling as the sword tugged free again.

Then, a sudden rent in the fabric of the battle. And there was Odin, flailing with the hammer like Thor in his youth, crushing all who would oppose him. Mjollnir ran crimson with elvish blood, swooping again and again to drink of it.

Father!

Lightning seared the sky, and thunder droned.

Odin's head swiveled in Vidar's direction.

A change of heart? suggested the Valfather.

No such thing. A challenge.

Odin's lips parted in a death's-head grin.

I understand, he said. *You'd rather die by my hand than some other.*

Vidar battered away a blow aimed at his face, brought Angrum down sharply across his assailant's bony chest. The Nidhogg staggered backward, collapsing around its wound.

But it's not time yet, continued Odin. *These others must be slain first. Then I can give you the attention you deserve —as my son.*

Ironically it was another of his sons who almost got to him then. In a burst of fury Hod fought his way within a sword's breath of Odin. He got in one stroke, one only—and the All-Father warded it off.

A moment later the sweep of battle had separated them. Vidar cursed out loud—felt a truncheon graze his shoulder, brought his blade up to stop another.

Don't worry, Odin told the dark one. *Your time will come also. You need not rush it.*

As if that were a signal, the creatures pressed them even harder. Vidar moved back a step, another, traded blows with a Nidhogg before Half came out of nowhere and stabbed it in the armpit. An elf finished it off, plunging his stake into the monster's concave belly.

Vidar's arms felt like lead, heavy with the strain of hacking at bone and gristle and thick, leathery hide. But there was no time to rest. The Nidhoggii swarmed all over them, pushing them back the way they came. An elf was lifted off his feet, thrown high into the air to plummet toward the chasm below.

That was when Vidar glanced down—and saw the battle brewing on the bridge beneath them.

Someone had gotten out—either Modi or Vali. Maybe both. It meant they had a chance.

Jawbreaker?

It was Vali.

No time now, said Vidar. *I see you. Below me.*

Not below, returned Vali. *Above. Hang in there. I'm coming.*

But Vidar's troops were getting thin. Too many of the *dwarvin* had been ground up already under the merciless strokes of the Nidhoggii, or within the deadly ambit of the hammer. And those left to him were covered with blood, much of it their own.

Catching a glimpse of truncheon out of the corner of his eye, Vidar whirled and split it into flying fragments. But his attacker still held the jagged stump, and he kept coming with it.

As Vidar brought Angrum across again, his foot slipped on something wet. The stump missed his neck, where the Nidhogg had aimed it—but it didn't miss him altogether.

Pain erupted in his shoulder as the shattered club tore flesh and muscle. Vidar fell back, strangling a cry.

Through the red haze that closed down over his eyes, he saw a black-and-silver fury leap forward. A moment later the Nidhogg was shrieking, holding aloft the spurting stub of its forearm.

Someone grabbed him, raised him to his feet while a circle of elvish warriors closed about him. Shoots of agony ran through his shoulder, and his left arm dangled at his side. But as the haze cleared from his eyes, he realized that he still held Angrum in his good hand.

Was it he who hadn't let go, he wondered—or the sword?

"I'm all right," he said, shrugging off the *dwarvin* who'd helped him, though it roused his pain to a frenzied pitch. "I'm all right."

And he waded back into the battle, swinging his blade one-handed.

Ah—you're up again, said Odin.

Vidar couldn't see him, and he didn't dare look. With one arm it was that much harder to batter aside a truncheon. And though he tried to hold his shoulder still, he could feel the splinters grinding together.

Good, said the Lord of the Ravens. *I thought I'd been cheated.*

Vidar didn't answer. He deflected one attack, confounded another. Whirled in time to take a third blow and return it.

But he knew he couldn't stand much longer. He could tolerate the pain, perhaps. But he couldn't ignore the loss of blood.

A dark elf fell at his feet, the back of his head turned to pulp. Another slumped against him, ribs crushed, eyes wide with pain.

Their resistance was failing. They were giving ground

more freely now, unable to match the Nidhoggii stroke for stroke.

From behind, suddenly, there were cries—elvish voices raised above the din. Vidar's heart lightened.

Modi? Vali? He turned for a moment, to see who had come to their aid.

It wasn't help, however, that came for them from the far end of the span. It was another pack of Nidhoggii, cutting off their retreat.

Hod bellowed a curse and went charging through the ranks, rallying the *dwarvin* against the new threat at their backs.

Lightning cut a jagged path through the heavens. Thunder moaned.

Without warning, there came a rain of bodies from above. Some of them, Vidar thought, were Nidhoggii. Their screams were swallowed by the abyss.

Slash, parry, hack, and thrust. Vidar heard himself cry out with each impact of sword and club, each reawakening of the fiery agony in his shoulder. He seemed to be surrounded by enemies everywhere he looked, everywhere he turned. There was no respite now, no time to think.

Something slashed him—long claws raking across his face. He pulled away, tasted blood, spit it out.

Cut and turn, batter and stab. Something struck him in the ribs, forcing the breath out of him. He gasped for air, fought the darkness, even as he raised Angrum against the next blow.

But a different one struck him, one he had not seen. It spun him around, robbed him of his equilibrium.

He reeled, felt the hardness of stone against his knee. Saw as if from a great depth the truncheons poised to finish him off.

There were lights before his eyes, particolored lights. He was losing consciousness. The clamor of battle seemed far away. As far as Woodstock, as far as the hills of Samsey.

With what will he had left, he lifted the sword. The truncheons fell.

Vidar felt a terrible white heat, a conflagration that seemed to burn his eyes out of their sockets.

When he opened them, however, he could still see. The skin of his face was burned and blistered, but he was alive.

Nor were his enemies towering above him. On all sides bodies lay burning, and their weapons along with them. Beyond the corpses the other Nidhoggii had drawn back.

And not just from him, he realized. They had turned away from the dwindling force of *dwarvin* to face some threat at their own backs.

Vidar staggered to his feet, sucking tainted air through the vise that had closed around his chest. Broken ribs, he told himself as he peered past the smoke and the ragged flames.

On the far side of the bridge, past the Nidhoggii, Vidar saw the lumbering forms of the Utgard thursar, the smaller forms of Aesirmen and humans. They issued from the mountain like a river, in great numbers, and they were armed like warriors with swords and axes.

Vidar turned, to help Hod defend their rear. But there too, things had changed. There was a battle taking place at the door itself, where those who had been so long in Hlymgard were trying to fight their way out.

And those in the middle, the dark elves and the two *hjalamar*, Ullir and Hod—they all looked at each other, disbelieving that they could be so unmolested when just moments ago they were so hard beset.

Finally they looked to Vidar. All of them, even Hod.

"Which way?" cried Ullir, over the singing wind. His tunic was splattered with blood, but he looked whole enough.

Vidar didn't hesitate. The choice was obvious. Gritting his teeth against the grinding pain in his shoulder, he loped past the burning bodies, headed in Odin's direction.

But before he could reach the clot of Nidhoggii, before he

could get close enough to bring Angrum into play, there came a sound even louder than the thunder.

And blue sparks filled the air.

And the bridge shuddered, sending them sprawling.

It took Vidar a moment to realize what was happening. By then there was another crash, and more sparks, and a worse shivering of the stone beneath them.

But the third blow was the charm.

With a huge and deafening roar, a section of bridge came away—just where the Nidhoggii and their former prisoners had come together.

True lightning raged, as warriors from both sides rode the chunk of rock down into the abyss. Their cries were sharp at first, but they faded quickly.

And when the wind swept away the cloud of flying grit, there was Odin, shaking his hammer at the heavens. The thunder shouted its approval, raving as if it were as mad as he was.

There was a blue web of tiny lightnings about Mjollnir, a play of power. And why not? It was created to smash, to destroy. In Odin's hands, it had done just that.

Beyond Odin, on the far side of the gap, there were figures rising to their feet. Vali was among them, with a sword in his hand. And Modi as well, with one of the leatherskins' bludgeons.

But they may as well have been miles away. With neither a spear nor a bow among them, they had no way of reaching Odin.

The Valfather grinned, stretching taut the livid sheath of flesh over half his face. His mane bannered on the wind.

Now there is no one to help you, Vidar. No one to stop me from crushing you.

The Nidhoggii about him hung back, as if awaiting his order. They outnumbered Vidar's company almost two to one. But even if it had been the other way around, they would have had the advantage.

You won't reach me without loss, said Vidar. He had the sense that they were all listening, all who could—

Hod, Vali, Modi, and perhaps some others among the Aesirmen, those who claimed Odin's blood in sufficient measure. *I've still got the sword. I'll roast you as I roasted the others.*

Odin laughed, a bark that carried despite the storm.

How many will you roast, Vidar? Not enough. And it will be worth it, however many you take down with you. You have proven too tenacious, lordling.

Then he turned, fixed Hod on his gaze.

And you, my son? What will you do? Stand by Vali, for the rewards he has in store for you? Will he even let you live? Or will he kill you slowly, as he vowed to long ago?

Vidar saw Hod's features harden. Perhaps he was remembering the words Vali spoke, outside his prison chamber.

Don't listen, Vidar told the dark one. *You'll face no better at Odin's hands.*

The Lord of the Ravens spat.

Join me, Hod. Of all my sons, you are the best—were always the best. Join me and rule at my side, as you were meant to, and I will give you Vali to do with as you will.

Hod's eyes narrowed. Was he thinking about the long nights spent in frigid darkness as he fled Vali's vengeance? The bitterness at knowing how little his own kinsmen loved him?

No, said Vidar. *Remember what he did to you. How he killed Baldur and blamed it on you. How he slew him with your bow and shouted fratricide into the night.*

He turned to face Odin.

Isn't that true, Father? Isn't that the secret you carved into my flesh, the words you whispered to Baldur on his funeral pyre? "Odin is to blame," you said. "He dreamed too high, he loved too much."

Suddenly Odin looked stricken. Like an old man, nothing more.

Aye, he said. *I had dreams. But he proved unworthy—too weak a vessel.*

The world turned a shade grayer.

I couldn't stand looking at him, bent and broken as he

was. It was a reminder of how I'd misjudged him—of how he'd failed me.

He was angry suddenly, as angry as Vidar had ever seen him. His free hand clenched into a fist, shook.

So I removed him from my sight.

So intent was Vidar on his father's visage that he noticed nothing else. Thus, when the cry of pain rang out in his mind, he knew not whence it came, or from whom.

Then he saw Modi whirl, away on the other side of the gap, like a discus thrower just before his release. And suddenly there was a figure aloft on the savage winds, emblazoned against the gray sky and the black flank of the mountain.

In that moment Vali was a thing of unholy beauty, an angel of retribution. For after all these years, he had finally learned the truth.

Modi's aim was true, nor did Odin see him coming. He was still peering into his soul, trying to stifle the fury erupting inside him.

But even with surprise on his side, Vali had no chance— not without help. Just as he bowled into the Valfather, driving him to his knees, Vidar bellowed a war cry and bolted forward.

A moment later his companions followed. He could hear their ululations.

The Nidhoggi seemed confused. Their leader was down, at least for the moment. And when Vidar unleashed Angrum's fire, away from Odin and Vali, the disarray became complete.

Some of them went up in flames. Some were shoved off the bridge as others attempted to save themselves.

Vidar had just loosed another barrage when he caught sight of Odin and Vali. They were struggling together, each with a hand clamped fiercely around the haft of the hammer. A shower of sparks erupted from it.

Vidar spun about, spewing flame at a couple of leatherskins who had gotten too close. The bridge was littered now with burning carcasses, awash with dark, waving tendrils of smoke. And the elves, heartened, were pressing the Nidhoggii as he'd never imagined they could.

Vidar turned again, peered in Vali's direction. The smoke stung his eyes, blinding him. And by the time he could open them again, it was too late for him to help.

For Vali and Odin, in their dance beneath the hammer, had staggered too close to the side of the bridge. They teetered on the edge, muscles straining, feet shuffling for position—the only two lords Asgard had ever known.

One of them lost his footing—it was hard to tell which one. They started to go over.

Vidar cried out, lunged in that direction. But he was too far away. It wouldn't even be close.

Then Hod came out of nowhere, cutting through the flames and the smoke, darting like a dark bird of prey. Just as Odin and Vali toppled off the span, he reached out.

Caught something.

Vidar got there a moment later, ready to drag whomever had been saved back up onto the bridge.

But it was only a strip of Vali's cloak that Hod held in his hand. And Vidar watched as his kinsmen, still locked in a struggle for Mjollnir, plummeted into the abyss.

A moment later they were gone, swallowed, without even a fading cry to mark their passage.

XXX

THE snow was melting. It sent the rivers rushing, gurgling, swollen in their beds. Birds sang from their branches, flushed with the change in the weather as well.

The sun's light was warm on his face and hands, stirring needles of pain where his burns hadn't healed yet. His shoulder hurt also, with every untoward movement of his horse, and it would probably be that way for a while. But he accepted the pain with the pleasure, and was glad for the chance to feel either.

N'arri rode up ahead with a couple of the other *dwarvin*. The berry juice had worn off, finally, leaving his skin as pale as his companions'. And his hair was starting to come in black again, though it was still straw-colored for the most part. He looked like a housewife who'd gone too long between dye jobs.

It had taken him days to get over his missing the battle for Hlymgard. He'd probably never forgive Hod for it.

Nor would Eric. He said he'd almost gone insane, knowing that Vidar had continued his quest with only Ullir to protect him from his enemies—having wheedled the story out of his guards.

But the boy looked content enough now, basking in the familiarity of Utgard's hills, naming the rivers and the woods and the villages they passed while Sif sat patiently and listened.

When they came in sight of G'walin, she took particular notice. "Aye," she said. "I can tell it's the *lyos* who dwell there. It has an air about it." She turned to Eric, then to Vidar. "Perhaps we might stop there, just for a little while?"

Eric chuckled. "There are places I can think of that would be a bit friendlier to us." And he recounted what happened the last time they'd passed near G'walin.

"I see," said Magni's daughter. She shrugged. "I'll wait a little longer, then, to meet the *lyos* of Utgard."

"When we reach Dundafrost," he said, "you'll say it was worth the wait."

Sif smiled. "I trust you," she told him. "I think."

Vidar smiled a little too, and might have laughed if his ribs weren't so sore still. They were brave and compassionate, these two young people, and they'd been through much hardship at his side. They deserved as much happiness as they could gather between them.

It was a long shot, of course. Eric was human, Sif a mixture of Aesir and elf. And they lived worlds apart—literally. But they'd faced greater odds, and beaten them, in the search for Frey's sword. Perhaps they'd overcome these obstacles as well.

And what of Vidar himself, and the elfqueen who awaited him? Would *they* find a way to beat the odds?

He looked around, at the *dwarvin* who'd followed him into Asaheim and Alfheim, at those who'd fallen into Odin's trap in Jotunheim. Many had died, but many more had not.

They were loyal, these dark elves, cheerful in the face of danger. It was no wonder that Baldur had come to love them, and one of them in particular.

But as much time as Baldur had spent among the *dwarvin*, he had not made their caverns his home.

Could Vidar? Even for B'rannit?

Nor was it any easier the other way around. Could he ask her to leave her people, her underground realm with its own array of wonders, for the strangeness of Midgard?

What would she say when he told her what he'd been thinking? Would she call it foolishness?

He had waited this long to find out. He could wait a little longer, he told himself.

So the rivers rushed, and the birds sang their songs. There were moments of careless laughter and moments of grim remembrance.

It was late in the day when they found the stones that marked the entranceway—one of the many that led to under-G'walin. Torches were lit, horses tethered. And N'arri led them down into the earth.

Vidar shuddered a little at the bobbing flames, at the fierce interplay of shadows on the smooth-hewn walls. For it reminded him of what he'd done in the corridors of Hlymgard, and he would have given anything to forget that.

But these were not the corridors of a fortress, the work of warlike giants. They were the hallways of a gentler place, where the air was sweet with the smells of roots and living earth. And though swords were forged here, these passages had never seen the spilling of blood.

Deeper and deeper they went, until the chill seeped into their bones. But after the gnawing cold of Jotunheim, it seemed like nothing.

They passed through a chain of caverns, each hung with its own set of tapestries. And as the dwellers in these caverns saw them, they sent up cries of gladness and sorrow. For not everyone could find his or her kinsman among those who'd returned.

By the time they'd reached the throne room, and Vidar recognized it—with its icy-blue marble floors and its fiery rain of stalactites and its flaming braziers on either wall— his heart was pounding in his chest.

Nor was he disappointed, for he found her where he had first seen her. On a golden throne that curled lizardlike about her, encrusted with rubies and sapphires and limned in fire-light. Her face was half hidden in dragon-wing shadow, though it could not conceal her beauty.

They filled the chamber, Vidar and his company. And

when B'rannit saw them, a fiery tear traced its way down her shadowy cheek.

Ever so slightly, she leaned forward. Suddenly her face was cast into the light.

Her eyes were the deep and dazzling green he remembered. And they clung to him, as if they were still bidding him farewell before Indilthrar.

N'arri and the others stepped aside. Vidar came forward, knelt.

"My lady," he said, looking up at her.

She smiled.

They walked through tunnels, over floors of hard-packed earth, and Vidar held a torch to light their way. He might have used Angrum instead, but he chose not to.

It wasn't long before they reached the cavern, the one that housed the great underground lake. Darkness reigned there, the water an inky blackness, with only a few stars reflected in it through the crack in the ceiling.

Boats were moored along the sandy shoreline, tied to wooden posts. They hardly moved, so still was the lake water. A breeze from the world above barely ruffled the torch flame as Vidar wedged it between two rocks.

B'rannit touched his face where Angrum's backwash had burned him—where the skin was still raw and rough with scabs.

"I'm listening," she said. For she knew, of course, that there was much to tell, and much he wanted to be purged of through the telling.

He told her, told it all. The torch had burned down halfway before he came to Vali's death, and Odin's.

"My father was mad, evil. Some of him died, I think, when he put the arrow into Baldur. And the rest withered ages ago, in the heat of Loki's flame. What fell into that abyss was a husk, a shell with nothing but poison inside it. Yet I feel a sadness at his death, for he was my father. I cannot help it.

"Vali was cut in Odin's mold. He was a war monger, a

conqueror—one who decimated entire races for the sake of glory. Nor did we ever truly love each other, as brothers love. But at one time we loved the same things—Asgard, and Baldur. Perhaps that is enough to explain why I mourn the bastard.

"I can still see him, B'rannit, soaring over the gap that Odin made with Mjollnir. Did he know what he was doing —laying down his life to save the rest of us? Or was he blinded by the need to finally avenge his brother's death, as he'd set out to so long ago? I suppose we'll never know. But they'll never call Vali a coward, in any case. Not in front of me, they won't."

When he went on, it was like a swimmer against the current. The closer he drew to the end, the harder it became.

"With their leader gone, the Nidhoggii seemed to lose heart. They swarmed over the face of Hlymgard like ants driven from their hill, and set out across Vigrid Plain. Some of the more vengeful among us wanted to pursue them, to wipe them out even as the hrimthursar had been wiped out at Ragnarok.

"But there were wiser heads there as well, and they were happy enough to see the monsters go. For if we'd gone after them, out there on the open plain, we'd have gotten the worst of it."

Vidar licked his lips.

"I thought it was over, then. But some of the Aesirmen urged me back into the tunnels, back into the deepest recesses of the fortress. And there, the mystery was solved as to how Odin had transformed the Nidhoggii—from peaceful creatures, such as Hod had described, into vicious predators.

"It was a chamber full of dark brown eggs—each perhaps a foot in length—stretching row upon row until they vanished in shadow. And there were Nidhoggii tending to the eggs—not the marauders we had battled, but females and younglings. It was a nursery, a breeding place for monsters.

"How long had it taken Odin to fashion his warrior race? To make them hate the Aesir, even as he hated them? It might have started with only a few eggs, stolen from a nest in Niflheim—back in the days when Vali was rebuilding Asgard. A few younglings, raised by Odin himself—fed the meat of fresh-killed wolves and eagles, until they acquired a taste for raw flesh."

Vidar swallowed.

"They cried out for me to destroy the eggs, as I had destroyed their warrior fathers. With great blasts of flaming chaos. Almost, B'rannit, I did as they asked. I raised the sword, held it out toward the females and the young. Almost, I let the sword have its way.

"Never had I felt such hunger in Angrum. Never had I felt such a pure urge to destroy. But in the end I held the fire back. And plunged the sword, still hungering, back into its sheath."

Vidar shook his head, sighed.

"Perhaps I should have made an inferno out of the place. Maybe those who brought me there were right—and those younglings will take our lives one day. I don't know. I just couldn't bring myself to murder children—no matter whose they were."

Gently B'rannit touched his face. Her fingers were cool against his skin. She turned him toward her. Kissed him.

"You doubt your wisdom, my lord?"

"Aye. I doubt it."

"Do not. If you'd destroyed those eggs, you'd have been as much a murderer as Odin."

Vidar nodded. "But when the eggs become warriors, they'll swell the ranks of those we allowed to escape. And in the next generation there'll be even more of them. Eventually there'll be too many for barren Jotunheim to sustain. And then the bloodletting will begin again."

B'rannit shrugged.

"Not if you send them home, my lord."

Vidar looked at her. She was smiling.

"Damn. Why didn't I think of that?" The logistics

started coming together in his mind. "There's no way the Nidhoggii would accept the adults raised in Jotunheim—they'd be too destructive. And besides, the warriors would dominate—in time, maybe even convert the peaceful ones to violence. But the unborn children—they haven't been taught Odin's way yet. They'd grow up like everyone else in Niflheim."

He snapped his fingers.

"And I know just the guy to transport the eggs—Hod. He knows his way around—even speaks the language. And he's familiar with the gate that leads there from Jotunheim. All he's got to do is take his *hjalamar* into Jotunheim, with plenty of supplies . . ."

B'rannit was laughing. It sounded like tiny silver bells chiming in the wind.

"You're laughing at me," he observed.

She pressed her hand over her mouth, but she couldn't stop.

Suddenly he lifted her into the air. She yelped, clutching at the hands that encircled her waist.

He let her down slowly, and slowly her laughter subsided. They held one another in the torchlight, by the shore of that star-speckled lake.

Vidar breathed in the smell of her—honey and musk. He caressed her raven hair, tracing the golden strands that began at her temples and ran back past her shoulders.

"You are a sorceress," he told her.

"There's no such thing," she said. "You should know that." She tilted her head slightly, gazing into his eyes. "But you haven't finished yet, have you?"

He grunted, releasing her bit by bit.

"No," he said. "I haven't."

He frowned.

"Is it the Vanirman?" she asked after a moment. "The one you vowed to set free?"

"No." He shook his head, smiling. "Asvit survived, though I had little to do with it. I saw him on the trek from Hlymgard to the Asaheim gate. He glared at me, seeing me only as the murderer of his brothers—knowing nothing of the pledge I'd made to Irbor."

Silence. Vidar picked up a pebble. Tossed it into the water and watched the ripples radiate from it.

"If not the Vanirman," asked B'rannit, "then what?"

He turned to face her, having decided at least where to begin.

"First off," he said, "there's no need for me in Asgard. I know what I told you—that I'd get involved in Asgardian politics again, do my best to oppose Vali's empire building. When he died, it occurred to me that I should step in, take the reins before someone else comes along—and carries on in his tradition.

"But there's no one about to do that. Modi would have been the popular choice, but he's never wanted to rule anywhere. That's why Vali abided his presence in Asgard for so long—he knew that Modi was content with the role of champion, just as Thor had been in his day.

"There's Magni, but he's in no condition to lead a coup—even assuming he would want to. I'd be surprised if he came near *any* crown—even Alfheim's. Especially since that seems destined to fall to Skir'nir.

"G'lann would probably love to rule in Asgard. He's always dreamed of seeing the place, and now that Vali's gone, there's nothing to prevent him. With Modi's help, he might rise to some prominence there. But he's half *lyos*, and Asaheim would never brook an elf on the throne.

"Nor is there anything to fear from Hod. For one thing, his name is still hated in Asaheim—and even when the truth goes out about Baldur's death, it'll take a long time for him to be accepted there. For another thing he's already got a kingdom. Hod's the real ruler in M'thrund—the Queen's just a figurehead. Of course that could all change if the *thrund* discover that he's a pale-of-flesh—but I've a feeling that Tofa and Half will keep his secret."

"Yet someone must rule in Asgard," said B'rannit. "If not you, or any of these others . . ."

"Someone will," said Vidar. "But maybe it's time that

Asgard picked its own king—time that the family stepped down and let the people find their own destiny. Ullir's father would make a good ruler, I think. Or another chieftain I met there—one called Gagni. Perhaps even Ullir himself. None of them seem inclined to be conquerors. Eventually they might even release the tributary worlds—free the slaves who've done their dirty work for so long."

"I see," said B'rannit, "that you've thought long and hard on this, my lord. Nor can I say I disagree with you. But . . ."

"But I make it sound like it's all a prelude to something else." Vidar nodded. "It is, my lady. It is."

Starlight glittered on the dark expanse of the lake. The water lapped softly at the sand.

And he told her of his dilemma.

By the time he finished, she was looking out over the water, her profile traced in torchlight. She was smiling a little, but sadly.

"I understand now," she said, "why it was so hard for you to come to this. I understand quite well—for I have considered these things myself, Leathershod. And come to the same conclusions." She cleared her throat then, as if there were something caught in it.

But when she spoke again, her voice was as low and melodic as before. "I could not bear to abandon under-G'walin. Not because I am queen here—but because it is my home. Nor can I ask you to dwell here with me—for as much as you may enjoy my company, it is not enough for you. It would never be enough." She paused. "So I resolved to content myself with those times your travels brought you here. And to fatten myself on your love, as a bear fattens herself against the winter sleep—so that I might endure the long night without you."

Vidar came up behind her, rested his hands upon her slim, strong shoulders, and his brow against her head.

"But what if there were another way?" he asked.

She turned then, slipping out of his grasp. Her eyes were soft and liquid, and it made them flash even brighter.

"Another way?" she asked. "What way, my lord?"

He shrugged.

"In Midgard I once heard a tale—not of the Aesir, but of a girl named Persephone, whose mother was a great priestess. It seems that the girl was picking flowers one day, when suddenly the earth cracked open and a god emerged in his chariot. Stealing the girl from the midst of her companions, he descended into the earth again. The ground closed up after them, nor was there a trace that the girl had ever existed.

"Her mother raised her voice to the sky gods and told them of her grief. Their hearts softened by her, they took her part, and asked their brother god to release the maiden.

"But he prized her too highly to release her just like that. For she relieved the darkness of his world below the ground, and made his heart glad as nothing else could. On the other hand, he couldn't stand against all the gods of heaven."

B'rannit's brow creased a bit. "My lord, I—"

"Hush," he told her. "I'm not finished yet." And he picked up where he had left off. "In the end, the god of the underworld had to agree to the girl's release—but he made one condition. If she ate even one piece of fruit on her long trek back to her mother, she would have to return to him, and be his forever.

"It was agreed, and the girl began her climb. But it was hard work, and it made her throat dry. In time she felt she could go on no longer unless she had something to give strength to her limbs.

"And so, when she came upon a fruit—something called a pomegranate—she couldn't help herself. She bit into it and drank of its juices. But she only ate half, remembering the deal the gods had made for her.

"Had she not eaten of the fruit at all, she would have been free. Had she eaten it all, she would have been the god's companion forever. But since she ate only half, she only had to live half the year in the kingdom below the ground—and she could spend the other half in the warm embrace of her mother."

B'rannit's eyes narrowed. "Truly," she said, "it is not a pleasant picture you paint of underground realms—or those who rule them."

Vidar laughed. "You've got a point there. But you see what I'm saying, don't you?"

She nodded. "Aye, Leathershod. I see it."

"And?"

Her features softened.

"And I am willing," she told him. "If you are."

He took her in his arms.

"*If* I am? Damn it, B'rannit . . ."

But he never got to say any more, for she'd pressed her mouth against his.

They lingered there until long after the torch had gone out. Then Vidar made one last request of the elfqueen—for there was one matter that still plagued him. And she granted it without questioning.

The cavern they entered was thick with billowing smoke, and the air was bitter with the scent of molten metal.

The *dwarvin* worked at a row of blazing hearths, raising a clamor each time they struck with their mallets, and a hissing each time they cooled a blade in their water troughs. The elves themselves were black with soot, exotically patterned with long streaks of sweat.

To N'arri, of course, this was nothing new. And Eric had seen it all the last time he'd been here.

But Sif had not. She looked around a little like a trapped fawn, wide-eyed at the violence of creation.

"He is the last one," said B'rannit, taking Vidar's arm. And he wondered if she meant the last one in the row—or the last one capable of doing what they needed done.

Eg'gun looked up as they approached him. His face gave away his age as his hard, smoke-blackened body did not. Wisdom gleamed in those emerald eyes, and more than that—a slyness, reminiscent of the *dwarvin* of Svartheim.

"My lady," said Eg'gun, stopping his work. He bowed his head slightly.

"I need your help," said B'rannit.

Eg'gun's eyes flickered over Eric and Sif, then Vidar.

"I see that your friends all have weapons, my lady." He made a harumphing sound. "So it must be a gift you'd have me make."

B'rannit shook her head.

"No," she told him. "No gift. Nor is it a making I need of you."

Vidar drew Angrum free of its sheath. It streamed blood-red with reflected light.

"This sword," said the Aesirman, "must go out of the world. There's no need for it anymore—no place." He held it out to Eg'gun. "It must be destroyed."

Eg'gun gazed at the blade. He put down his tongs and took Angrum in his hands.

"This is no ordinary sword," he said, noticing the runes. "It is the one made by the elders, in the time before the crossing."

"Aye," said B'rannit. "It was forged by one called Ival'di, for a prince of the Vanir."

Eg'gun hefted it, considered it with a craftsman's eye. "Do you know what you ask, my lady?"

"I do," said B'rannit. "I ask you to destroy the greatest sword ever forged." She paused. "For as the lord Vidar says, it is too dangerous to be allowed to exist."

Eg'gun ran a finger over the runes twisted into the hilt, over the dark and mysterious symbols carved into the blade itself.

"Yet it served a purpose, if I've heard right," said the *dwarvin*. "It brought down a great and powerful enemy. Who can say," he asked, "that such an enemy will not rise again? And such a sword not be needed?"

"No one can say that," agreed the elfqueen. "But without a sword such as this in the world, there is less chance of evil rising. And should it rise anyway, the swords we make in Utgard will have to suffice."

Eg'gun nodded, shrugged. He tilted the blade, so that the firelight flowed over it anew.

"It seems a shame," he said. "But if it is your wish, my lady, it shall be done."

He laid Angrum down, point first, in the fire at which he worked. The flames leaped higher for a moment, then subsided again.

At the other hearths the elves had stopped their work. Even if they had not guessed what was about to happen, B'rannit's presence alone had stirred their curiosity.

Vidar saw his companion's faces dance with firelight. Eric met his gaze, but Sif was intent on Frey's blade. After all, she had reason to fear it—she'd seen what it had done to G'lann.

But Eg'gun seemed to hesitate.

"What is the matter?" asked B'rannit.

Eg'gun considered the blade.

"I need blood, my lady. This sword was forged in blood as well as fire. And both must be present if I am to break the magic in it."

Eric started to step forward, but Vidar stopped him. "No," he told the boy. "I think he means me."

The *dwarvin* looked up. "Aye," he said. "The stronger, the better."

Vidar nodded, came closer to the flames. His skin burned again with the memory of Angrum's backwash.

He held out his left arm, palm up.

Eg'gun was quick and deft. Taking out a knife he carried at his belt, he slid it across Vidar's forearm. There was a momentary prick of pain, and then blood was running down toward his hand, collecting in the shallow cup of his palm.

"Now," said the *dwarvin*, "let it fall into the fire."

Vidar held his hand out over the hearth, turned it over. The blood dripped, thick and red, and as it dripped it hissed.

Suddenly the flames geysered, scorching the very roof of the cavern. And they remained that way—a pillar of fire, fueled by Vidar's blood.

Angrum lay half in and half out of the blaze, its blade glowing ruby red, its hilt a sullen purple.

Eg'gun set to work, his back to the rest of them. His skin seemed to crawl beneath that roiling light, to flow like lava down his shoulders and his sides.

Before long Vidar heard a muttering, a string of harsh, whispered words that sounded like tiny explosions. And try as he might, he could make no sense of it, for it was the ancient language of the dark elves—not meant for the ears of other races.

Someone—N'arri perhaps—held Vidar's arm out, used a shred of cloth to bind his wound. But the Aesirman never took his eyes off the sword.

You cannot be rid of me, it seemed to say. *You can never be rid of me. You have tasted my power. How can you forget that?*

How indeed?

Almost, he reached into the fire then. Almost, he plucked Angrum from it.

But he held himself back. And after a while he felt B'rannit's fingers entwining with his own, cooling the desire there.

Still, Eg'gun muttered. And as he did this, he picked the sword up with his tongs. Plunged Angrum into the red-orange fury, hilt and all.

The column of flame seemed to roar, as if in agony. Sparks leaped from the blade, ruby sparks that scattered and died.

For a long time—or was it an instant?—the dark elf held the sword in the maw of the flame, turning it. His arms began to tremble, as if he were struggling with something alive and powerful.

Then, abruptly, he slammed Angrum down on his anvil. The weapon glowed a dark, molten red.

"The mallet," he rasped. "Strike it, Aesirman! Quickly!"

Vidar saw the mallet, picked it up in both hands. And raising it over his head, he brought it down on the sword.

Angrum shivered with the blow, but remained intact.

You see? You can never destroy me. Never be . . .

A second time Vidar raised the mallet. A second time he brought it down.

The sword cracked a little. A hairline crack near the hilt.

"Hurry, Aesirman! Before the magic can harden again within it!"

. . . be free. Never be . . .

Vidar brought the mallet up.

. . . free. Never be . . .

With all his strength he hammered the sword, striking it just where he'd seen the crack.

There was a great flash, and a terrible shriek, and the mallet came apart in his hands.

Strange things erupted from the vicinity of the anvil— awful, fiery things that left trails of flame and keened like lost souls. But after a moment, spent, they burned away into smoke.

As the pillar of flame began to shrink, to collapse in on itself, Vidar peered at Angrum through smoke-stung eyes.

The sword had broken into a dozen pieces. Silent and ordinary now, the fragments began to cool.